STANDING ON THE GIANT'S GRAVE

STANDING ON THE GIANT'S GRAVE

PAUL DUTHIE

For Margaret

First impression: 2011

© Paul Duthie & Y Lolfa Cyf., 2011

This book is subject to copyright and may not be reproduced by any means except for review purposes without the prior written consent of the publishers.

Cover image: Chris Illiff

ISBN: 9 781 84771 355 1

Published and printed in Wales
on paper from well maintained forests by
Y Lolfa Cyf., Talybont, Ceredigion SY24 5HE
e-mail ylolfa@ylolfa.com
website www.ylolfa.com
tel 01970 832 304
fax 832 782

And the deeper secret within the secret:
The land that is nowhere, that is the true home.

The Secret of the Golden Flower

1

I am thirty-one years old. I have in one of my drawers a purse with eighteen guineas and two seven shilling pieces; there are two twenty shilling notes in a pocket book; in my workbox is my Will. I must be careful with every penny until I learn how far thirty-six pounds a year will go.

And I have this journal. I like to feel its weight and to smell its green leather binding. Like my future its creamy-white pages are blank. What will fill them is as yet unknown. I'm quite sure it is of little consequence to the world who I am, let alone who my parents were or what my life holds for me, but it will occupy the lonely hours ahead when my only other employment would be a tedious piece of sewing. In a month I leave and I am determined never to return. So I shall begin by writing an account of my life here. The fire sparks and flares. It is very quiet. It must be cold outside. I reach for the subtle comfort of the quill, the intoxicating smell of ink, the pleasure of paper. I search for my earliest memories.

Up Holland 1784–1808

At the soft knock at the door, my mother rose immediately but let the servant answer it. Her face was full of apprehension at the sight of Mr Hinde whose son she knew was abroad in the Indies. He was a corpulent, wine-faced man with snowy hair and whiskers. Self-conscious before my mother, he coughed unnecessarily.

'We have heard from James, Mrs Weeton. He writes from Jamaica,' he said in an unsteady voice. He took a letter from his breast pocket. Its whiteness made it something almost obscene in the room.

My mother crumpled onto one end of the sofa and shielded her face with both hands. She seemed suddenly smaller as if deep within her something had collapsed or broken. Her lips had turned almost as white as the letter Mr Hinde held. His fingers trembled. I remember his big strong hands shaking.

My mother's voice when it came was strange. I would not have recognised it if I had been in the next room. 'Laura,' she almost croaked, 'please take Ellen upstairs and check that Tom is still asleep.'

My mother would never be young again.

Laura gently bundled me out of my mother's sight. I was frightened. My mother had frightened me. Mr Hinde's trembling fingers had frightened me. 'What's happened, Laura?' I asked when we were in my tiny room.

She put her good, kind arms around me.

'Something dreadful, Missy.'

I hid my face in her starched apron smelling of soap and cleanness. I had seen that Laura too was frightened.

She stayed with me for some time sitting quietly on the edge of my bed. When she rose to leave, she picked up a little book from a chest of drawers where she had placed the candle and put it under my pillow. My father had given it to me the last time he was at home. When I sat for my portrait so that he might take it to sea with him, the artist thought it would look too stiff in a painting, but I would accept neither dolls nor dogs, and insisted on Papa's little storybook. In the darkness my fingers sought its hard comforting edges.

I woke to find my mother sitting on my bedroom chair near the window. She was crying quietly. Her grief-drawn face was like chalk in the half-light.

'Poor Nelly,' she said, 'you have no father.'

My mother had never called me Nelly before. It had always been my father's pet name for me.

★

The house was changed. My mother was changed. Men, their faces solemn and carrying papers tied with ribbon, came one evening and spoke in serious undertones to her at the big table. I was told that we were now poor. The few pence I offered my mother from the battered tin I kept in my drawer did not bring the response I had anticipated. I was rewarded with no more than a sad, forced smile.

★

It was a long time before I was able to piece together the stories my mother told me about my father's life. His parents had both died when he was still young and he went to live with his Aunt Gibson and her avaricious and miserly husband. He soon tired of drudging for them and bound himself as apprentice to a ship's captain in Lancaster as soon as he was old enough to run away. When he married my mother he was captain of a merchantman engaged in the African slave trade. With the outbreak of the American War, Rawlinsons, important and wealthy merchants, commissioned him to command a vessel carrying a Letter of Marque. In this vessel he sailed and took many prizes. He returned and was loaded with congratulations for his bravery. My mother told us that they were as happy with each other as any couple in existence. I was born on Christmas Day 1776, and although I was always called Ellen, I had been christened by the name of Nelly. My father was at sea on his favourite ship *Nelly* and my mother thought to win his affection for me by naming me after it, as she had heard him say that he wished all his children to be boys. I was for some time the only child. We lived in a smart new cottage at the top of Church Street in Lancaster and my mother was anxious for my father to realise his fortune so he could resign from such a dangerous employment and settle at home. When I was four my brother Thomas was born. My father did not see him for over a year, but he now intended giving up seafaring for good. Unfortunately, Rawlinsons would not hear of it, but promised that if he would embark on one final voyage he should find on his return all the accounts settled and his prize money ready for him. My father accepted. A half-remembered scene remains in my mind. It was the evening before he sailed. I see my parents, standing before open, long windows. There are distinct sounds – a band in the street – people, colours. Voices give repeated cheers from outside in the dark-grey air. I see, or perhaps I want to see, my mother peering up into my father's face, smiling her pride. We never saw him again.

For some months merchants brought glowing accounts of my father's valour and successes. What my mother thought and felt during this time, I have no notion. I cannot remember her being critical of my father – not ever – but she attached no romance to his life at sea. She told no tales of ships lurching and creaking under full sail or of fluttering pennants, shrill whistles or of cannons belching smoke. When at last she received a letter fixing the date for my father's return and his solemn pledge never to leave her side again, she was all quiet practicality and tense with nervous anticipation. Perhaps, some superstitious dread prevented her from whispering, 'Your father will be home soon.' But on the night of Mr Hinde's visit, every comfort was prepared for his return. The flagstones were scrubbed; the iron grate gleamed with black lead polish; his linen put at the fire. The warm room held the soft fragrance of lavender and was aglow with cleanliness. The

Jamaica packet arrived – she waited, sitting quietly by the fire playing with her infant son in her lap until he fell asleep and was carried to the nursery. I was nearly six years old.

★

I heard the circumstances surrounding my father's death from my Aunt Barton. I cannot remember any phrase exactly, but an uncompromising voice comes back, intimidating and unkind. Her truths were harsh and unembroidered, insinuating, self-serving. She could have been a preacher standing above a sober congregation giving a lesson on the theme: 'They that take the sword shall perish with the sword.' I can give no sense of my father's personality, but the imagined scene of his death is a distinct memory, thanks to Aunt Barton. It is from her that I have learned to loathe bullies and cowards.

He had wreaked such terrible damage on American ships during the war that a vessel of superior strength was expressly ordered to seek and engage with my father wherever he could be found. They met him and ordered him to strike. He was incensed to discover the Captain was an old school fellow of his and he refused to strike to a traitor and a base rebel to his own country. He was answered with an ear-splitting cannonade from the American ship. His antagonist's vessel was so large and so close that it could not bring its guns to bear upon the hull of my father's ship but did terrible damage to its masts and rigging – and to the men stationed there. The English vessel directed its fire directly at the hull of its opponent between wind and water and it was soon reduced to a sinking state and struck. My father raised a cheer from the men who had survived in the shrouds. At that instant, a chain shot came sweeping past my father and took off half his face. He dropped convulsing uncontrollably on the open deck. The American ship made off and my father was taken to Jamaica near where the battle had taken place. He died within hours. He was thirty-four.

★

Rawlinsons never paid my mother the promised prize money or the property my father had accrued, a fortune of at least twelve thousand pounds. She had recourse to the law, but this she was not prepared to do in case it jeopardised the little she did have from a small estate at Sunderland, near Lancaster, which my father had inherited. And even with the strictest economy this soon proved inadequate. My mother sold most of the furniture and removed to Up Holland. Its narrow, cobbled streets and medley of stone houses had been her mother's native place. The cost of coals and rents was also much lower than in Lancaster. We lived in a pretty cottage across the street from St Thomas's churchyard and priory. From my window I could look over the street through the iron railings to headstones, which leaned this way and that under yew trees. At one end of the house was a small, painted, iron gate: the sharp clack as its spring drew it shut comes back to me as I write this. It is now rusted and moss-tufted, but then it gave entrance to the garden. I see myself – small, dark – standing in the centre of a great space, my eyes open and my arms outstretched, whirling around and around beneath leaves, flowers, clouds, until I fall to the grass, my head still whirling like a spun top. In reality the garden was small, but through my childish eyes it was extensive, romantic and beautiful. In spring apple trees were matted in a foam of blossom; in summer it was ablaze with nasturtiums. It gave me a peace of mind, a feeling of security in the world that I have not been able to recover. The upper end contained an arbour of roses with a stone table and benches where my mother gave little tea parties, for she was soon acquainted with the principal families of the district: Doctor and Mrs Hawarden from nearby Wigan; Mr Braithwaite, the rector of St Thomas's and his wife; Mr and Mrs Prescott, who were what my mother called people of considerable property. I think of that time and strawberries come to mind, and cream, and twirling white parasols, laughter. When the weather was fine Tom and I played in our garden. I joined him in his games of marbles, helped to sail his little boat in the water tub or to trundle his hoop. When it was cold or raining we would write letters to each other, compose riddles or try to build a kite from an assortment of thin sticks, glue and brown paper. I don't remember one ever flying.

An incident surfaces unbidden, another garden scene. Tom, shamefaced, shaking, glares at me; he is holding a stick in his hands. A round cup of mud and straw is broken at his feet, a tiny, too-heavy head wobbles on a thin neck, and a beak opens soundlessly. It is blind, blue skin covers its bulging, veined eyes. I run from the horror, but stop and turn to see swallows flit and arc above the eaves near the water barrel.

★

Mr Braithwaite had transformed part of his house into a boarding school, which he called The Academy. He taught the sons of the rich who lived in the dark, red-black priory almost directly opposite our cottage. Tom was permitted to attend as a day student and could soon spout a little Latin, which of course was too much for me. He enjoyed this small triumph and revelled in his superiority by quoting Latin phrases at every opportunity. He would never tell me their meaning. I don't think he was particularly clever, nor did he enjoy learning, but he had a strength of mind and a deep determination to succeed. He liked to compete, but only if he were confident of winning. I can remember clearly how he would rage if I were the first to bring the last of my stones into my corner and win a game of backgammon. But when he was fourteen and articled to Mr Grimshaw of Preston, his leaving was like a death. I felt sure I would never see him again as he then was. He passively accepted our hugs and kisses. He was a little pale, but with a show of manliness he settled his cap, pulled his scarf closer, and climbed the ladder to his seat behind the driver.

'Goodbye Mama. Goodbye Ellen. I will work hard.'

My throat constricted with emotion and my voice broke to a half-sob. I could say nothing even as he disappeared from our view with a clatter of wheel rims on cobbles. I felt entirely alone.

My mother's voice was at my elbow, quiet and reassuring. 'We must do all we can for Tom. One day he will be established in business and he won't forget us. I know it's a long time to look to, but it will pass and then we will be together again.'

The house seemed unnaturally quiet, the garden deserted. Tom's room remained neat, lifeless. I missed his demands, his banter, his noise and his untidiness. My mother began to deprive herself of comforts, even of necessities, to support Tom – and I suffered with her. Visits to the butcher were infrequent. We lived on little more than bread and potatoes and talked and dreamed of the time when Tom would be an attorney at law. Then there would be veal pies, smoking rounds of beef, and green goose! It was a vain expectation, but she did not live to know it.

★

My education was not entirely neglected. Mr Pollard, an usher from Mr Braithwaite's school, taught me Writing, Arithmetic and a little Geography. However, I showed such interest in my lessons and made such quick progress that my mother, who had initially been delighted with my abilities, grew less certain about the project and Mr Pollard's visits became noticeably less frequent. I think she was afraid that I would be ruined for any useful purpose in life if such inclinations were indulged. She was happier to see me shelling a trug of peas in the elbowed seat under the pear tree than to be there reading one of Mr Pollard's books.

I had helped her in the village school she had worked so hard to start since I was eleven years old. I now taught for nine hours a day, sewed a little for hire and helped with the work of the house. We had no servant. There were days when I had no one to speak to. I had no real companion. My mother's pupils were all too young and most of the village girls my own age were so vulgar that my mother would not have allowed me to associate with them even if I had wanted to – and I didn't. I was shy and diffident. Looking from Tom's low-beamed room across the churchyard and beyond the houses to the fields below, I would have gladly gone for a solitary walk, but under no circumstances was I allowed to go beyond the village unaccompanied. I looked, longed and sighed, but kept my wishes to myself. Of necessity I was much alone, but in time it became a matter of choice. Even at the age of eighteen, on the now rare occasion an acquaintance of my mother called, I would flee upstairs rather than join them. I didn't know why. I would often imagine having conversations with men who could discuss science and literature or be deeply moved by music. I would have liked to be thought clever, well-informed, elegant and witty, but I could not afford books and I lived almost entirely amongst the coarse and illiterate. I craved company but avoided society.

Day followed day in dreary routine. I became ill. For months I suffered from a sore throat, extreme fatigue and stomach pains. A bilious complaint further weakened my digestion. I would heave up quantities of yellow stuff after eating meat. It would eventually contribute to another of my oddities – I eat no meat given the choice – much to the puzzlement and even amusement of the beef and offal eaters of Up Holland.

When I felt I could barely crawl, Doctor Hawarden ordered that I was to have more air and exercise. He was adamant that my very life depended upon it.

'A holiday, Mrs Weeton, is what you both need. Liverpool – a change of scene would work wonders.' He settled his substantial frame into a chair with a professional calm and direct gaze. 'I have a niece in Liverpool who is about the same age as Ellen. You would get along famously with Ann, I'm sure,' he said, nodding at me kindly.

'We could stay with the Chorleys,' my mother said, her voice suddenly more hopeful.

The Chorleys had been friends of my mother in her Lancaster days and although she had corresponded with them for years – every Christmas without fail – I had never met them. I knew they too had a daughter, but to me they were merely names. They were the Chorleys of Liverpool. The thought of actually going there had never occurred to me before. A deep excitement stirred in my very soul. Liverpool!

But later that night, my mother decided she could not afford the time away from her school and that the necessary expenses could not be justified given Tom's circumstances. Instead the aid of the Prescott girls was enlisted. I was to accompany them every afternoon on the walks considered by

Doctor Hawarden to be necessary for my health. They were young ladies with whom my mother took every opportunity to nurture an intimacy on my account because of their affluence and standing in the community. And their manners *were* superior to mine, but only in the presence of my mother. Alone with them, they never tired of showing me that they considered themselves to be vastly superior to the daughter of a schoolmistress. I'm sure I was no better or worse looking than any other sample of young women, but beside them in their graceful, high-waisted, low-bodiced, sleeveless dresses, I felt self-conscious about my appearance – my worn face, my thinness, my tallness. On one painful occasion we were hardly through the front door before their taunts and snobbish banter began.

'Well, Miss Dowdy Draggletail,' said Miss Prescott the elder, glancing at me quickly with undisguised hauteur, 'you look so smart this morning I feel sure you could pass for our maid.'

Delighted at this first volley, her sister, Elizabeth, was only too happy to continue the assault.

'No, no, no, silly, she is looking for a man, aren't you Ellen? Tell us what he must be like.'

They were both evidently pleased with their cleverness and smirked with self-satisfied laughter at my expense. My shyness they took for stupidity and because I so rarely took part in their vacuous chatter, they assumed I didn't understand half of their crude hints and barbs. My anger was a fire, but it was too smothered by exhaustion to leap and be dangerous. They walked too quickly for me. My head swam with barely suppressed nausea and I felt sure the added exertion would only slow my recovery. There was a stark stench of rotting vegetation from the choked gutters, which added to my distress. I reeled a little from dizziness. A rat disappeared up a dripping water pipe dragging its naked tail in behind it. I hoped it would not climb into my dreams.

'Oh, God! Hurry up a bit,' said Catherine. 'Well, for my part,' she soon continued blithely, tossing her light siren curls which fell luxuriantly over her neck and shoulders, 'I have two criteria which must be satisfied. He must be handsome, that goes without saying, and he must be as rich as Croesus.'

'Are you sure you wouldn't settle for an only son of very, very elderly parents of slightly more than modest means?' asked Elizabeth knowingly. She turned briefly in my direction. 'Now Ellen, no doubt you have been inspired by the exploits of our romantic Miss Porter,' she said mockingly.

Laughter again. I knew something of the Porters of Ackhurst. Towards the end of summer, Janet Porter, who was only seventeen, had gone to Gretna Green and married Mr Saunderson of Preston, who was upwards of forty. He had made frequent visits to Ackhurst ostensibly as a friend of Mr Porter's. Out riding together one afternoon, Mr Porter almost fell off his horse with astonishment when he was asked for his daughter's hand. Without a word to Saunderson, he returned home, bundled his distraught daughter into a chaise, drove to Wigan and placed her under the protection of his brother. Her uncle was very fond of her and well-to-do, but she had only been there a short while when one evening she claimed to feel so unwell that she couldn't dine out that night with her aunt and uncle. Saunderson was waiting a short distance away and their elopement was not discovered for hours.

'They say,' said Miss Prescott, 'that the once prosperous Mr Saunderson now works in a warehouse and earns so little he can hardly support himself let alone a wife.'

I remembered my mother telling me that Mrs Saunderson had returned to Ackhurst only once since her marriage – to ask her father for his forgiveness. He granted it, but left the house immediately without another word. When he returned, his daughter had gone. 'Poor Mr Porter has hardly been seen since then – not even at church,' she had added sadly. But I knew the good church people of Up Holland. They would show no mercy in such circumstances. After Sunday service, they would be like hens in a circle squawking and pecking at the lacerated dignity of the Porters until the last scraps of the scandal were gobbled up. There would be much solemn head shaking and pious solicitude: 'Oh, it's a shame,' someone would be bound to say, in an almost sincere voice. 'Did you know that Mr Porter would not see his daughter for fear of upsetting his brother?' someone else would assert, convinced she possessed the truth in every detail of the case. 'Old Mr Porter is quite well off you know – he can't afford to upset him,' would come from a third, secure in his worldly wisdom – and his wealth.

★

In spite of my walks with the Prescotts, perhaps because of them, I did slowly recover. As the season turned and the days grew shorter and cooler, my strength increased and I throbbed again with the pulse of life. However, fate was only readying me for impending tragedy. My mother had long suffered from a breathing difficulty that Doctor Hawarden called the asthma, and as the chilly, dank days of late November wore on, she became increasingly listless and pale. The mornings were bone-white with fog and damp with droplets of rain. Frills of yellow fungus appeared in the garden and unless a bright fire was kept the very walls ran with moisture. She would wake wheezing and choking in the hours before dawn and be racked with a cough that could not move the congestion on her lungs. She continued to go to her school – until the morning Bill Ramsey confronted her.

The day before, a worthless glass brooch that a child had brought from home had gone missing. Eventually, it was found in the pocket of Edward Ramsey who, rather than endure the gentle wrath of my mother fled to his home in tears. What story he manufactured to explain his early arrival, I never discovered, but he now stood silently, his heavy, round head bowed and his shoulders hunched, while his father shouted angrily at my mother. He had lost all control. Spit flew from his thick purplish lips and tiny muscles in his face worked and twitched, before he turned on his heel taking his son with him.

My mother remained outwardly calm, but I'm sure the shock of the incident triggered the acute attack she suffered that afternoon. She was suffocating for lack of air. Her chest ached. The balsam inhalations Doctor Hawarden prescribed for her had little effect. Her breath rattled painfully as she bent her head covered with linen over the steaming bowl. It soothed, but did not cure. The next morning, the fog turned to grey rain and she was much worse. Doctor Hawarden sat her upright, propped by pillows, and she made noisy little gulps at the air.

When he was leaving, he stopped at the door to pull on his gloves and said with a frown, 'Ellen, if there is a change for the worse, you must send for me. I am well used to venturing out at all hours.' The note of seriousness in his voice betrayed his unease. 'I will call again tomorrow.'

I wished he could have stayed. I missed the kind, grey light of his eyes and the reassurance of his calm decisiveness. I felt very much alone.

The Braithwaites visited in the early afternoon. Reverend Braithwaite, tall, slender, educated, was formal, but he was not the stern, self-sufficient preacher one may have expected. Behind the lectern on a Sunday, he was all authority and learning, but he enjoyed company and was alive to the beauty of the world. He insisted on caring for the little garden beside the priory himself and early summer saw phlox and roses, red and white, flourishing there. To her husband's strengths, Mrs Braithwaite added tenderness. To the poor of Up Holland, those bruised by an unaccommodating world, she was a familiar figure with her basket, a piece of linen covering her offering of bread or some freshly picked vegetables. My mother used to say that the Braithwaites were two halves of the same whole, they were so well suited to each other. In their presence she seemed to rally a little – I too, began to feel more hopeful. But the thin, blue veins in her temples and the dark shadows under her eyes betrayed her fragility, her invalid state. She soon fell into a restless sleep.

'Remember, Ellen, we are just across the road,' Mr Braithwaite said when they were leaving. Mrs Braithwaite wordlessly put her arms around me with a strength that spoke eloquently of her silent concern.

★

The night closed in, wet with steady rain and my mother grew agitated.

'You're a good girl Ellen. Oh, and poor Tom,' she groaned, 'no matter how hard he tries he won't have enough money now. I was going to have everything settled in a new Will when you turned twenty-one.'

'You still can. It's not long till Christmas,' I said, trying to be encouraging, but my voice was little more than a whisper.

She shook her head and desperately tried to rouse herself. It was a struggle for her to speak at all. Her voice was weak and tremulous with an edge of urgency in it.

'Ellen, listen to me carefully,' she said between gasps. Her eyes were unnaturally bright. 'Tom must have the money from Sunderland. You can keep the school going. Please – will you promise me that? As things stand, the house is yours and you will have the interest from a hundred pounds. If you marry, promise me the hundred pounds will go to Tom.'

I promised. And I will keep my promise.

My mother had exhausted herself. She lay back and closed her eyes. Her breaths now came in slow, harsh sobs, which hollowed and whitened her cheeks. I think my earliest memory is of my mother. I was a little girl. I am not sure how old; she was dressed in white muslin. We were walking amongst birches and alders besides a stream. Late autumn leaves carpeted the ground. She was holding my hand and talking to me. I was happy. I have no recollection of what she was saying. She was a felt presence only.

My thoughts turned to other scenes: my mother with Mrs Braithwaite in her kitchen where there were white cups, slices of cake and laughter; I saw her hurrying along the cobbles to her little school. I remembered her the afternoon of one of Miss Dannett's visits. Miss Dannett, poor simple soul, was in the habit of being frequently bled for fear of becoming fat. The apothecaries of neighbouring villages refused to bleed her any longer, but Jackson of Up Holland was prepared to – for a fee. She had convinced herself that if she were not bled she would become swollen and so lethargic that she would not be able to move. And this was not her only fear. She had a dread of a terrible presence in the old Mill-house just below hers.

'In the dead of night,' she said, 'the mill wheel turns of its own accord. True as I am sitting here.' She rummaged in her bag and placed a small jar of homemade jam on the table. She would never visit us without bringing something: half a teacake or some stewed fruit that my mother would inspect suspiciously before consuming. 'And other folks hear things too,' she said, 'the tongs, the poker, even the chairs are set a-dancing by it.'

When she had gone, shuffling her bulk along the path, a little pale and wheezing slightly, Tom spread his coat wide and ran through the house moaning eerily. My mother would have none of it. This in a place where hardly a stile, or crossroad, or mossy boulder did not have some old story associated with it – usually grisly. She would not permit us to ridicule Miss Dannett nor to accept her story, but sat us down and urged us to apply our reason to the matter.

'Remember the Lord himself tacitly allowed for such a possibility when the Apostles saw him walking on the water and thought he was a ghost,' she said, so seriously that it precluded so much as a giggle from us. She found the passage in our heavy black-bound Bible and made me read the line she was tapping with her index finger: 'A spirit hath not flesh and blood as ye see I have.'

She was rarely so solemn. Perhaps she had some inkling of the years I would spend alone.

She lapsed into sleep – perhaps it was unconsciousness. The cold night hours passed. I was gripped with the icy fear of certain knowledge. I wanted to send for Doctor Hawarden, but I was frightened to leave her. I stayed – holding her hand. I wanted her to know that I was still there – that she wasn't alone. I grew strangely calm, almost peaceful and listened to her breathing quieten. The shock, when it came, as I knew it must, came as noiselessly as a petal falling. Her breath left her; the colour of her face drained away and was stilled. I gently folded her arms across her chest and kissed her on the forehead. Eventually, I moved to the window and looked out at the chill misty morning, the curdled sky and the sweep of rain.

★

Old Mr Prescott had died three days before my mother. In a few weeks Mrs Prescott and her daughters left Up Holland. Catherine promised – perhaps superciliously, perhaps because of mutual grief and loss – to write occasionally. I had no legal guardian. Tom was too young and had four years to complete before he could practise law, and the entire care and support of him was now my responsibility.

★

My mother was buried in Up Holland churchyard. Her grave is only yards from her old school house. It was a cold, blustery day. The last of the leaves on the near-naked boughs were being tormented by the wind and were black against the fish-coloured sky. They would soon be torn from their uncertain anchorage, leaf by leaf, and be swirled and lost amongst the gravestones. Tom, taller and heavier, stood stooped in misery. He was cheese-white. I tried not to dwell on the gaping dark earth in front of me – the dull thuds the wet sods made on the coffin lid – what lay inside the coffin. Mr Braithwaite gently intoned the final words of the service. And then the living turned their backs on the dead – as they must. I felt a terrible need to be alone, but Aunt Barton was beside me.

'We have a Saviour, child. Dry your eyes,' she said briskly and without emotion. I winced inwardly. Not a wisp of hair protruded from under her bonnet making her look prim and severe. Even as a child I disliked her – her baggy jaws and narrow, critical eyes. Being respectable was my aunt's true religion. It was far more important to her than merely being respected – what people might think had guided her unerringly through life. Now in her sixties, with her carefully guarded reputation for moral uprightness in the parish unblemished, she was able to reward herself with the subtle pleasures of judging the failures and weaknesses of others with impunity.

'You have suffered a great loss, but you are also fortunate that you have a respectable home with me and your good uncle.'

'No, no, Aunt,' I stammered. 'Thank you, but I will stay in my own house and I will keep the school now.'

'Alone? That would hardly be proper at your age. Why, you are not yet twenty-one. And my health is not what one could wish. Surely your duty lies with me?' I felt her observant gaze on me. Tightly dressed in black, her eyes missed nothing – not so much as a stray cotton thread or a frayed hem. How constricting life would be in her house, enduring her affectation, her discipline! Even in the depths of my grief a part of me chose the freedom of lonely solitude in my own cottage. 'Well?' she persisted.

'It was my mother's wish that I should continue with the school, Aunt. And the Braithwaites are close by if I need them. I think I will be able to manage.'

She grimaced sniffily and a look of annoyance came into her eyes.

'The Braithwaites,' she spat out condescendingly. 'I have heard he plays cards of an evening, and that he is a little too fond of a glass of port on occasions. Are these the people…'

She stopped speaking. She had noticed Mrs Braithwaite coming towards me, her face full of undisguised compassion.

She put her arms around me, searched my aunt's face briefly, before saying, 'Mrs Barton, you will of course join us at the priory for a cup of tea?' We began walking together towards the group gathering in the cold shade between the heavy church tower and the angular, dark brickwork of the Braithwaites' home, but my aunt did not follow.

★

I had hardly, if ever, been alone in my cottage. Its mood changed, the rhythm of its life, its rituals, its sounds, and especially its silences – made heavy with the weight of age and the coldness of winter. I was alone with my grief and crushing loneliness. Mrs Chorley had written, kindly inviting me to stay with her for as long as I liked, which was generous, but hardly possible. As I sat at my window looking across at the dark tower of St Thomas's, Liverpool receded in my mind to become an almost make-believe place, as far away as it had been when I was a child. I had the school now. And there was another difficulty. Tom had returned to Preston, with three pounds in his pocket that I could ill afford. I was starving. I had no money at all. One poor meal a day had to suffice. Then, one of my girls paid me a penny for some thread. A treasure! 'Well, I will have some dinner today at least!' I thought. No doubt, if my good aunt were there, she would have warned me about the sin of presumption. I gleefully bought some potatoes and boiled them with plenty of milk. When they were ready I put them above the oven while I fried bacon for the children who often brought their own dinner to be cooked at school. All was nearly ready when a child hurried past and knocked the dish off the stove and onto the floor. Covered in dirt, they were utterly unfit to eat. It was only a few potatoes and I had borne everything bravely until that moment, but it was too much for me. I placed the pan on the floor without a word, left the room and cried bitterly in my frustration. The guilty child stood looking at me in wide-eyed, silent amazement. That afternoon, in Mrs Braithwaite's kitchen and sitting before a scalding hot cup of tea and freshly baked scones, I laughed as I told her of the disaster. I realised with a quick pang that it was the first time I had laughed since my mother had died. It brought to an end one phase of my life and the faint, uncertain beginnings of another.

My aunt visited me only once in those first weeks. She seemed almost disappointed to see me as clean as a cat in my own house and at least outwardly content. The painted, garden gate shut with a sharp clack as she left and she did not stop at the corner to wave to me.

★

I remember very clearly one summer's evening about six or seven months later. Mr Braithwaite's little garden was again burning with the cold fire of scarlet flowers and I went for a walk past the jumble of slate roofs and the stale shops and along sun-washed lanes to Tower Hill. The air was so clear I could see the Welsh hills quite distinctly in the distance. Honeysuckle had tangled with pink dog roses in the hedgerows. A pair of plovers called to black-faced sheep. The dull routine and the petulance of the classroom drained away from me as if I had drunk wine. When I returned, I went upstairs to take off my bonnet and shawl. Every window in the house was open to the warm light. The sky had deepened to indigo and the few clouds of tarnished silver were edged with rouge by the setting sun. The evening was so beautiful I was reluctant to leave my window. Some children were playing on the road beneath it. At a little distance from the iron railings of the churchyard, a group of people had gathered around a man who played a flute. He kept time with the help of his hobnailed boots on the cobbles. So infectious were his rhythms that a passing labourer removed his straw hat and a rush basket of tools from his shoulder and began to dance. There was a mood of perfect contentment and harmony as the daylight became more muted and slipped away. The shadows of night drew on and a white thin mist began to fall. The laughter, the music, the distant voices fell quiet. I looked out at a soft, silent moon haloed in cloud. It seemed that all living things had gone to their rest. And I would too! In a moment I was in my bed where sleep as soothing as rain on water washed over me.

It could only have been an hour or so later when some sound startled me into complete alertness. I heard the muffled sound of a voice – someone was in the house! This sudden realisation took my breath away and I felt a weakness in my chest and knees. I was out of bed in an instant and drew the sword, which had belonged to my father, from underneath the bolster. I had put it there for just such an occasion as this, but it was with a sense of unreality that I crept down the stairs holding the horrible weapon and dressed in nothing but my nightdress. I still wanted to believe that I would discover no one, but to my horror a few steps from the bottom I could see the dark shape of a person walking towards me! I momentarily faltered, but found my voice.

'What are you doing? Who are you?' I demanded in a near scream, lifting the heavy sword in front of me.

The response was a loud shriek that frightened me even more, and the person, whose scream had identified her as a woman, bolted to the other end of the room. Another heavier voice shouted from outside the parlour window.

'Ann! What's going on? Are you alright?'

'Oh God, Ellen, put the sword down. It's me, Mrs Braithwaite.'

Mr Braithwaite then clambered noisily through the open window with a lantern. I stood in amazement, my chest heaving and unable to say a word. My mouth opened and gaped like a carp's, as I tried to fathom why they were there.

'Miss Weeton,' said Mr Braithwaite, looking uncharacteristically embarrassed and flustered. He put the lantern on a table and went to his wife's side. 'We saw your windows open and thought you must have been out or forgotten them. We waited a good long while, but as there was no light, I thought we'd better come over.'

'We did knock,' said Mrs Braithwaite, recovering a little from her fright, 'but we couldn't make you hear, so I climbed through a window to shut them for you. My goodness, I didn't expect to see you in that white nightdress with a sword!' She laughed a little in nervous relief.

'We will be a little more circumspect before intruding on your privacy again, Miss Weeton,' chuckled Mr Braithwaite. 'You could have been Boudicca herself when you were on those stairs brandishing your sword.' He now laughed a rich, ageless laugh. 'Doctor Hawarden will hear of this young lady!'

I could still hear them laughing over the night's exploits on their way home. At first I felt nothing but relief and amusement. It was not until I had locked everything securely, and had gone upstairs again that I reeled at the thought of what could have happened. What if I had struck Mrs Braithwaite with the sword in my terror? What if they were not my well-intentioned neighbours, but were in fact burglars – or worse? What crimes could they not have committed without so much as a lock or bolt to contend with? I would never be so careless again!

But the Braithwaites were to see me again in my white nightdress and with my dark hair all awry in the moonlight.

*

People have commented to me that they would not like to live alone so close to the churchyard, but I don't feel any closer to the ghosts for all that. I have looked at the gravestones at all hours of the night when I have been unable to sleep. I have stared at their grey shapes, but they have not turned into men dressed in cowls, or ravens or monsters of any sort – they have remained but gravestones. My brother and I as children were quite prepared to wander through the house at night without a candle to find some item or other we wanted. I am not superstitious. What a miserable time I would have endured alone in my empty house if I too easily granted a supernatural agency to explain all my petty frights and starts. But that is not to say I am entirely free from such fears. One night I was almost completely unnerved at the prospect of climbing the stairs to go to my bed – because of a sound I dreaded – a sound I only heard at night. *Sounds* can do me no harm I reasoned, and comforted myself with the thought that there would be few in my situation as little afraid as I usually was. But my blood turned as cold as an icy stream when I heard it again. Someone was breathing rather hard as if asleep in the room next to mine – my mother's old bedroom. I crept as quietly as I could and listened outside the closed door trembling in the blue silvery darkness. The breathing was quite audible – rhythmic – even peaceful. The church clock began to strike eleven. I ran in blind terror down the stairs, clawed the bolts on the door open and fled from the house. I had no candle and nothing on my feet. I can only imagine what a sight I must have made standing there in the night outside the Braithwaites. I hesitated, about to knock. 'They are probably in bed,' I thought, 'and what explanation can I possibly give of myself?' Just then, the bolt on the other side of the door was slid home into its hasp. Mr Braithwaite was on the point of retiring for the night! Fear of being left alone overcame my inhibition and I rapped loudly on the door. Silence. Then again the scraping of a heavy bolt and I could see Mr Braithwaite's tall form frowning and peering tentatively into the darkness from behind a candle.

'Oh, Mr Braithwaite,' I said. I was shaking uncontrollably.

'Ellen! It's you,' he said, opening the door wider. 'Whatever is the matter? You quite startled me.'

'I am very ill,' I answered. 'Would you be kind enough to send up to my Aunt Barton's?'

'Of course, come in. Please come in.'

As soon as I heard his voice I revived. The fire in their parlour was almost out and was starting to smoke, but it rallied with the cool air when the door was opened and with Mrs Braithwaite's help it was soon a congenial blaze. She brought me a warm rug and urged me to drink a small glass of brandy that Mr Braithwaite had found for me. He offered to go to my aunt's himself, but my fears now seemed terribly childish. Rather than disturb my aunt's entire household at such an hour it was decided that Mrs Braithwaite would spend the night with me. But by the time they walked home with me, I was perfectly calm and was quite capable of returning to my bed alone. I'm sure it was only want of company out of school hours that had so unsettled me.

I still hear the sound of breathing most nights. I have got up and gone into the room, turned down the quilt and looked behind the curtains but to no avail. I have found nothing. I had almost concluded the brood of owls that lived in the church tower made the sound until I learned from Mr Braithwaite that they had recently deserted the neighbourhood. It must be a mere fancy – but it was a strong one! It was to become another turning point in my solitary life, for I decided it would be folly to live in a constant state of fear because of a noise – because of what *might* happen to me. I continue to rise in the morning uninjured and refreshed in body and sound in mind. I have even entertained myself with the sounds when unable to sleep by counting their quickness or slowness while holding my own breath at the time. Perhaps I have a defect in my hearing and the sounds can be accounted for in a physical way. But I have the better of it now and I am no longer afraid.

★

At length the time when my brother would be free from his clerkship drew closer. The thought that we would soon be living together again encouraged me in my weary routine in the schoolroom, and the deprivations I suffered on his account were borne more cheerfully. I was still plagued by the megrims – very often. But aren't most people employed in activities very different from what their inclinations or talents would naturally lead them? When I received a note from Tom, or some trifling gift, or a book he had borrowed for me, I was encouraged to further efforts. I thought I was lucky to have such a brother! I would write as long a letter as I possibly could to him in spite of the barrenness of my life. I also began to write to Miss Chorley of Liverpool. She was so worldly and refined I was sometimes puzzled by her interest in me, but she proved to be a faithful correspondent. I was so pleased with my 'epistolary conversations', as I dubbed them, that I painstakingly made copies of every letter that I wrote and kept them in a large quarto book. They will one day, no doubt, sit on someone's musty shelf and await destruction from the dusty finger of time. I also had my flageolet. It was my one act of selfishness during all that time. I bought the little flute and a book of simple instructions for a few shillings. For a long while I was restricted to a few psalm tunes I knew from church on a Sunday and played them very badly because I was completely baffled by sharps and flats and played all the notes natural. But I loved it and in the quiet of the evenings its sounds filled the house with a contented longing.

As winter tightened its grip I daily expected to see or at least to hear from Tom. Trees bent to a knife-edged cold, puddles in cart-ruts froze and ice underfoot shattered into shards as hard as broken pottery. Villagers spoke with white puffs of winter breath, but I remained buoyant with expectation. And then at last, there came a letter from Tom! He was in London! He had gone to London confident of finding employment without bothering to see me first. I thrummed with anger and hurt.

It was to be another three months before I saw Tom. The snowdrops had bloomed and the young yellow-brown foliage of the oaks was nascent when he suddenly arrived without any warning. I came home from school to find him staring sightlessly into a smouldering coal fire, his eyes shining as if from raillery and his thin lips a drowned blue. There was an extraordinary pallor about his mouth and his brow – knotted in either pain or anger, I wasn't sure which – was greasy with sweat as if from exertion. His trousers were torn and his wet coat, which he had not taken off, steamed from the heat of the fire. I quailed before his squalid appearance and his dark, threatening broodiness, but he stood up when I came in and embraced me weakly.

'Ellen, I have come home.'

'I am glad, Tom. I am glad. I will not be so lonely. But what's happened to you? Are you ill?'

'What's happened to me? Well, Ellen, let me tell you what's happened to me,' he said bitterly. He threw himself heavily, almost violently, onto the sofa and his face twisted with insincere amusement. 'I have had a most wonderful time. I have jostled with the very sweepings of the great city itself for a place in hell. I have been liberally dosed with opium and am presently in need of more. Jackson would give me nothing. I have also enjoyed the most genteel of English pastimes in my forlorn search for a profession. Let me tell you about the bull baiting. I lost all my money. The wretched animal was supposed to be ferocious and I had managed to get a seat quite near the stake. They waved red flags at it, threw pepper up its nose, twisted its tail. They even poked viciously at it with iron pikes until it bled, but the brute refused to defend itself against the dogs. It was soon pinned and fell to its knees bellowing. I swear to God, Ellen, tears as large as peas ran from its eyes and down its nose. And the smell, the filth!'

'Oh Tom, Tom,' I bleated.

'Oh Tom, Tom,' he mimicked in a bitter falsetto voice. 'Don't go Tom, Tom-ing me, Ellen. Mind you, I don't expect much else from you really except complaints and whingeing about your noble sacrifice and how lonely you are and how hard you have to work! God! How I looked forward to those long cheerful letters of yours!'

I was stunned, and could do nothing but stand there dumfounded. He must have taken my empty silence for calm, which further enraged him. He stood up abruptly and paced in nervous anger about the room like something caged. He looked ill.

'How can you complain about being lonely all the time when there are people all around you?' he demanded. 'What's wrong with aunt and uncle? The Braithwaites are close enough, aren't they? Or aren't they good enough for you? You know, unless someone is a lord or a visiting professor of mathematics they're not good enough for you, are they? I bet no pimply hobbledehoy has had his hands over you, eh? How old are you, Ellen? Twenty-five, isn't it?'

He was vicious and unfair and crude in his accusations, but I managed to say, 'Tom, you're not yourself. Don't talk like that. Why are you being so cruel?'

'I have been lonely too, you know. But the great city has much entertainment to offer.'

'Tom, I don't want to know. I don't want to hear any more. You're not yourself.'

Suddenly, he shut his eyes. The corners of his mouth drew down tightly and he wept noiselessly, drawing his hands up in an attempt to hide his face. I put my arms around him and tried to comfort him.

'Tom, you need sleep. I'll help you to bed. I am glad you are home.'

His weakness and defeat made me strong and he offered no resistance as I helped him up the stairs and led him to the room, which had been his as a child. I got some warm water and put it into a basin and fetched a towel and some dry linen for the bed. He sat on a chair; his face was sallow and flecked with moisture, but he was calm again.

'I'm sorry, Ellen. I'm sorry. Forgive me.' He stifled a sob or a cough before he could continue. 'I have broken God's law, true enough, but thankfully not man's law. I'm safe.'

He grimaced from the bite of shame and looked at me directly for the first time. There was something haunted and frightened in his eyes. What had he seen?

'Go to bed, Tom. You must rest,' I said, closing the door gently.

'Ellen,' he called quietly.

'Yes, Tom.'

'Ellen, I have no money.'

★

There followed three weeks of perfect happiness for me. At first Tom was full of remorse but soon his leaden self-disgust was lightened. His lined face relaxed and was smoothed, his grey-blue eyes cleared and his dark good looks returned – not another word was spoken about London. He was assiduous in his efforts to be cheerful and to please. Tom, I believed then, was tender hearted, only a little weak in the company of those who would prey upon him. I mended his linen and bought for him pocket-handkerchiefs, neck-handkerchiefs, stockings and cambric for ruffles.

He settled in Wigan, but visited me every Saturday returning that night or the following one. He often talked of the time when I could live with him and he spoke of taking a house in Wigan for that purpose. It was also in Wigan that he became acquainted with Jane Scott, the daughter of a prosperous factory owner, and they were married within two months of their first meeting. They married in secret without the knowledge of her friends or with the approval of her parents. My brother had no house where they might live, so I offered them mine. They came on the day they were married with no prospect of living anywhere else for the coming months. Mrs Weeton! The name seemed odd to my ear and in truth there was a certain vague oddity about her. Not in her appearance, for she had the attractiveness of youth, although she was large boned and her features had a slight coarseness – she would be prone to fatness in the years to come. No one though could deny the beauty of her hair, which, when sun-rinsed, was the colour of melted honey. She spoke in a thin, papery voice and rarely to me, even when Tom was away. She did no household work, either because she was too indolent or too slow or was simply unused to it. I made no complaints. My brother now had responsibilities and again he needed my help.

They had been with me for about a month when I arrived home from school one afternoon to see Tom talking to a man holding a horse. I saw Mrs Weeton's face at a window with a look of passive anxiety. The man was dismissed but he left on foot leaving the horse with Tom who glanced up at me briefly as I approached but said nothing. He was intent on a letter he held. Breaking the wafer, he read it right through before speaking.

'It's from Jane's mother,' he said in a slightly unsettled voice. 'She says she has been persuaded to recognise her daughter in spite of what she calls such an imprudent match and she wants us to come to her as soon as possible on the horse.'

It was soon concluded best to accept the invitation. They left that same afternoon, were reconciled, and I was once more a solitary thing. Tom continued to come most Saturdays, ostensibly to see me, but it was really in the hope of drumming up a little business for himself in Up Holland. He talked of little else except his need for money. I thought of little else except leaving the schoolroom and joining his household.

★

I saw no more of Mrs Weeton until one overcast Saturday when she and Tom arrived in a gig that rattled and jingled in the still humid air. She *is* Mrs Weeton now. It suits her. I will never call her Jane. Although it was mid-afternoon the light was weak and unsavoury. Distances were blurred into bleached shades of indistinct grey. The street was lifeless, the houses dull and heavy. Up Holland. Poor drab Up Holland. And there was Mrs Weeton unbuttoning her gloves of good kid. Her dress was coloured an intense marine-blue and it was as smooth and as delicately patterned as the porcelain teacups I put on the table. Her extraordinary hair was parted down the centre, curved and ended in ringlets near her chin giving the china whiteness of her face a heart shape. There was a constrained silence about her that was not eased by Tom's few desultory remarks, nor by the rich aroma of my freshly baked plum cake.

'How is the school going, Ellen?' he asked without any real interest.

'I have fourteen students, but I have a werreting time of it, Tom. I earn little from it.'

He grimaced. Gave a short laugh, a brief, 'humph'. Local words now irritated him and I immediately regretted my blunder. Silence again. He seemed to be choosing his words carefully, perhaps for that reason when he did speak it was with such direct bluntness.

'Must you continue with the school, Ellen? You do own your own house and there must be some interest accruing annually.'

'Tom, this is Up Holland. I long for something more! I thought, I have always thought, that I might live with you.'

There was a quick glance exchanged between them.

'We have concluded, Ellen, that if you are to live with us you must pay thirty guineas a year for board.'

I studied my cup – my mother's from Lancaster – with its scalloped edge and its eggshell fineness. I couldn't think for a minute. Thirty guineas! It was my entire income exactly. How could he know that? Had he been speaking with Aunt Barton? What would I do for clothes? I would have to ask Tom if I wanted so much as a packet of pins. They did not want me with them.

'The house could be rented or sold and some of the furniture could be taken to Leigh,' Tom said flatly.

'To Leigh?' I asked in confused surprise.

Mrs Weeton now spoke for the first time. Her soft, perfectly controlled voice irritated me. 'Tom has secured the bulk of a legal practice in Leigh. He is now Mr Thomas Weeton, Esquire, of Avenue Place.'

'The fact is, Ellen,' continued Tom as if his wife had not spoken, 'your stubborn determination to persist in your degrading position as a teacher is becoming something of an embarrassment to the Scotts – and to me. God knows it's hard enough to make my way without having my miserable past continually on display here in Up Holland.'

I wanted to crush the cup in my hands and watch the spreading stain of my scalding hot anger seep across the white cloth. I wanted to fling the pieces at his head.

'I am perfectly willing to leave the school, Tom,' I gasped. 'Nothing would please me more. But I must be able to live by some means!' My voice was unsteady, almost husky with the emotion I felt. I was struggling to breathe, struggling to control my terrible anger.

'Of course it's not your fault – your father's misfortune, I believe. But to descend to the level of selling oneself in a classroom to make one's living.' This from Mrs Weeton – her voice was clipped and precise, almost sibilant.

'Would you have me winding bobbins for a shilling a week?' I said, angry to the point of ugliness. 'You're unfair! What choice do I have? I think I could have been something better than I am. Something might have been done. I think I had it in me, or might have had. It still wells up inside me sometimes, but what can I do? Would you like me to study divinity? Medicine? I *could* perhaps do these things, but who would employ a female physician? Who would listen to a female divine – except to ridicule? I could almost laugh at the idea myself!'

'No dear Ellen,' said Tom scathingly, 'we thought perhaps you might manage a small farm with a few cows.'

Mrs Weeton smiled.

I felt vain and foolish and was close to tears. 'I will go to Leigh,' I acquiesced. When all is closed off, a small opening can be a great freedom. I could sew, I thought, for my clothes. If Tom has taken a house, thirty guineas would pay for the rent and taxes. I would be with Tom. I would no longer be lonely.

Tom seemed taken aback. Again a knowing glance passed between them. Tom coloured slightly, but said steadily enough, 'Ellen, Mrs Scott and ourselves have concluded it would be better if you didn't live with us at all. Such a kind of family is always unpleasant and there would only be dissension at every turn.'

Must I live, as long as I do live, I thought, here in this place – without any hope of change? Each day much like another – each bringing its crowded empty routine – stretching out endlessly into the future. How could I face it? A life of insignificance is surely worse than death! I didn't know at the time that it had already been agreed amongst them all that Mrs Weeton's younger sister would live with Tom and his wife at Leigh.

★

Saturday afternoon. I gaze from my window at the ceremony of sadness that is Up Holland. Rain is letting down swirling veils of pearl-grey. It shrouds the slate tiles of roofs in white smoking air. The trees drip and stone walls are stained with moss. Mr Braithwaite hurries across the sodden churchyard sheltering under an umbrella. A man cloaked and hooded in an oilskin curses as he drives three geese with a stick; they crane their necks low and hiss indignantly. He passes a drayman in a leather apron straining his hairy arms to load barrels in the wet while his horse steams and stamps. It is the most ordinary scene in the world. Each player in the little drama has been drawn by a purpose clear to him and all have been brought together in the frame of my window by the workings of blind circumstance. I feel my separateness – my littleness. The long, listless years since Tom's removal to Leigh have settled into a painless but joyless pattern. I have few vexations, but little affection from others. Tom now has children of his own. I have no one. Adam, even in the Garden of Eden, was discontented and wanted a creature like me for company. If I could meet with a man I could esteem and love, I would marry him tomorrow, but there is no one. There is no mate for me in Up Holland.

The bulk of my furniture has been sold and my house whitewashed. I have arranged to let it on the 12th of May to a Mr Winstanley, a small middle-aged, slightly dapper man. His wife and children are above the ordinary and they are unlikely to misuse the house. He is a watchmaker and will, hopefully, be on time with my rent! I will give up my school before then. Many of the children have whooping cough. Some are pitted and scarred from smallpox. I will stay with the Chorleys in Liverpool and look for lodgings. Doctor Hawarden has written to his niece, Ann, who is also expecting me. My great hope is to be a governess with a genteel family, but I fear my lack of accomplishments will be a handicap. I have no piano or singing, no French, and no fine manners. On the subject of my departure my Aunt Barton remains silent. The Scotts, who have been at least civil to me over the last twelve months, have also set themselves against it. Perhaps they fear that Mr Tom Weeton's sister may be more publicly known if I leave. As it is, I am buried alive in Up Holland – unknown and forgotten. Tom, though, has promised to place an advertisement for a situation in the papers for me.

In a month I leave Up Holland – scene of my childhood and home of my mother's grave – for Liverpool! I must leave or I will go mad. Desperation gnaws at the soul of this place. It is in the rheumy eyes of the weavers hunched in conspiratorial groups at street corners on their day of rest. It moves and scratches like rats' feet vitiating the mind. It contaminates and spoils. There have been two suicides. One, an old man of seventy, hanged himself in his orchard. Two small boys found him in the clear light of the following morning. He had had a little property, which had fallen into bad hands. He had allowed it to oppress him and was thought to be the reason for his dreadful escape. The other was an old woman crippled with arthritic cramp. She was found suspended from the tester at the foot of her bed by a thin red cord. They say she could not have done it herself, and are suspicious of her husband – a much younger man – but no proof can be brought. She was buried last Thursday. Scandalous rumour, illegitimate births – ignorance is not bliss in Up Holland. And all the while the Reverend T Meyrick, the incumbent of Up Holland Church, dutifully obeys the injunction to 'increase and multiply' – with his servant – and Miss Dannett continues to visit Jackson.

2

Dale Street, Liverpool
14th May 1808

He looked as tough as a coalminer. And below his dark blue cap with its insignia of gold, which declared his occupation as bargeman, his hard lined face was so brown it could have been stewed to make it keep.

'You should be comfortable enough there, Miss,' he said while gripping an evil-smelling clay pipe between discoloured teeth. 'It's a lot slower than the coach, but cheaper and on a day like this it's a lot more pleasant.'

'Thank you,' I said, trying not to show too obviously my excited nervousness. I settled myself on a cushion at the stern, placed my copy of *Gil Blas* on my lap for the sake of appearance and opened my green umbrella as a parasol against the bright warm day. I was dressed in sober grey and white bonnet and was only going to Liverpool but I felt my entire life up until that moment had been nothing but preparation for what was ahead. Consider what state a person's brain must be in, who for twenty years has been imprisoned in a poor village school and has just been set free! I was almost drunk from gulping in huge draughts of liberty from the morning air and would rather have been deprived of food than of such a beverage. Like Lesage's hero leaving for Salamanca on his mule I felt as if the whole world was spread before my feet waiting to be explored. I was setting out! I was leaving Up Holland! I smiled – a long quiet smile just for myself.

I began to study some of the boat's company. There were six or seven at the front end, who were travelling as a group;

eight others were all we took in. Places were found, bags were stowed, and farewells were waved. A short, bustling woman with the most amazing bumps and lumps on her face sat beside me. Without a word or glance in my direction she produced wool and needles and started knitting a stocking in stony silence. A clergyman came on board. He wore a quizzing glass, which at first I thought was simply an imaginative addition to his face, but soon concluded it was an attempt to soften the keenness in his eyes – he would be exacting of his tithe. There was a cry from a diminutive scarlet-coated boy who jockeyed the huge towing horse, the rope drew taut and with a creak the boat began to move passively along the canal. As if this were a signal, the passengers seemed to relax, and there were nods and smiles and exchanges of pleasantries. The cook began her operations in the cabin at about ten o'clock and fried bacon, eggs and mutton chops. Another signal! People stooped over baskets and rummaged in them for a veal pasty or a bottle of stout or pigeon pie with which to further the ambience of the morning. Most people in the tail of the boat seemed to think that eating and drinking was the chief amusement of travelling, but obviously not those in the upper end. They appeared almost offended by such vulgarity and it was early afternoon before they brought forth their dainty pieces of chicken, ham or game, pots of shrimps and little tarts, as if to prove to the rest that they did eat sometimes. I was beginning to think that the various odours of tobacco, spirits and hot meat must have been quite enough for their subsistence.

Below Heaton's Bridge a rough-faced journeyman saddler, I suppose from what he said, produced a cracked flute. On impulse, I reached into my carpetbag and took out my flageolet. Like street-fiddlers we were soon the centre of attention in the stern of the boat and – would you suppose it? – he and I attempted several duets! He had red hog-like bristles on his chin and wild copper hair turning to flame. How some in my acquaintance would have reacted if they saw such a contrasting pair piping and playing together! Ellen Weeton who doesn't dance; Ellen Weeton who dislikes cards and who was such a frump at the Braithwaites' little farewell party was now a common busker with a fiery flute player in a canal boat! 'Now, do you know this one, girlie?' he would ask, his florid face beaming. He would play a few notes, stop, and look expectantly at me. The man behaved civilly as far as it lay in his power, but his exterior betrayed him cruelly – he was as ugly as a gargoyle.

But our little concert came to an abrupt end when a girl, distressed and in tears, came aboard when the bargeman was negotiating a lock. She put her bag between her feet, nursed her knees and cried inconsolably. A gentleman – that is, a man with powdered hair, but in a rather worn coat and dusty shoes – did his best to cheer her up and eventually succeeded in raising one or two weak smiles. He asked her questions, which she, from want of experience did not evade. She had come from Richmond in Yorkshire; had been at Lancaster and Wigan; and was going to Liverpool. With a faintly desperate expression on her face, she said the family she was going to was not expecting her and that she had no idea where to find them. The gentleman who, I began to sense, may well have been little more than a cheapjack, offered to take her there, and I suppose he did – they left together. I think more of the girl now than I did when she was on the boat and feel guilty that I had not accompanied her myself. His idle appetite, his pouting sensuous mouth and soft effeminate hands disturb me still. The light was failing and a dense fog was starting to fall when they left the boat. It was not right that she, an innocent simple girl of little more than seventeen, should leave with a stranger in a strange city. I was trying to catch another glimpse of them amongst the blackened brick of Liverpool when I heard my name being called and saw the rather imperious form of a woman who I assumed was Edith Chorley come to meet me. She stood in the strangely-coloured light swathed in a sable cloak and hood, which revealed little more than a patrician nose.

Giving me a tentative hug and a terse greeting, she said, 'It's best we hurry, Ellen, before this fog becomes too unpleasant. It's not far.'

A step behind her with my bag and portmanteau, I tried to pick my way carefully through the muck and street litter. I could taste the fog in the warm, damp air – acrid, gritty. My eyes began to water and my throat prickled. Lights glowed luridly in the dusky yellow and pedestrians in black looked like lost souls wandering aimlessly for eternity in some lost twilight world.

'It's a wonder people don't become lost just crossing the street,' I said in an attempt at humour. The hem of my dress was already wet and grubby. Miss Chorley made no answer.

*

We were soon at a small, decent house and were ushered into a room, which served as both parlour and dining room. It was comfortably furnished but without any attempt at adornment. The table was laid for a meal. The wavering light of the candles was harsh on my now tired eyes and I could feel the beginning of a headache.

'I cannot tell you how grateful I am for your kind invitation,' I said taking Mrs Chorley's hand and bowing slightly to Mr Chorley who remained seated at the table. 'I hope one day I will be able to make some return.'

'Nay,' said Mr Chorley, stroking his smoothly shaven jaw. 'If you wish it you can stay until the end of the winter.'

Mrs Chorley, dressed in a serviceable grey with her hair tied up in a coif, said restrainedly, 'It will be nice for Edith to have a companion. You mustn't think of leaving before next spring.'

'Or, if Edith has occasion to leave home,' Mr Chorley chuckled with a mock-sly look, 'you can nurse us in our encroaching old age.' His features were remarkably plain showing no strength of understanding and his manner was blunt, but he seemed to be good tempered and honest-hearted enough. He drew deeply and noisily from his pewter mug of ale as if for strength to face the next battle of life.

'Oh, father, really!' said Edith with annoyance.

'If I could stay a week or two at most until I can find some modest lodgings of my own I will be most grateful,' I said, sensing a building tension in the room but unable to locate its source.

The conversation stumbled and fell into an uncomfortable silence. It revived when Mrs Chorley brought in a simple supper.

'I thought you were to buy some oysters for supper, Mr Chorley?' she asked accusingly as she ladled some eel soup to her pursed lips.

'And so I would have, but there were none in the market except those great dirty things that I would not have for any price,' he retorted defensively.

'Why, no, I suppose not,' said Mrs Chorley.

'Do you pay more for large oysters than for small ones?' I asked, oysters being practically unknown in Up Holland.

The question went unanswered, but I could not have been looked at with a greater degree of indignation from Miss Chorley. How I had offended her I still have no idea.

My spirits sank. Little else was said. Pleading tiredness and a headache from the day's travel, I said goodnight to them as soon as I thought it polite to do so.

My room that night was as confined and airless as a cabin below the decks of a ship. And although it was so hot, the small soot-stained dormer window was fastened down and stuffed with sand bags. A chimney board prevented any circulation of air by that means. I was so shut in that I thought I would perspire myself into a fever. But at last, exhausted, I fell into a fitful sleep of confused dreams. I remembered little of them in the morning, but I was left with the sensation of being in a strange light, as if I were under the sea. My nightdress was damp with sweat and I felt drowsy and weak. I washed my face at a small washstand, dressed and made my way downstairs in the sickly darkness to the tiny back parlour. They keep no servant so I riddled the grate, threw some coal in and placed the large copper kettle on the black top of the stove. 'So these are the Chorleys of Liverpool,' I said quietly to myself while gently biting my lip.

★

I will not forget my first day in Liverpool with Miss Chorley. In her wake I was introduced to what she called refined society. At 10 Princes Street, I was confronted with delicate Staffordshire cups of camomile tea, thin slices of shortbread and light syrup dumplings in Miss Winkley's drawing room. I was so afraid that I might show some awkwardness in my expressions or manner that I could hardly breathe let alone eat. I was sure I would forget some little ceremony, or transgress some rule of etiquette and embarrass Miss Chorley. But I liked Ann Winkley. She is Doctor Hawarden's niece and is amiable and welcoming. Her large blue eyes were flecked with the grey of clouds and she spoke to the former mistress of an obscure day school with the familiarity of an equal.

'Tell me, Ellen, what have you seen? What do you think of Liverpool? We must take you to the theatre – we must take you everywhere!' she pronounced with authority.

I soon relaxed in her presence and was not silenced until Miss Chorley lifted an expressive eyebrow – no doubt in surprise at some petty impropriety I had committed.

And I liked Ann Winkley's drawing room. Lace curtains moved at the clean windows and there was a fresh fragrance of starch, soap and tansy in the room. Violets in a bowl of Venetian glass exaggerated the whiteness of the snowy damask cloth.

That afternoon, we visited Bullock's Museum. I cannot describe everything I saw, but there were several things which particularly struck me. There were two pictures in sand – one of a tiger, with a jungle behind it; the other was of an eagle darting at a hare. The trees, talons, eyes and every part were composed of nothing but different coloured sands. I was also drawn to a wax figure of Voltaire, which was very small – perhaps only six inches – but every detail of the dying philosopher, the wan, grey face in the agonies of death; the hollow eyes and toothless gums; were all faithfully depicted. Entering another room, birds, beasts and fish were all stuffed in a life-like manner. A huge rhinoceros as large as life stood with its head down, and surviving his charge, you immediately faced a springing panther! How little of the world I have seen!

★

And I did go to the theatre. We entered a vestibule resplendent with gilt-edged mirrors, oak staircases and scarlet carpet to a very comfortable seat in the gallery. There was a strong odour of liquorice cordial and pomade, which combined smelt like damp straw. A haze of yellow light haloed the auditorium above the confused sounds of the expectant audience. I can feel some of the excitement rising again as I write this. Mrs Siddons played Lady Macbeth. When she emerged robed in a voluminous dress of rich velvety green, she appeared rather small – until she spoke. Then the audience was wonder struck. In the sleepwalking scene, she *was* Lady Macbeth – not just in appearance, but also in her very being – or Lady Macbeth had become her. It was a transformation as real and material as any in nature. *I tell you yet again, Banquo's buried. He cannot come out on's grave.* The witches had seemed such a merry lot; the ghost quite substantial – but so completely did she concentrate on her role that she seemed possessed by it and was oblivious to all else around her. She was the sole object in that immense space as she felt the pain of a meaningless world. It was as if she spoke directly to me alone. *The Thane of Fife had a wife. Where is she now?* I hardly heard the applause of the audience and ignored Miss Chorley's dismal complaints about smuts falling on her dress during our dark drive home. My mind was full of the mysterious power of the theatre, where the past could be made present, and the present made to vibrate with emotions centuries old. Life was an endless process of transformation. My future lies ahead of me trembling with possibilities.

20th June 1808

More than a month has gone by, and I have neglected this journal. It is an odd household I have come to. Both parents treat their daughter with a marked diffidence and defer to her taste and opinion on all matters. Clearly the meagre, dry-featured Miss Chorley is to the household what Bonaparte is to Europe! Perhaps I have grown too rustic altogether in Up Holland, but she makes me feel my inferiority of birth, fortune and talents most painfully. She is so continually severe that I am sure she would rather die than be found guilty of the vulgar perpetration of so much as a laugh in the street.

The continual darkness of the place is depressing. The windows remain shut against the burning yellow fogs and soot. I am hemmed in, trapped, almost smothered in their petty domestic world. Miss Chorley went out this morning. I was not invited to go with her, as she used to do when I was in favour. I was not sorry – I should have been in tears again as there is no pleasing her. I told Mrs Chorley I, too, was going for a walk. And I did so – alone. The noise, no, it was the *movement* in the streets that cheered me a little. A costermonger pushed his handcart and called attention to his vegetables by crying out in a hoarse rhythmic wail. An expensive phaeton clattered past full of self-importance with two footmen in bright yellow livery standing solemnly on the footplate and the driver smacking his whip. I had to dodge a man in a wine-coloured waistcoat pacing the cobbles in patent leather shoes. His pouchy eyes were fixed on the stone facade of a bank building and his small expressive hands were clasped in anxious supplication to Mammon. And it was the act of walking itself. The freedom, which allows the pedestrian, even in the precisely mapped and solidly defined streets of Liverpool, to walk down those yet unexplored paths scratched so lightly and freely across the surface of the mind. But my little pleasure in going out was short-lived. The smell of damp yellow smoke soon became too unpleasant. It is very likely I will sit for the rest of the day without stirring, except to move my chair, or fetch *Gil Blas* from my room. I will scarce speak a dozen sentences before supper.

So why write here at all?

For the reason that my journal is a thread on which my empty life hangs. It is a distraction from gloomy, debilitating thoughts. It makes me believe that although so little happens to me, my life does have a shape and may yet have a purpose – that I still have a mind even if it is asleep. It is an act of hope. Taking it up, I sniff its Morocco binding and its creamy pages with an animal pleasure. It smells of cleanliness, like beeswax, or mountain air, or pine shavings and turpentine.

23rd June 1808

I fancy she is tired of me. Perhaps she had formed too high an opinion of me, as I did of her, and now that she finds me frail and mortal she cannot help venting the bitterness of her disappointment. I have been quietly making inquiries about lodgings at a small, white, shabby-looking house close to the shore just below Kirkdale. It is called Mile-End House and is almost opposite to the Black Rock. It is quite isolated. A man, his wife and a little boy of about six years old live at the house. Miss Chorley, no doubt, would consider it fit only for crossing sweepers and footpads. But I could afford the eight guineas a year and I think I would like it better than being buried in the town. If I knew what to say to Mr and Mrs Chorley, I would be gone. Blame must rest somewhere and I no more want to throw it at them than to take it to myself. That my health suffers from lack of air I can say – so that will have to do.

25th June 1808

Sunday.

'We can make a start, at least, and give it to the mantua maker to finish,' said Miss Chorley, unrolling some taffeta, 'but I am determined you will have something fit to wear to Christ Church *next* Sunday.'

'Well then Christ's Church is not what it was formerly,' I said peevishly.

Ignoring my comment, perhaps she failed to understand it, she produced from the assortment of reels and packets of pins scattered about on the table a little box and opening the lid showed me nestled in the blue felt a pair of highly polished scissors, completely finished, but no more than three quarters of an inch long. For some vaguely felt reason I rebelled at the exquisitely-wrought curiosity.

'Is it chiefly to the rich that the gospel is now preached?' I continued querulously. The scissors floated in the air in front of me. I tried to ignore them. 'There was a less fashionable time when it was otherwise,' I offered, my pride stung. I was surprised at the depths of my anger. It was those little scissors! I could feel my throat constricting and my heart beating in protest against them.

She lifted her hawkish nose and met my gaze steadily, breaking it when she snapped shut the little box. 'The rich and poor do not have to *meet* together. The poor go to pray – who knows where? – and any scrubby fellow may instruct *them*,' she said brusquely.

I stood up – too quickly. 'Well I am going to set off to see if St Catharine will let me pray in her house,' I said, leaving her there, impotent, her mouth agape and still holding the box with the ridiculous little scissors in her hand.

But pleasure met me along the way.

Sitting on a bench in Temple Square trying to regain my composure – I was watching a sparrow hopping amongst some litter of orange peels – I heard my name.

'Ellen, how are you?'

Ann Winkley stood before me with a young gentleman in a frock coat and carrying a silver-topped cane.

'We are just going to Eastham,' said Ann pleasantly with

a fresh smile, 'can you come with us? It's such a wonderful day. Look at the sky,' she said, lifting her blue eyes to gaze at the larger blue. 'Look at the clouds. Poets must love clouds like that.'

'Please, come if you can,' said the young man, 'we are to meet my sister there. And we are well supplied to have a picnic,' he added, smiling affably and raising a basket before me.

I went, and enjoyed the afternoon. After all, I reasoned, *any*body may go in a packet boat. Mr Lucifer has not found it worth his while to tyrannise there in the appearance of fashion. He probably gains more converts by coming in the guise of a bottle of wine with the colours of a warm autumn light trapped in its depths, or in the laughter from the strong throats of young men or in the music from a well tuned fiddle.

1st July 1808

I am shut up in a box seven feet by nine, with a bed, a plain chest of drawers, two straight-backed chairs and a washstand and jug. I have put a tea tray over the washstand to serve as a desk. Here I sit, a lonely recluse, from six in the evening until eleven, or sometimes twelve, before I get into bed.

I had written no more than this when Edith Chorley entered my room after a peremptory rap on the door. She had rarely sought the intimacy of its scant comfort and confined space – nor did I wish for such condescension. I started like a guilty thing. Her small dark eyes fell immediately on my open journal.

'What are you writing?' she asked, her voice quavering with barely suppressed emotion.

I hesitated, loath to tell the truth and wary of telling a lie. Had she been into my room before without my knowing and

read what I had so carelessly left in view? Or, did she only suspect I had been writing about her? She was well aware, I dare say, she had given me good reason.

'Is it a letter?'

'No.'

'A journal?'

'No. Well, not really.'

Her hungry little mouth tightened and became thin-lipped. Anger surged up into her eyes.

'What is it then?' Her voice was becoming thin and unpleasant. 'I am determined to know,' she added petulantly.

She was trying to read it as I held the book half open. Shutting it I tried not to give way to my bitter resentment.

'I don't see,' I replied, 'what right you have to insist upon seeing anything I write. I would never ask you such a question, or pry into your personal affairs.'

'I am determined to know by some means or other,' she said, 'or you will not write another line.'

'Very well,' I said, wiping my rather tattered quill clean and screwing the top onto my inkwell. 'If I cannot write now, I will take some other opportunity.'

'Let me see it, or read me a line or two – go on, it will be something perverse and cruel about me I'm sure.'

'What makes you think that?' I asked, looking steadily at her.

'Read me some then!' she almost screamed, 'and convince me that it is not.'

'Perhaps you have already seen it,' I rejoined, standing to face her, 'and if so, there is no need for me to read it.'

'You will let me read it, or tell me about it, or I will not leave this room,' she said at the point of tears and sat heavily on the edge of the narrow bed.

I was becoming calmer. 'I will do neither,' I dryly replied. 'I am not a machine to be moved by your force, or a child to be commanded,' I asserted with steel in my voice. 'Will you please leave my room?'

'*Your* room,' she sneered, her lip curling and her cheeks reddening. 'I'll see what you have written first.'

She lunged towards the book and we both struggled for possession of it. I was the stronger and the book suddenly came away from her grasp and glanced off my face, a corner of it cutting my cheek just below the eye as if by a piece of jagged ice or broken porcelain. Miss Chorley stood in stupid amazement gabbling frightened apologies. I touched my cheek with the tip of a finger. I was not greatly hurt and turned to the washbasin.

★

I was dressed and ready to leave by breakfast time. I could stay no longer. I would take my chances amongst strangers at Beacon's Gutter. Noisily and ostentatiously I placed my belongings in the small entrance hall, banging my portmanteau against the door for effect, and then turned to face the rigours of the parlour. I had decided on being perfectly civil to Mr and Mrs Chorley – I had no quarrel with them – but I made no effort to conceal the puce of my cheekbone or the small zigzag of red at its centre.

'Good morning,' I said brightly, superciliously. My confidence was stirred with the anticipation of escape.

Miss Chorley stared mulishly at nothing and refused even a curt nod. She simply raised her chin in a magisterial gesture worthy of Mrs Siddons.

'Please call to see us, Ellen,' said Mrs Chorley earnestly, her voice quavering a little.

Her husband cracked his knuckles nervously. 'I am sorry that...' he began kindly but he trailed off into an embarrassed silence.

25th August 1808
I am the new lodger of Mile-End House, Beacon's Gutter. As I write about the day that has passed, nothing disturbs the intense silence of the house. I breathe in the cool, night breeze from the open window and settle to my task.

★

Early morning. So early that the sandy, serpentine path, which ribbons down to the shore, is still dew-damp in the still air. I have crushed a snail underfoot and crouching down I can see thin silver slime-trails leading from moist ferns and across the sand of the path. I find them strangely disturbing – feel the soft crimp of unexpected desire – something that will linger – return. A bell-like bark fans out across the morning – and another! Roger, the Smiths' Dalmatian, thinks I am playing a game with him. He rushes at me butting his bony head up under my hand demanding affection. The great lout of a dog is all impatience and hurry and launches himself off amongst the ground ivy and tussocks disturbing a hare. Its fur is stained dark with the wetness of the early morning. It hesitates, quivering, and then flees in bewildered terror full pelt swerving and zigzagging to disappear in gorse bushes. Roger gives chase, stops, barks once unconvincingly and then waits for me further down the path. As I approach he draws himself up in a show of dignity, with a whimsical cast of expression – something between an intended frown and an involuntary grin – 'For shame! For shame!' I admonish him laughing and pat his extraordinarily hard head. He would soon tire himself out and retreat unnoticed to his sunny alcove in the broken garden wall near the house.

★

I have been happy here. The days and weeks pass so pleasantly compared to what they used to do. Mile-End House is only about two miles from Castle Street where I walk every Saturday to the vegetable markets and to see Ann Winkley, but it is very retired and can only be reached by paths through the fields. There are no neighbours, except rough farmers more than half a mile away; but we seldom or never see them, except when we go for milk and butter. At low tide I sometimes see people walking on Black Rock, and people on the Cheshire shore are clearly visible when the weather is fine, but no one has disturbed the solitude and isolation of this place. The Smiths sometimes take in lodgers or a genteel family during the bathing season, but there has been no one but myself to watch the ships and brigs coming and going this summer. There was a particularly high tide about a week ago and near a hundred sail embarked on some great venture. Liverpool mustn't be suffering too much from the abolition of the slave trade when I can enjoy such a sight. Tom has not visited me, despite my entreaties, even though his embarrassment about my employment is hopefully at an end. I wish he would come for a day or two – alone – and pretend he was not a married man. Away from his wife, the fresh air and the varying moods of the sea might restore some of his old friendliness towards me.

Betty Smith, the mistress of the house, is a plain, stocky woman of twenty-seven. She is chatty and cheerful and no disagreeable companion. Her voice is rougher than her appearance suggests and I have learned that she is not only capable of chopping the head off a rooster at the worn chopping block, but also of releasing her headless victim to enjoy its antics as it flaps and runs around the yard spurting and splashing blood on the clumps of green nettles. She is a combination of generosity and good-for-nothingness just as the mood takes her. She is frequently in Liverpool with her little boy Henry, and as her husband works there, I am often left alone with Roger as my only companion. Edward Smith is a journeyman tobacconist in his early thirties. The fingers of his right hand and his strong even teeth are noticeably stained with his trade. The house is never entirely free from the stale smell of pipe smoke. He is affable in any company but particularly so in the taprooms of Kirkdale. I hear him in the morning hawking and spitting into the fireplace before he sets off in his large black hat and Hessian boots as raffish as a Toby Philpot jug.

*

A tumble of light floods through pearl-pink cloud and a line of large birds, ice-white, arrows across the sky as I reach the bathing machine. It has long been abandoned and it is partially buried in sand. One of its doors is missing altogether and the other is stuck fast. There is the tangy, pungent smell of old wood and rotting seaweed. I hesitate. I have a sudden irrational fear that someone may be inside – waiting. Roger, of course, is nowhere to be seen – but I am being silly – it is clearly empty. I enjoy the feel of the sand on the coarse floorboards under my bare feet as I take off my dress, leaving on the long flannel chemise I have underneath. It is lightly weighted with little leads sewn into the hem. I walk towards the sea, become conscious of the waves gently slapping the wet beach before falling back with a hushing, hissing sound over the tumbling sand; the sad squeal and scrape of gulls; the distant piping of long-billed shorebirds – the sounds heard here at dawn for hundreds of years. The distant air is now burnished bronze and soft. A black cormorant wings its way urgently across the waves, almost touching the surface. The sea is fresh and clean and sharply cold at first. I gasp for breath and shiver like a horse – then comes the elation of warmth, the taste of salt water. The small fragments of clouds brighten to silver, turning the dimpled skin of the sea into soft hues of blue and neutral grey where it was not sparkling with innumerable points of bright light. I move further from the shore.

The flannel balloons shapelessly around me in the water. I have been tempted to decorate it with seaweed and shells as a pagan offering to Neptune. It makes me as amorphous as an Antipodean jellyfish or squid. I could take it off altogether. If I was sure no one was about I would. I slip away from its wet weight. I am as free as a ghost – drifting, floating – seeing but unseen. My limbs go limp in the peaceful pull and tug of the tide. I revel in the emptiness, the draining away of personality, the pleasant pressure of the swell and suck of the waves on my body. The water is mottled with shifting brightness. My face too must be dappled with reflected light. The brine is in my hair – it stings my eyes.

Bundled back into my obscuring clothes, my hair loosened, my arms bare, I glow from towelling and weak sun as I sit with the broken and rusting bathing machine behind me and face the sea. My flannel chemise is spread blankly on the grass drying. The waves gently rise and fall – rise and fall – like breathing. *And tomorrow, and tomorrow?* My dash for freedom can't go on forever. The future drags shapelessly in front of me – clings to me with its leaden weights. There is no discarding it. It is beyond my control, implacable. I must make something of my life. But what can I do? There is only

Tom. And he won't come here. I hear nothing from him. Unexpectedly though, I have been forwarded a letter from Catherine Prescott. Ah, the clashing silences, the anodyne responses, the sheer melancholy of those horrible walks with the Prescott girls seem far away. They are almost lost now in the whorls of memory. Catherine writes at a time of victory – she is soon to be Mrs Singleton. Mr Singleton is a linen draper and apparently a very respectable young man indeed. I smile, as I remember Miss Chorley speaking of a certain lady in Liverpool, 'She is too sensible to marry,' she had said. A consoling idea. I mustn't forget to repeat it to single ladies of my acquaintance. It seems to insinuate that all married women are – but the whole world knows. Cloud shadow, a breeze, I feel chilly. It is nearly September. Betty Smith assures me that Beacon's Gutter will be a very different place in winter. No matter. With a fire in my room I will be content to listen to the wind and tramp the dusty vineyards of Spain with *Gil Blas* or amble along quiet English lanes with William Cowper – if I cannot walk the shores of Kirkdale. I often think of Cowper. I think I am a lot like him – not in talent! – but in disposition and sentiment – and I fear I am as ill-suited for this world. *I was a stricken deer that left the herd*. Cowper turned to the hedges and garden-walls, the ploughland and the ponds of the countryside because he loved them – and because he was afraid to turn anywhere else. Catherine Prescott, soon to be Mrs Singleton. She will give the occasional pleasant tea party, receive little unexpected gifts from Mr Singleton, perhaps an ornament for her little drawing room, to be set on the mantelpiece and quickly forgotten about. Mrs Singleton, safe with her linen draper.

Standing, I look at the distant grey tints of the horizon before I stoop and pick up my bathing dress. It is still wet, cold and heavy.

2nd October 1808

Betty Smith was hoeing vegetables in a patch at the rear of the house. Her movements were slow, heavy, deliberate.

'I must say you are looking a picture of health, Ellen. Must be all the walking you do,' she commented, as she rammed her old garden fork into the dark resisting soil and pulled up what would be the last cabbage for the year.

'Yes, I could run faster than Henry here. Couldn't I young man?' I said, tickling him on the ribs with both hands. He squirmed and twisted away from me laughing.

'Could not neither,' he chortled.

'You know, Betty, I have a wild notion to travel through Wales — on foot — even if I were wealthy I would rather walk.'

'What alone? In Wales? No. You mustn't be going and doing a thing like that. Think of the insults you might receive — a woman travelling alone. And you wouldn't be able to understand a single word over there! Not a word.'

'I could get acquainted with a decent Welsh family and by their means get to know another, and so on — as long as the chain would last. I could dress like a man. I'm tall enough. Edward may be kind enough to lend me his big black hat,' I added playfully.

'Now you mustn't go thinking of such a thing! Lord love us, you would be in even greater danger then if you were discovered,' the poor woman said in a concerned voice. She bit her lower lip and shook her head at the enormity of my proposal. Again she reached for the grey weathered handle of the fork with her large rough hands, applied the weight of her cracked and laceless boot to it, and slowly levered it back towards herself.

A biting breeze cooled and hardened my cheeks and I pulled my shawl closer. The days were growing shorter, the afternoon shadows longer and colder. Large, shabby thistles growing among broken cucumber frames in the neglected end of the garden bent their faded purple heads against the wind.

'In the spring I would love to plant some things, beans perhaps, or potatoes, leeks,' I said.

'Now that you *can* do and welcome!' she said straightening and leaning back with one hand at the small of her back.

'Race you to the apple trees,' said Henry.

'Wait for me,' said Betty Smith, abandoning her fork and putting the cabbage on the coping of the rough brick wall, which gave some protection to the garden from the wind. 'I'll beat the lot of you tired as I am!'

The apple trees were spilling their autumn bounty beside an ancient outbuilding just beyond an old unused swilling trough. Like mad things we ran off squealing and laughing. Roger realising he was too late to join the fun gave a loud bark from somewhere in protest. Letting Henry run beside me and telling him I was sure to win, I leapt over the trough. Mrs Smith tried to follow, but shrieking she fell heavily and lay sprawled like a frog in a ditch. She sat up with her legs apart and looked blankly at her knees as if for the first time. I feared for a moment that she may have gashed her leg on one of the many pieces of rusty iron lying about. There were tears – but only of laughter as she rocked back and forth slapping her hands on her ample knees, and smelling of the earth and onions.

5th December 1808

Misery. A tooth pulls threads of pain through my cheek and down into my jaw. Half of my face is swollen and puffy with throbbing pain.

'I fear the brandy was of little service to you last night,

Ellen.' Edward Smith's broad forehead was knitted in a frown below his coal black hair. He coughed wetly and spat into the fire. 'I stopped at an apothecary for you,' he said, knocking out the dust from his pipe against the hob and placing it on the mantel.

He then took a tiny brown bottle with flat sides from his pocket and held it in his grubby yellow fingers. 'Some laudanum.' He loosened the cork a little with his thumbnail and put the ugly little bottle beside a glass for me. 'He said to take at least twelve drops but on no account more than twenty. Hopefully you will get a good night's sleep, at least for tonight.'

'Thank you, Edward,' I said gratefully enough. But I had no intention of taking it. I thought of Tom the day he came home from London. 'I will have to go into Liverpool tomorrow and see what can be done.'

I stood up to go to my room but started in fright. A heavy shot rang out in the troubled twilight, lengthened, hollowed and died leaving the air vibrating.

'Who's that?' I asked, a little unnerved.

'Someone down on the gutter most like, after some game I suppose,' said Betty, putting down her sewing to listen more intently. The small sounds of the night had returned. 'It will be dark soon in any case. Take yourself off to bed now. There's nothing to worry about. Ned's here to keep an eye on things.'

Two more shots spread out through the fading light of the estuary and echoed over the dark reeds and still water as I prepared for bed. My face pulsed and jumped in sympathy with the pain of broken wings and the cruelty of crumpled birds tumbling lifeless from the last light of the sky. My eyes ached and I massaged them with the thumb and second finger of my left hand. When I opened them again I was looking at Edward Smith's little bottle glinting soft amber in the wavering candlelight. I would take only a little, just this once. I uncorked it and carefully poured some of the thick reddish-brown liquid into the glass and drank the bitter stuff off in a single gulp.

*

I woke with a start in the livid gloom before dawn, stagnant and apathetic and as cold as a fatal truth. The baffling dreams of the night lingered with a preternatural vividness. And such dreams! I still felt a confused sense of loss and fright. I was at the theatre piled high with red twisting galleries. I remembered thinking that I would never be able to find my way out. Staircases arched and spiralled; intersected – led nowhere. I was alone. I could see myself as if from a distance, a solitary figure moving through vast halls encased in shadowy grey stone. An alabaster bust toppled from its pedestal and smashed noiselessly. Pieces flew up like wave spray over rocks. Smoky clouds uncovered stars. The roof was open to the cold night sky! I could see the cavernous depths of the theatre revolving beneath me. I was flying. I was above an ocean of bright turquoise. The lightness was in my blood making me as buoyant as air. I looked down from a vast height at a cataract of water – a cliff of water plunging into the sea. No. It was not the ocean at all, but mist or cloud below a white mountain spangled with diamond-hard frost in saffron and violet light. I was falling through the drifting snow, the white air. Yet in all this swirling cold I was as warm as blood on my aerial voyage – except for my feet, which were as cold as stone. Strings of wet, black kelp – cold and slimy – clung to my legs. Leeches! I had struggled to get them off.

Shivering uncontrollably, I sat on the edge of the bed, my

dank pillow across my lap and held my poor jaws in the palms of both hands to stop my teeth from chattering. I dressed slowly determined to go to Liverpool to see Mr Aranson of 21 Princes Street, who, according to the *Manchester Guardian* specialised in artificial teeth 'without the use of wire or ties of any sort' and in performing extractions 'with the greatest care and safety'.

★

'Next October, yes I know, but meetings are already being held and plans are being made,' said Mr Aranson, as he placed a jug of water, a metal basin, a cup and towels on the table beside the chair. 'Fifty years is a long time for our King George. They say there will be brass bands and a procession the length of Princes Street.'

'But there is a good long wait for us yet,' I said, sick with fear. I loathed the room in spite of Mr Aranson's affable smile and professional air – the sickly light trickling through the yellow windows above the door, the specially designed chair, the hard clinical metal.

'Now let's have a look at this tooth of yours.'

He was a strong, thickset gingery man with faded orange hair turning to grey with a vague smell of wet leather about him. His bushy eyebrows were the most salient feature of his face and I closed my eyes against them as he put a thick finger in my mouth to test the looseness of the tooth next to the molar in my lower jaw and the tenderness of the gums.

'Yes I will soon have that out for you, Miss Weeton. I don't think it will need any hammering to start it on its way.' He tied a white towel around my neck and picked up some heavy forceps from a metal tray. 'You can help me a little by gripping underneath the arms of the chair and keeping your feet firmly on the floor. Hold your head back as far as possible please. That's it, good. Mouth open a little wider if you can.'

He began tugging at the tooth with a violence I didn't expect. The muscles in the back of my neck ached and his strong ropey wrists bulged. There was a cracking sound – surely my tooth was breaking, or my jaw! My head started to swim and I felt nauseous and faint. He rocked the tooth in its socket bruising my lip between his thumb and my lower front teeth. I had a moment of anguished panic; my forehead was damp with cold sweat. I was sure I would faint. He started to pant. I could feel his warm breath on my face. And then with a final wrenching twist the tooth came free from the jaw sideways tearing the gums. Blood filled my mouth and I leaned over the basin and spat streams of gore.

He held the inch-long bloodied fang in the forceps to the light like a trophy. 'It is completely whole, Miss Weeton, and there is no damage done to the upper teeth.'

I could not reply. Trembling and feeling horribly ill, I clamped a towel to my face. It was soon so blotched with blood that it coloured my fingertips.

'Here is another towel, Miss Weeton,' he said kindly. 'I will give you some wadding to bite on, and some more to take home with you. The bleeding will soon stop. Some laudanum tonight will help with the pain.' He moved to the grey light of a window, drew a crumpled handkerchief from his pocket and blew his nose.

16th January 1809
As I write this, can hear the harsh squeals of nearby gulls and the childish squeals of protest from little Henry as he resists the efforts of his mother to wash his hair.

★

Poor Aunt Barton. If she only knew! Yesterday I went to church in the morning, the Presbyterian Chapel in the afternoon, and a Methodist meeting at night! However, it was not a display of free thinking, nor of piety, I simply wanted to hear a sonorous voice of some authority. Beacon's Gutter is a quiet place. But I would rather be a servant here than what I was.

2nd March 1809

She is singing at her work. And she works hard, desperately hard. At times I know that Betty Smith is afraid — afraid of the future. Afraid of the dingy streets of Liverpool, the dim alleys of shapeless sullen houses, the haggard faces of workers blanched and unhealthy. 'Better the Gutter than Liverpool, eh Betty?' Edward was wont to say of an evening. But she can't smile away her fear. Can she see Henry trudging amongst them, his tread heavy as he plods along, his limbs aching, his eyes swollen and burning, and the maddening whir of machines still ringing in his head? I try to teach him what I can but his ignorance is astonishing. He is not unloved, nor is he neglected, but he does not receive so much as the travesty of an education — and this in Liverpool, where science and literature should make so great a noise. An immense wealth is brought to this city from all over the globe and flows through its noisy factories and degrading workrooms before coming to rest in the hands of those few for whom life is smooth and easy. No wonder Mrs Smith's eyes gleamed bright as gin when I placed a shilling beside her on the washstand. She smiled her acknowledgement, plunged her red soapy arms into the frothing copper tub, and continued to hum quietly to herself.

14th March 1809

Yesterday afternoon was unnaturally dark with roiling, inky-black clouds and thunder so intense that it rattled the row of blue china plates propped on their edges along the old, battered sideboard in the parlour. Betty Smith dressed in an oilskin much too large for her knocked on the window closest to the door and beckoned to me.

'Ellen, there's a ship on the rocks,' she shouted over the noise of the wind and rain.

In an old greatcoat of Edward's, I followed her to the shore slipping and skidding in the leaf mould and wet. My cheeks were hard cold marbles in the bitter volleys of wind and I flinched at the forked, steel blue lightning tearing at the sullen skies. We went into the old bathing machine from where, partially sheltered from the violence of the wind, we could see the vessel in distress. The sea heaved it up and beat it repeatedly against rocks no more than two hundred yards away. A small crowd began to gather on the shore and I could see an open boat in the shallows, its oars were awry in the wash, and a wave burst against its bows violently slewing it sideways.

A man lifted a speaking trumpet in his ungloved hands and shouted defiantly against the wind, 'There will be a guinea each for any six or eight men who are able to fetch the crew!'

The ship was dying. It lay down on one side and the waves crashed over the decks washing away everything moveable. Men hacked furiously at its masts with axes and there was a wrenching crash as timber and rigging fell overboard, but still the ship stuck fast on the rocks. The shore boat set off but was almost immediately swamped by the waves and current. A second attempt was made but again it was forced back despite the tremendous efforts of the men – strong men who knew the sea – knew the fear of those on the stricken ship. One man with a face like a washed potato and arms like a blacksmith's tied a rope around his waist and boldly, or foolishly, waded into the water. He disappeared, appeared again, his black head bobbed like a seal's in the waves until he too was driven back and lay exhausted on the wet sand spluttering oaths. The boat set off a third time and fortunately reached the ship and took out the men. Soon they were landed safely to a shout that could be heard as far as our cottage. The vessel was too high to sink and remained on the rocks bleeding its cargo of Irish linen into the sea.

★

Just before midnight, Mr Smith left the cottage to prowl the shore for plunder. The rain had stopped but the wind was still high. In the morning I asked him what he had found. 'Nothing but a pillowcase filled with ruined bread,' he had answered, as he poked at the smoky fire. If he had found anything more I doubt he would tell me. The Smiths are not people of the strictest principles in many respects.

29th March 1809
The storms have brought days of chill and mist to Beacon's Gutter, and a most singular visitor. I saw him standing near the old stone outbuilding under the leafless apple trees, their dark branches funereal against the leaden sky. Roger sniffed inquisitively at his heavy boots, unafraid of them or the stout stick the man carried. He was tall, lean and sinewy, perhaps forty, with a red kerchief around his neck. His weather-beaten face was framed with strong whiskers but his chin and lips were clean-shaven making his face appear elongated. A faded blue peaked cap indicated that at one time he may have been

a seafaring man but he now looked more like a farm labourer in his rough coat fraying at the sleeves.

'That will be grand now,' he said, tapping his stick against the aged doors of the building, which may have once been a barn. 'Hides and tallow,' he continued in a soft, lilting, almost musical accent. 'I bought them from a wreck near Hoy Lakes near a week ago. They will find their way to Manchester, but if my men could land them here rather than take them further upriver, that would be most convenient.'

'They will be safe enough in there, I dare say,' said Mrs Smith. She was wearing a woollen scarf around her head against the damp rather than her usual bonnet. There was a glint of hard silver in her eyes as she took measure of the stranger. 'For a small sum – to cheer my husband, you know.'

'Oh, aye, it's an ill wind that blows no one some good, eh?' the Irishman laughed as he strode away holding the rough stick across his broad shoulders as if he were about to lift imaginary weights attached to its ends.

★

That same night I awoke to Roger's sharp, cold bark ringing out in the fog, the sound of muffled voices and heavy knocking at the door. I called up Edward, who took a lamp and directed them where to go. They came again with their carts the two following nights. The Irishman was not among them that I could see, but they were well rugged up against the mist and were largely silent as they went about their work. It was strange that they came on the night tide only. The Smiths made no comment, but I began to suspect the cargo had floated out of some wrecked vessel and the people who had taken the hides out of the water had sold them to the men who brought them here with the intention of defrauding the owners.

Two uninterrupted nights followed, and then on the third evening at about six o'clock there was a knock at the door. I was home alone and half expected to see the red kerchief and peaked blue cap, but the man who stood before me was a complete stranger. There was something wintry about him despite his heavy greatcoat. His corduroy trousers were flecked with mud and the watery eyes, which met mine steadily, had a frosty certainty about them. As he removed his hat revealing a strong nose and chin under a thatch of dark hair, I noticed his hands were red and chaffed from the cold.

'Could I trouble you for a candle, Miss? We would like to look at those hides in the barn,' he said without any further ceremony.

His manner was so indifferent I assumed he was one of the men who had been before and gave him a lamp and the key. Just then, Henry arrived. I could see him near the dilapidated barn where the four men were milling around under the bare shadowless apple trees. But there was no sign of Mr and Mrs Smith. The stubborn heavy doors of the old barn were dragged open, and Henry ran breathlessly back to me, his face pallid with sudden fright.

'There's goin' to be trouble,' he said, his eyes widening, 'yon men is not them as brought the hides here.'

'Why, how do you know? Who are they then?' I asked, feeling my throat tighten in the quick grip of fear.

'I don't know, but there's four of 'em, and that man as took the lamp asked an old man to stay by the hides while he went with t'other men to fetch the constables. "Nay", said the old man, "I dare not stop. They'll know me!" Without another word, he put the lamp down and grabbed the old man by his coat collar and swore at him. A younger man said he would stay and keep watch. And they asked me such a deal of questions – who you was, and how long you've been here; where my father was, and everything. And if there was any hides or any tallow in the house.'

I knelt down and took Henry gently by the shoulders. 'Henry, listen to me carefully. You must run and meet your mother and father, they cannot be too far away, and tell them what has happened. Go down along the Gutter so the men will not see you.'

As soon as Henry set off – he seemed more than happy to be gone – I set about and fastened every lock, bolt and bar in the house. But within ten minutes, Henry was back tapping anxiously on the window. He had met his parents coming home along the path through the fields, but they were so alarmed at his news they had turned and hurried back in the direction they had come from as fast as they could.

'And will they stay away all night, Henry?'

'I don't know,' he said, close to tears.

I could hear the man they had left behind pacing backwards and forwards occasionally stamping his feet like an old dray horse in the cold. The stink of the hides was so intolerable that it had driven him away from the barn. There was no other shelter and the night was deathly cold with a chill white fog creeping along the ground. At about eight o'clock, several more men arrived. Through the window they were little more than grey blurs moving in the darkness. Their lanterns haloed in yellow, misty light. I was terrified. 'They are here with a search warrant and will shortly break into the house,' I thought. There was a loud knock on the door. I froze. I could neither speak nor stir, but held tightly to little Henry, who began to sob quietly against my side. The knocking continued. It would be answered. I mustered enough courage to enquire tremulously what they wanted.

'We must speak with Mr and Mrs Smith.' I recognised the cold, decisive voice of my visitor from earlier in the afternoon. 'It is a matter of grave importance. Please open the door.'

'They should not be long in coming,' I said, my heart thumping almost audibly. 'I am hardly at liberty to open the door in their absence.'

'There is no need for you to be frightened, Miss,' came a younger, friendlier voice from outside the window. 'We know Ned Smith well and will wait for him – all night if necessary. But there is no need for you to be alarmed if you hear us about.'

It was past eleven o'clock when I heard Mrs Smith's voice outside. She strode past the men declaring brazenly that she knew nothing of the business and that they would have to speak to her husband wherever he may be, as she didn't know. There was another woman with her. I hurried to the door and let them in. Henry rushed to her embrace while I tried to suppress my sudden anger.

'How could you leave me here alone all this time?' I demanded.

'I was frightened,' she said. 'I am still so frightened I hardly know what I am doing.' She gave a long, querulous sigh. 'And Edward is more dead than alive.'

Her face had a sickly pallor and her eyes were swollen from lack of sleep. Her thick sausage fingers trembled as she stroked Henry's hair.

'But you will stay now?'

'Mrs Oulston durst not go back by herself,' she answered, 'and she can't possibly stay all night on account of her little one. I am obliged to go back with her.'

'You will surely come back then? These men may break into the house during the night once they procure a search warrant. Or they might be plunderers themselves for all I know. You must promise me you will come back. Please!'

'Well,' she said, 'I'll take Mrs Oulston as far as Lunts' farm, and then come back.'

The lumpish and no doubt mercenary Mrs Oulston stood behind her in shabby silence. Her dull eyes roved blankly about the room as if she were totally unaware of the situation. She took a few stolid steps to look more closely at the few tawdry ornaments on the mantelpiece. I felt sure that Mrs Smith had brought her only by way of excuse to go back again – and so it proved. I did not see her until nearly midday the next day. I was left alone in the house with Henry. He eventually fell asleep, but there was little for me. I heard the men about all night and whenever Roger gave a desultory bark or whined in his confusion, I caught my breath and stared wide-eyed and expectantly into the darkness. At last, just before morning, I drifted off into confused dreams of a lonely shore. The monotonous waves were rolling over dark rocks and cold shifting sands, tumbling what seemed to be a black sodden greatcoat in the shallows.

★

When Mrs Smith did return, two gentlemen, who I assumed were merchants and the owners of the hides, had brought two teams of horses and were taking the stuff away. She did not escape their notice as she hurried towards the house.

'Mrs Smith, I would like a word with you, if you please.'

She stopped to face the speaker, who was a portly well-dressed man in a brown jacket and matching cravat. There was a stern, resentful glint in his eyes as he drew himself up to his full height and put his thumbs officiously under his waistcoat. His companion, a large balding man, stood arms akimbo nodding in agreement.

'Now, you got nothin' against me,' said Mrs Smith, raising

her right hand towards them. 'I had no idea whose property that was, and for that matter, I still don't.'

'You might have been sure it was not honestly come by,' he said, still holding his waistcoat importantly. A gold watch chain could be seen leading to his fob pocket.

'As to that,' she sneered, 'how can I tell that you are not taking it unjustly away?'

His face reddened with anger and he stepped forward towering over the suddenly defeated Mrs Smith. She stood with her head down as if expecting a blow; all the fight had drained from her robust frame.

'I could take legal steps to ascertain certain proof of ownership, Mrs Smith. That I could, and I tell you it would mean transportation for you and that shy husband of yours.' He shouted so imperiously that the workmen paused from their labours and glanced towards them.

Mrs Smith quailed terror-stricken before him, but she was allowed to make her way tearfully to the house, and as they got the goods quietly away, they were content, I imagine. We have heard no more of them.

*

Mr Smith returned quietly during the afternoon. Fine nets of red thread covered his eyeballs and his voice was thick. He brought with him a stale smell of cheap brandy as acrid as curds. He said little and sat morosely brooding and smoking by the fireside. Soon he had surrounded himself in a heavy blue haze. When Mrs Smith entered the fuggy parlour carrying milk and a pat of fresh butter from the Lunts, I was sitting at the table helping Henry to form some of the letters of his name. His face was twisted in concentration as he laboured with a newly sharpened pencil as if it were the heavy ash haft of a workman's tool. He jumped when his mother thumped the pail heavily on the bare table and landed the butter carelessly down beside it.

'So you have condescended to come home, have ya?' She walked over to the hearth and taking up the heavy brass poker violently raked and pushed at the coals. 'Let me make up the fire for you, poor thing,' she said with mock concern, ending with a mordant little laugh. 'You are still pale and shivering with fright.'

I had never suspected that sarcasm would be one of Betty Smith's weapons, but she continued to goad and needle her husband like some harsh-featured Lady Macbeth. Edward Smith reacted with no more than a phlegmy cough and a scoffing snarl until he suddenly stood up, so violently, that he knocked his chair over.

'Shut ya gob, damn ya!' he bellowed, lunging towards her, his chest heaving and his eyes awash with anger.

Never had I heard him speak so brutally. Henry whimpered piteously, and the tears welled up, out and down his cheeks. Mrs Smith, still holding the heavy poker in her hands, was not to be easily subdued this time. Even when she caught a heavy smack on the side of her head, she managed to bring the poker down across her husband's temple. He fell heavily onto the already overturned willow chair, which cracked under his weight. The poker clattered on the flagstones as Mrs Smith staggered backwards towards the open doorway where she paused.

'Get out!' he roared. 'Bugger your eyes! What have you done to me?' He put both his hands against his forehead for a moment. 'Get out, you dunghill! You'll look like pigs' chitterlings if you don't!' he almost sobbed, struggling to his feet.

Mrs Smith slammed the door with a shuddering blow.

And her husband holding his purpling brow in his left hand shot the bolt to with all the strength of his right arm.

★

Fearing that he might turn his anger on me, I spent the rest of the evening in my room leaving him to nurse his injuries and fend for himself as best he could. But he did not disturb me in any way. I heard him calmly settle Henry for the night and soon the house was silent. I was completely worn out and slept deeply and dreamlessly. I heard him again in the morning clumping awkwardly around in the kitchen in his Hessians, clanging and banging pots and pans. The result was the unmistakeably strong odour of onions and the hissing of frying liver – he obviously intended to treat himself well during Mrs Smith's absence. The door closed with a sharp bang and I looked down from my window to see him striding off into the clear day of capricious sunshine with Henry doing his best to keep up with him. For some inexplicable reason I felt sad watching the pair of them trudging along in the weak morning light, their heads down, oblivious to the lark, which had risen from a tussock near them and was spiralling skywards. I ventured downstairs. Brown fat was congealing in the used pan and Roger standing up on his haunches, his forepaws on the edge of the table was noisily snaffling scraps of meat off his master's plate.

★

By the time he came home that evening I had made sure that the parlour was clean and orderly, and that a good fire was burning. Mrs Smith had still not returned.

'By Christ, she must have the headpiece of a sparrow if she

thinks I will stand for this!' he spluttered, his face twitching and jumping with suppressed rage. He grimaced and put his hand to his still swollen temple, which no doubt throbbed and pulsed with pain. Replacing his hat which he had only just discarded, he declared vehemently, 'There will be no home for her here now. Never! I will go this minute to my sister's at Kirkdale and get her to come with her family to keep house – and it will be rent-free too!'

Off he marched leaving the door open behind him.

'Keep the door well locked until I return,' he said peremptorily over his shoulder as he neared the broken masonry of the garden wall. He was silhouetted against the sky streaked with burnished attenuated clouds. It was almost dark.

Henry appeared as soon as his father had left and chatted away while I set about preparing some sort of supper. I was about to go in search of some ale against Edward's return when Mrs Smith rapped anxiously on the window and demanded to come in. Her dingy face looked stale and drawn, her eyes had a wild, frightened look about them.

'For goodness sake, let me in! Why is the door locked, Ellen?'

'I dare not open it, Betty. You will have to go to Kirkdale. Edward has gone to fetch his sister.'

'Ellen, you cannot keep me from my own house. Let me in!' she demanded desperately.

After some hesitation, I did so with my heart racing in apprehension of further strife. Edward came in almost on her heels.

'What are you doing here, you mutt?' he said, staring malevolently at her.

Mrs Smith stood dully before her husband, looking vulnerable despite her work-roughened features and her plump strong arms. Her tired eyes filled with treacherous tears.

'Edward, where could I go? What could I do?' she wailed, lost in a quagmire of hopelessness.

'You can sell watercress in Castle Street for all I care,' he growled, slumping into a chair.

Their anger slowly subsided and they grew quiet. Betty continued to stand, crying, sniffing rapidly. She made no effort to wipe her crumpled face – not even with the backs of her hands. Edward refused to look at her and began to tamp his pipe.

I left them and went up the narrow stairs to my room.

9th April 1809
Such a feckless pair! But where else can I get lodgings for less than twelve or fourteen shillings a week? I save little enough as it is. And Ann Winkley has kindly offered me asylum if anything unpleasant should happen again, but I think all will be well. Mrs Smith has behaved with more consideration towards Edward than ever before. Long may it last! I think she was terrified at being so nearly turned out of the house. Nor am I particularly sorry that I have heard nothing in regard to a situation in Wakefield, which was advertised. The school could well be the headmistress's own house and there would be a very great difference between working with my mother in a school of our own and working amongst strangers as little more than a hired labourer. Linen, combing, washing and some sewing were to be part of the deal – I am spared that drudgery for a while longer at least. And it's spring. Early violets are in the hedges and the path is bordered with snapdragons and hollyhocks. The weather is growing warmer, the days longer. I will soon be able to ramble for miles along the shore again – alone

and unobserved – without the least fear of danger. I must be content with Beacon's Gutter.

20th May 1809

Uncle Barton sat in Tom's low wainscoted parlour. His face still aglow from the ride with me from Up Holland on a double horse, he was relishing the last of the pale ale and Stilton that Mrs Weeton had so sparingly provided. We had not been invited. It had been at my insistence that we had come when I learned in Up Holland from my aunt, not only that Tom had a new baby girl, but that he was also recovering from a recent riding accident. The baby lay contentedly against my breast. I studied the large pearl-grey eyes and the delicate beauty of her little fingers as I gently stroked her cheek which felt as soft as cloud.

'You live in a place called Beacon's Gutter!' Mrs Weeton exclaimed thinly.

Her eyes widened a little under her mobcap, which did not entirely hide her fair hair. She had grown stouter, but still preserved a vague prettiness.

Without warning or apparent reason, the infant's face suddenly crumpled and she started to cry fretfully. She was quickly lifted from me and I felt a sudden pang of exclusion. Mrs Weeton made one languid attempt to comfort the child and then handed her to the nursemaid.

'Yes, I live very simply, almost entirely in the society of Edward and Betty Smith of Beacon's Gutter. I am often ill at ease in case I cannot find even their modest rent.' I turned to my brother. 'Tom, you must bring the family for a visit during the summer,' I said, affecting a brightness of tone I did not feel.

'The sea always has a very unpleasant effect on my bowels – makes me bilious,' retorted Tom, putting his pottery mug on the table and wiping his mouth with the back of his hand.

'So you prosper in Liverpool,' offered Mrs Weeton, with a touch of sarcasm, 'a single woman, and such connections!'

Her eyes, flecked with scorn or condescension, met mine. It struck me, not for the first time, that there was something peculiarly repellent in her manner. It succeeded in throwing a degree of reserve upon me.

'Well, I must return to your good aunt,' my uncle said standing. He patted me lightly on the shoulder, adjusted his curled wig, which he still wore despite the changing fashion and buttoned up his suede gloves. 'It's good to see you looking so well again, Tom.' He was a quiet, reserved man, more inclined to communicate with a kind gesture or reassuring touch of the hand than speech, but the ride from Up Holland had lifted his spirits. He had commented on the sweet scent of the hawthorn blossoms and hedge bells and had stopped at a mossy Norman church for no more important a reason than to listen to the ivy rustling in the breeze.

'Yes. I was in fear of losing my brother. I hurry to Leigh and just look at him!' I said teasingly.

'It was no laughing matter when he lay bruised and unconscious in a ditch,' said Mrs Weeton defensively. 'It could have been the death of him and what I would have done then, I don't know,' she sighed petulantly, gripping Tom's arm. 'Things are hard enough as they are if the truth be known.'

By this time, Tom's older children were leading my uncle's sturdy chestnut cob towards him under the watchful eye of a servant. Little Thomas, looking important, gave him the reins and Catherine happily took my offered hand.

'Thank you, young sir! Yes. How did you manage that little incident, Tom?' he asked, lightly throwing himself into the saddle.

A tone of annoyance had crept into Tom's voice. 'I was coming home from Wigan – fortunately I was not alone – when a wretched calf that had been lying down on the other side of the hedge, suddenly rose up and galloped away. My stupid mare sprang sideways nearly dismounting me. I managed my seat but I must have spurred it in the flanks accidentally. It set off like a Banshee eventually throwing me over its head.'

'Fortunately, he fell rather flat, or his neck would have been broken,' said Mrs Weeton. 'It was a full hour before he came to himself.'

'Take care, Uncle,' I said, 'and tell Aunt I will be back tomorrow morning.'

The humour drained from his eyes and he now spoke more soberly.

'I will. Tom, Mrs Weeton,' he said nodding. 'Give my regards to your sister.'

Mrs Weeton's sister was in Wigan staying over a night or two with her mother. I had not been disappointed to find her away when I arrived.

'I will visit Aunt too,' said Tom, 'when I can.'

'She would like that, Tom. She is far from well. She has been bled and blistered in the last week, but I fear she is in a sad decline,' he said, the corners of his mouth tightening.

The horse set off at a gentle walk. He was still an attractive man, tall and neat in his wig, which presided over dark, kind eyes, the jaw strong, clean-shaven, giving him a serious, intelligent mien. His clothes were dark too, and neatly cut without any consciousness of elegance or ostentation. Before today, it would have been some time since he had donned the thick leather gaiters he wore when riding. He had enjoyed his outing.

He had not gone fifty yards before Mrs Weeton turned on me like a graceless virago, abruptly ending my reverie.

'I do think it rather churlish of you to talk about the narrowness of your income in that way Ellen. You are too humble and open altogether.'

'Thank you for your sage observation,' I said, bowing with a mirthless smile. 'I strive daily to improve myself!'

I was determined to maintain my composure. Tom, no doubt, saw what he interprets as my snobbishness.

'I suppose you see your fretful complaints and petty grievances to the ageing Bartons as a little investment for the future, Ellen?' he quipped cruelly.

I trembled and felt myself turn pale with an indignant swelling anger. I became aware of not breathing and had to take two or three deep breaths before I could answer him. 'Tom, I live amongst complete strangers who, no doubt, consider me cheerful and fortunate. But who can I really talk to if not you? Who else but you seeing tears in my eyes would bother to ask why?'

*

I left early the next morning when the leaves were still wet and jewelled with humid sunlight. It had been an unhappy visit. Tom walked part of the way with me and although he was civil, the strain between us was palpable. I struggled with the resentment I felt but had not adequately expressed. Mrs Weeton would die before making a concession on the most trivial of issues, and Tom defers to her on all matters. Perhaps it is right that he should, but I was thoroughly tired of her quiet insistent cavilling and her constant references to single women. She would never have a good word for Ellen Weeton! Guiltily, I felt a sense of sad relief when I turned and waved to him on parting.

★

It was good to see the Braithwaites again and after leaving them I walked through the churchyard to visit my mother's grave. It was an odd feeling looking across the road from the priory at my own house where the watchmaker, Winstanley, still lives. Having squirmed into every nook and cranny of it as a child, I knew it intimately – its moods and noises, its garden, its draughts, its dust, its smells. But if I so much as went and peered into a window I would cause alarm. I would have to knock on my own front door and try to explain! It had been warm walking, but it began to rain steadily if lightly and I felt chilled. My mother's gravestone was stark and terse and deeply shadowed by yew trees shivering in the slight breeze. Already it was lightly discoloured with moss and lichen. Its whiteness darkened. I have asked Tom that if he survives me, not to place a stone over my grave, or to have my name put upon any that may previously have been placed there. If my friends cannot remember me without such a memento, let them forget me. The rain grew heavier, the clouds more leaden. I could not postpone my farewell to Aunt Barton any longer.

★

A maid led me up the creaking stairs to her room. I hesitated at the door. Propped up on her pillows, she looked gaunt and thin. Her ivory throat was sadly wasted and her lips were parted and drawn back slightly as if in disgust or pain. Her breathing was laboured and rattled noisily in her throat. A wine table had been brought near the bed and on it were corked bottles of various sizes, two small silver spoons and oddly, a tortoise-shell brush. The room had the sharp odour of camphor and red lavender, and the deeper sour smell of human waste. A large vase stood in the bay of the window, empty of flowers. She coughed wetly, opened her eyes and looked directly at me.

'Ellen. So you have come at last.' Her eyes were a watery grey above a prominent nose. On waking, her face had resumed its customary lines of thin-lipped severity. 'Ellen, I need to speak with you,' she said, coughing again and raising herself a little higher on the pillows with the maid's assistance.

I brought a soft velvet chair to the bed and felt I should take hold of one of her thin hands, but did not.

'How are you managing, Aunt?' I asked. The remark sounded shallow and trite. 'Is there something I can get for you?'

'I am dying, child. This is my final illness.'

The statement was well calculated and was forcefully delivered, but I noticed her hands did have a slight palsy on the snowy counterpane.

'But I have done my duty. I have not persevered in obstinate selfishness, when others needed me.'

'Aunt?'

The maid busied herself by uncorking a small angular bottle. 'Will you take your syrup now, Mrs Barton?'

'No, I will not! Leave us in peace for a moment', she ordered with peevish harsh emphasis.

'Thank you, Amelia,' I muttered. She had flushed down to her neck but managed to replace the medicine carefully on the table before leaving the room.

'Ellen, will you continue in this purposeless existence of yours, or will you come and care for your uncle and me? I

86

must be honest and say I do not understand what attraction there is for you in living with strangers of that sort, when you could live with your own kith and kin.'

How many reputations and lives, I wondered, have been blasted and withered throughout England by the ferocious respectability of pious ladies like my aunt?

'By *of that sort*, Aunt, do you mean that great anonymous mass of people for whom the world is devoid of opportunity? People who would be individuals like us if only they had made eligible marriages, or if their fathers had not lost a fortune, and as a consequence they must show respect for their betters?' I replied hotly.

'You know perfectly well what I mean, Ellen. There is no need to be supercilious. Will you answer my question? What are you going to do?'

'I am resolved to be happy, Aunt.'

'How?'

'I'm not sure, but I cannot stay in Up Holland. I have the good sense, or foolishness, to know that. Aunt, I have taken a seat in the coach and I must go.' She turned her face slightly away from me and sniffed. 'Perhaps hope, good intentions and a little courage will be enough,' I said more lightly and stood up. She offered no reply. 'Will you not say goodbye to me, Aunt?' She turned herself towards the opposite wall, brought hers knees up higher in the bed and closed her eyes. I waited helplessly a moment or two longer. 'Goodbye, Aunt,' I said quietly, and left the room.

★

'Amelia has prepared this for you, Ellen,' said my uncle, picking up a neatly tied parcel from the bench seat in the entrance hall.

'Thank you, Uncle,' I said and hugged him briefly.

'At least let me accompany you to the coach, Ellen,' he offered, opening the door and glancing at the heavy sky and drizzling street. There was the clink of pattens on cobblestones coming from somewhere nearby. 'It has turned into such a poor afternoon.'

'There is no need at all to do that. I have my wraps and my umbrella, but thank you all the same. I will write soon.'

'Goodbye, Ellen.'

★

My heart sank when I saw that the outside seats of the coach were crowded with livid-faced roughs. The wind blew with such malice that I could not open my umbrella, and I now regretted booking an outside seat even though it was half the price. Daunted, I hesitated with my foot on the first step and briefly surveyed my fellow travellers. Their clothes were soaked; their faces unshaven and bleary eyed. One had usurped my seat. His head lolled upon the shoulder of his equally unsavoury neighbour who seemed oblivious to the shadowed jowls nuzzling and snuffling against him. A small sample of that great anonymous mass of people, I had defended so ably against my aunt daunted me completely! Tom may be right. Perhaps I am a snob.

'Better come up here with me, Miss,' said the coachman, scratching his neck above the collar of his oilskin, which was running with water. 'We've had trouble enough with that lot already.' He briefly took off his broad-brimmed hat and shook the water off it before replacing it on his well-shaped brow.

'And, if we have any more,' said the lanky guard in his dirty scarlet uniform, shaking a clenched fist in their direction, 'I will have the pleasure of hurling one or two of you off the coach!'

One of the men bared his grey teeth and snarled an obscenity under his breath. Another lifted a half-pint bottle of brandy, as if he were defiantly proposing a toast to the guard whose square-bearded and hard-boned face clenched and flared with anger. I stepped back a pace or two from the coach. They were so viciously rude and uncouth I was frightened a brawl was about to erupt. And they were the sort who would have the last word, or blow, if they argued a week. Begging the guard to say no more, I took my seat beside the ponderous coachman. He began to rummage under his seat and produced a stout horse rug to cover my shoulders, and another to cover my knees, and in this elegant attire, the coach jolted forward and I left Up Holland amidst the hiss of rain and the pungent smell of wet horses, wedged between the burly coachman and the iron handrail as tightly as a cork in a bottle.

My hip was soon sadly bruised and although I had placed a thick cotton handkerchief under my bonnet, the rain soaked slowly through a little crevice between my hood and neck in cold little streams until I was literally wet to the skin. The air was so piercingly cold my wool-lined beaver gloves were a treasure to me. The countryside was an empty swirling grey of loneliness. Not a gentleman's carriage and scarce a gig was passed all the way to Rainhill where I stiffly descended from my elevated situation and made my way into an inn. My clothes were so wet that I found myself a woman of much greater weight – if not more substance – than I was in Up Holland. I steamed and warmed myself at a roasting kitchen fire while most of the other passengers busied themselves with hot porter and a helping of boiled brisket or shepherd's pie. Amelia had given me a good lump of cold tongue, but hungry as I was, I could not eat it. The very sight of it on the thick white butcher's paper, edged in brown congealed jelly, made my gorge rise. If only the inn could have provided some hot clear soup or if Amelia had given me some dry biscuits or a few of Peggy Hodson's buns – then I could have feasted! I could almost hear the jangle of the bell on her shop door and smell the warm, clean fragrance of freshly baked bread. No matter!

I again clambered up to my cramped perch beside the coachman, even though I had noticed there were now fewer passengers outside the coach. I enjoyed the sensation of his close physical presence – his warm breath, which occasionally fanned me carrying a hint of the cellar with it – the faint odour of his sweat. The ostlers were fixing fresh horses. One became terribly frightened and fell twice in the shafts. The second time, they had difficulty raising it. Protesting, the mare backed and twisted so violently among the other horses, that although there were plenty of men, they had trouble managing it. I expected an overturn and clutched the handrail fearing I would be dropped headlong onto the greasy cobblestones. The inside passengers knew nothing of their danger until the coach suddenly jolted violently backwards. There was a scream, angry demands, oaths. But at last, the men had the horse under control. The coachman gave a throaty 'Har!' and we were safely off. I winced each time the whip licked over the flanks of the recalcitrant mare on the way to Liverpool. Poor horse, it was made to wear the harness of life and was whipped for it!

Although I was wet, the rugs did help to keep me warm against the wind. When I took them off, I went smoking all the way to the coach stand, hired a gig, and went from Red Cross Street to Princes Street, where I knew Ann Winkley would have comfortable lodgings for me overnight. I was soon dry and snug, and with a scalding hot cup of tea before me, I have spent some time writing up this account. Tomorrow, a short walk will take me home to Beacon's Gutter.

15th July 1809
My old enemy has returned. For two days I have been scarcely able to crawl. My stomach knotted and cramped with pain after eating salad and vinegar and then drinking milk. The milk turned sour and came up again as black as ink. My appetite was quite gone until I ventured to get an emetic from a druggist. I suffered a drastic nausea the afternoon I took it but I have recovered quickly since then.

30th September 1809
I write this from 10 Princes Street, where Ann Winkley, soon to be Mrs Price, has given me refuge.

★

I enjoyed the constant trickle of summer visitors to the house until near the end of the season. All were respectable families. I was particularly sorry when Mrs Huntriss from Halifax left. About my own age, she had been terribly thin and sallow when she arrived, but after a month of living largely out of doors and walking on the sands with me, she had left as stout and energetic as I am myself. But earlier this month a gentleman arrived with a servant girl. He was adamant that he suffered such poor health that he required attendance several times during the night. Edward arranged a second bed in the room to this end, to be occupied by the servant – a pretty girl of about seventeen. I saw no appearance of ill health the following afternoon when he walked some miles on the shore. At the very worst he may have been a little hipped, or wished us to believe as much. And that evening after supper, as he turned his feet towards the low fire, stretching and sighing complacently, I felt even more uncomfortable in their company. His smile was neither mirthful, nor malicious and certainly not thoughtful. It was the sensual smile of the grown spoilt child, the self-satisfied satyr who was proud of his artful manoeuvres and the soft murmuring ministrations of his servant. She had a sensitive face and her full, almost bruised looking lips, were slightly parted, so engrossed was she in their whispering *tête-à-tête*. I began to think he was oblivious to my presence, or else he was simply ignoring me, when he pressed her unresisting hand to his lips and looked over it directly at me and smiled.

Nonplussed, I stood and left the room. Unwilling even to meet with the Smiths, I left the house to find some comfort in the damp cloudy twilight. Barely conscious of my surroundings, or of why I was so affected and affronted, I walked as far as the line of attenuated poplars marking the beginning of the path across the meadows to Liverpool. The dying sun was leaving a last smudge of smoky pink above a pale darkening sky when I returned to go directly to my room. I was relieved to find them gone and the parlour empty, but was arrested by a sound outside their door in the hallway. I heard what could have been the sudden intake of a breath or the muffled, suffocating cry of someone struggling under a heavily clamped hand. But there was no mistaking the words.

'Charles – no, please stop Charles! You're… you're tearing me!'

★

I complained and then appealed to Mrs Smith the following morning, but she simply shrugged her shoulders before leaving the kitchen.

'Well, I'll mention it to Edward, but he do pay so handsome like.'

Judas! No, not Judas, Betty Smith would never throw good silver away – not even at the heads of her tormentors. She would have carried it to her guilty death. I knew at that moment that I would leave and they would stay.

26th October 1809

'The King's grand parade! It was more like a funeral procession than anything else,' remarked Ann wryly.

'There were only two bands of music. There really ought to have been one to each company. Mind you, had there been twenty, it would still not have been enough for the length of the procession,' said Mr Price, who had just come into the room bringing with him his customary good humour and energy.

'Well, if our good King George reads the newspaper he will nevertheless be flattered,' I mused, folding the newspaper and placing it on the polished mahogany table. 'They report immense crowds who behaved extremely well and conclude that it was a huge patriotic spectacle.'

'Ah, that is the very purpose of my visit!' he exclaimed, quickly unbuttoning his gloves and striding towards the paper. He picked it up and started riffling through its large rustling pages, his eyes alive with a limpid intelligence. 'Not about our ageing king, but something else I feel sure will interest you, Miss Weeton. Yes, here it is! I stopped at Mr Nevett's, the bookseller in Castle Street on the way over this afternoon, and stumbled upon this advertisement.' He read it in his clear tenor voice: 'Wanted, in the neighbourhood of Kendal, a governess of considerable experience and competence in tuition, to supervise the education of a young lady in a gentleman's family. References as to ability and character are essential. Apply to Mr Montgomery.'

'Ellen, it sounds exactly what you have hoped for,' said Ann excitedly.

'If you wish, I could make inquiries at the publishers tomorrow, regarding the advertiser?'

'Oh yes please, and thank you!' I stammered.

'But what of our plans for a musical career?' asked Ann smiling for my happiness without the slightest trace of disappointment.

I was going to procure a guinea's worth of lessons on the flageolet, while a week ago a Welsh harpist had visited Princes Street in a valiant attempt to convert Ann to the pedal-harp.

'I have not even applied for the position yet!' I said. Their enthusiasm was so infectious that I felt a stirring of optimism in my blood. 'But if I am successful, my single regret will be leaving the two kindest people in Liverpool.'

'Accept nothing less than thirty guineas, Miss Weeton. Anything less would be an insult to your abilities,' he beamed, playfully tugging at the silk ruff of his shirt.

Walton near Preston
15th November 1809

I am too excited to sleep, although it is late at night and my bed is clean and comfortable.

I have told no one else except Tom in case the venture fails, but I am going to be a companion to a Mrs Pedder, about six miles beyond Kendal, somewhere bordering or at least not far from Lake Windermere. Mr Pedder has recently married a servant girl, in fact, a dairymaid, and has taken her into retirement in the country for a few years until she becomes a little better suited to his usual society. He has a little girl of eleven years old from a former marriage and I shall superintend her education at home. I have been told that she will have a maid, so her education alone will employ me.

I wrote to Mr Montgomery assuming it was for himself that he had advertised. An anxious week passed and I began to lose hope when he called in consequence of my application at Princes Street. Mr Price had wisely suggested that Ann's lovely drawing room would be the best venue for such an interview. After admiring the vase of red roses carefully arranged on the table, the elderly Mr Montgomery informed me he was only acting on Mr Pedder's behalf.

'I live at Walton and have known the family for many years,' he said politely, settling himself comfortably into the wingback armchair with the glass of port he had accepted. The lace curtains behind him allowed a shaft of soft moted sunlight to spill near his feet. 'You will be treated as an equal by them, you know, more as a companion to Mrs Pedder than as governess to Miss Pedder,' he said encouragingly. I warmed immediately to his kindness of manner. 'Regulating the management of the household as Mr Pedder wishes his to be would be your only other duty. Now, what salary would you expect, Miss Weeton?'

Brazenly, I suggested the unconscionable sum Mr Price had recommended. His clear hazel eyes behind the glinting spectacles expressed not the least surprise.

'Well then, if we are all in agreement, the coach leaves on Friday morning next!' he said with a ready smile, visibly more cheerful now that he was relieved of responsibility.

★

It was with mixed feelings that I waited, cloaked and bonneted for the coach. I would miss my good friends in Liverpool – and their wedding day. Not once have I felt the frost of withering criticism from them and yet I was excited by the prospect before me – the Lake District! The actual moment of departure was confused and sudden, and left me feeling sad and irritated for miles. The door of the coach opened and a young, handsome man alighted, bowed and beckoned me towards my place. At that precise moment amidst the fervent farewells to Mr Price and Ann Winkley, of all people to be passing on the pavement, Miss Chorley appeared at my elbow. A pregnant pause, an inquisitive glance at the gracious young man and a knowing look directed at me – and she was gone!

The polite young man, a complete stranger to me, was good company, but the coach made such a noise I had to bawl like a fishwife to be heard and my throat was soon tired from the effort. At Preston, Mr Montgomery met me at the inn and with his help we took another coach down to Walton. I have seen little of Mr Montgomery since, but his niece, Miss Rhodes, was an attentive and cheerful host for the afternoon. She is lively and effervescent and I am pleased to have her as an acquaintance. She is hopeful of visiting Dove's Nest, the Pedders' home, with her uncle sometime in the future so it is likely that we will meet again. Tomorrow, I will hopefully complete the remainder of the journey under Mr Montgomery's friendly protection. The mail coach passes his very door. I am anxious to see Lancaster again, and wonder if I will recognise any of the places I knew in my infancy.

3

Dove's Nest, Ambleside
5th December 1809

Mr Montgomery and I arrived at Kendal soon after four in the afternoon. We dined there, and then took a post chaise to Mr Pedder's of Dove's Nest; twelve miles from Kendal (not six – I was misinformed) near the head of Windermere Lake. I was so dulled by fatigue that recollections of my arrival there live as a sequence of dream-like vivid impressions. We passed through a gothic gate onto a broad gravel path so steep that I became alarmed. Mr Montgomery got out, but I preferred riding up because of the wetness of the ground. If the horses slipped even a little I was sure we would all end up in the lake! I got up safely however, and glimpsed shrubs, hedges, a stone fountain and large trees under the ancient light of early stars. The air was vibrantly cold and clear. 'What a garden it will be in the spring or under the burning tints of autumn,' I thought with a stirring of excitement. In my mind's eye, I could hear the ringing of a child's laughter and the music of water tripping and splashing over stone. The house itself was large and plain to the point of ugliness with turreted wings to each side. Shallow stone steps led to an entrance hall paved with black and white marble. Mrs Pedder, who could only be seventeen, was slim and pretty in pink muslin and was seated with her husband at their wine amidst damask cushions, green velvet curtains and the cheerful glitter of glass and silver in candlelight. I felt a little awkward, not knowing exactly what was expected of me, but Mr Pedder, a very little man of about thirty-four, gallantly stood and greeted me with deference and a pleasing smile. After some toast and a tureen of vegetable soup, Mr Montgomery settled himself in front of the yawning old-fashioned fireplace for talk and laughter, but I was more than grateful to be escorted by the light of a single guttering candle to my room in the upper storey, from where it overlooked the garden. The bed was fresh and dry, the pillow delicious, and I heard not another sound until the cold cawing of early morning rooks.

★

It was Sunday and when Mr Montgomery set off for Kendal in a hired chaise, Mr and Mrs Pedder and myself left in the opposite direction in the curricle for church in Grasmere some five or six miles away. Never have I been in such a dashing vehicle! It was a frosty morning of flitting cloud and pellucid air. My heart leapt with a sudden joy at the surrounding countryside of blue-green hills, woods and water. Lake Windermere was only two or three hundred yards below us. It was not blue as I had expected, but adopted the shadows of the sky on its ruffled surface. From my precarious perch in the curricle – higher than the upright horses' heads – I could see rocks, some naked, others tinted with lichen, tumbled to the lake's edge amongst sun-backed bracken.

Mrs Pedder was a little embarrassed and Mr Pedder obviously vexed when we found the service already over. I suspect they are not regular churchgoers. St Oswald's was as deserted and peaceful as on a weekday. Its earthen floor was strewn with rushes to keep it clean, fresh and warm. The ceiling, high above the village dead buried beneath it, was a tangle of oak beams supported by whitewashed walls. Mr Pedder soon recovered his good humour and, determined to show me some of the neighbourhood, drove on to Hawkshead, where we dined on whitebait before returning home.

Mrs Pedder is gentle and amiable. I am fortunate to have such a person under my care, for she is my pupil as well as Miss Pedder. Little Gertrude is nearly eleven and was presented to me that afternoon dressed in a crisp, white pinney. She is unnaturally silent and shy. She stood timidly before me uncertain of what to do or say, her wistful little face was confused and staring. She has fits, sometimes five in a day, rarely a whole day without any. However, she seems compliant enough and tentatively took my hand to explore the garden before it grew too dark and cold. There we met old Solomon returning from the fields with a hare over his shoulder, a double-barrelled gun broken in the crook of his arm and three Border Collies moiling about his heels, their tongues lolling and panting rhythmically. The household has five servants: two men who serve dinner in livery, a cook and two maids. They have treated me with such reserve that I expect nothing except cool indifference from them at best, perhaps even resentment. Old Solomon lives nearby and serves as gardener-cum-gamekeeper. He is of a different order altogether. Garrulous, kindly, polite in a rough workmanlike way, he is as much at home in his setting as an ancient lake stone or shaggy yew tree.

'Aye, this will be near the last for the season, if I am any judge with Christmas coming on,' he said, draping the dead hare, its eyes fixed and glassy, over the garden wall. ''Tis unlawful to hunt hares when snow is on the ground in these parts and that will not be long away.'

'It is a most beautiful place,' I said, slowly inhaling the moist, clean air and looking down at the lake towards Windermere.

'Aye, that it is,' he replied readily, stroking his rough chin with an open hand. 'But nothing like it was twenty, thirty years ago. The timber has been so much cut about. Now they are slashing away at the woods under Loughrigg,' he almost growled. 'But 'tis not a good time of day for you to be out in the garden, Miss.' He then added in such a matter of fact tone that I started, 'I have just seen old Benson's ghost down near the woods.'

'Benson's ghost?' I almost laughed aloud, but there was a seriousness in his face that stopped me.

'Aye, he were the former owner of the house. They say he were a great miser in his day and has a considerable sum laid about here somewhere. 'Tis said it keeps him from his rest. Aye, his ghost can be seen often enough near the house when the mist gathers towards nightfall.'

'Near the house? He has not been seen in it?' I asked a little dubiously, letting go of Gertrude who had knelt to pat the dogs. She had not spoken a word since leaving the house despite my efforts to be friendly, but now she stroked the white noses of each dog lovingly and smiled for the first time.

'Nay. Never,' he said, producing a brilliant red handkerchief and wiping his nose, which was of a similar hue. 'But they do say he makes strange noises on occasions – all over it sometimes.'

Touching his worsted cap briefly, he whistled sharply for his dogs, collected the stiffening hare and left me amongst the darkening trees near the silent, waterless fountain.

'Come along, Gertrude. It's time to go inside,' I said airily and retrieved her small gloved hand.

★

In the early hours of the morning, it must have been about two o'clock, I was woken by a noise as if someone had opened the window in my room and had forcefully let it down again. I looked at the ivy-darkened pane, but saw nothing unusual. But the noise came again, its loudness magnified in the still cold heart of the house. Dead fingers of fear touched the back of my neck and I shivered. Surely if there were robbers, they would not be such fools to make such a noise! Every moment I expected to hear Mr Pedder or the servants. But the hope was vain.

Getting out of bed, I went to the window. The room was cold, very cold. There would be a frost sharp enough to ice the ponds by morning. I lifted the window and looked out. The grass-plat, the gravelled driveway, the naked trees were in perfect quiet – not a soul was to be seen – not a leaf of ivy stirred. Shutting the clear little pane, I stood for some moments, my chest heaving and my heart racing. I had expected to see someone out there. I had looked for him – a man, darkly clad – standing still in the nimbus of blue-grey light, staring at me, silently, from the leafless grove.

Again! A sharp jarring sound came from Mrs Pedder's room to my right. I then heard quite distinctly, at least I thought so at the time, someone in heavy boots walking in her room. My fear drained away into annoyance. Surely if Mrs Pedder could not sleep, she need not disturb everyone with such noise! My bare feet were numbing with cold and I hurried back to restore the warmth of my bed. I lay there listening for an hour or more. Someone, it seemed, was carrying chairs from one part of her room to another; drawers were dragged open and then abruptly shut. I heard a scream. Not a loud scream, but high-pitched and dreadful enough in the night. Realisation dawned on me at last – rats!

Oh God! Rats! I loathe them. They make my flesh creep. And there must have been dozens skirmishing and skittering and squeaking just above me in the low ceiling. I knew their vicious little teeth would tear at anything, and in such numbers they would tumble and squirm and claw at each other to burrow their way into the living or the dead. I was rendered so completely helpless in my terror that it was impossible for me to get out of bed again to assure myself that there were none at least actually in my room. I hid under the blankets like a frightened child and somehow endured the hours until morning.

★

'Their noise began before one o'clock and continued until five,' agreed Mr Pedder. But he seemed more concerned about the temperature of his bacon and the strength of his coffee than the events of the night. 'Pat, would you please put some more coal on the fire. You know I like a good blaze in this weather.'

Patrick, his hair already powdered, solemnly bowed and did what he was requested. It had struck me before that Mr Pedder was always very relaxed in the company of his servants and he enjoyed talking to his workmen without any formality whatsoever.

'Were you not alarmed? Did you get up?' I asked eagerly. I dreaded the thought of spending another night in the house; that the creatures might perhaps be resting just behind the wainscoting at that very moment.

'No,' said he, laughingly. 'I was far too comfortable to do anything of that sort.'

He has, to date, been good-natured, liberal and hospitable. So much so, that I must be cautious not to assume too much, but I was determined that some action must be taken.

'I was so frightened I couldn't sleep a wink,' I said pleadingly.

'Yes. Well perhaps it is time for Mrs Morley to prepare her little specialty for them again, although in my opinion it is a waste of good brandy. I'll get the men to see to it today, if you like.'

★

The loft immediately under the roof, I was told, was perfectly dark, and there were no stairs leading into it. Mr Pedder had organised a ladder and a candle, and followed by the tittering domestics, I mounted the ladder and ascended through a small square hole left in the ceiling. I remained on the ladder, but judging by the heaps of filth and the amount of litter, the rats must be enormous in both size and number. The boards were loosely placed as flooring and no doubt provided ample hiding places and would easily have been moved about in the battle during the night. The men spent much of the morning nailing the boards down firmly.

'Here, let the greedy beggars feast on this tonight,' said Mrs Morley dryly, handing an opened bottle of wine up to the men.

'Wine?' I asked, completely puzzled.

'Oh, aye, and a potent brew it is too,' she laughed, wiping her hands on her apron. Seeing my confusion, she proceeded to enlighten me. 'Melt one pound of hog's lard with a gentle heat in a bottle plunged into warm water; then add half an ounce of phosphorous and one pint of Mr Pedder's good proof spirit; cork the bottle securely and shake it to mix the phosphorous uniformly; when cold pour off the spirit, and thicken the mixture with flour,' she recited mechanically. 'It's the brandy that draws 'em and the phosphorous that guides 'em. And they have just enough time to take 'emselves off somewhere and die,' she added by way of conclusion.

We have a versatile cook at Dove's Nest!

★

The rats are still there. I hear them at night and I dread seeing a sharp uplifted nose quivering in the corner of my room, but they are nothing compared to what they were like on that first night.

20th December 1809

The novelty of my situation begins to wear off a little. I am calmer, more at home, and grow more and more pleased with those about me. But there are times when I feel I am not equal to the task. Not only am I responsible for the improvement of Mrs Pedder and the education of little Gertrude in language, manners, books and work, but I also have to attend to the direction and management of the servants and household. I am particularly ill at ease during dinner. There is such a display of plate, cutlery, silver nutcrackers and cruets; I confess some ignorance as to their use. Miss Chorley, I have need of thee!

I am very fond of Mrs Pedder. Her father is a respectable farmer at Holms Head not five miles away. He has another daughter and a son. Mrs Pedder is the youngest and has a quality of mind and a dignity of character, which make her more than equal to the rank to which she aspires – at least in my opinion. Mr Pedder's father, a successful Preston banker, has vowed to have nothing to do with her, but she tries so desperately hard to improve herself that I am confident she will soon win him over. Mr Pedder is probably what people would call a good husband – he would be a better one if he were less fond of the bottle after dinner. But I have no personal complaint. He is full of praise for my efforts with Gertrude.

Anyone can see that she is no ordinary child. She is silent, remote; her eyes are a little strange. Her fits, I think, have a terrible effect on her disposition. She is frequently lost in a dull reverie, which at first I mistook for a lack of concentration. The poor child vexed me to such an extent that it almost induced me to give up my situation. But I am now convinced she suffers from momentary lapses of consciousness even though her eyes blink rapidly at such times. On awakening, she has a frightened look in her face and seems confused and lost. The fits start and end so suddenly that I cannot always save her from falling. She will bruise herself cruelly, and, shuddering with convulsions, will claw repeatedly at her clothes. She seems to have no recollection of what has happened when the fits subside and they leave her tired and listless. The inner creature of her being could be deeply responsive and alive but I am faced continually with a hard, impregnable shell. The only time of the day she shows any excitement is when we are in the garden for our late afternoon walk and she is obviously anticipating seeing Old Solomon coming home and the rough greeting she will receive from his black and white dogs.

16th January 1810
Today we walked to Ambleside in weak sunshine and light showers – the sort of rain that lifts one's spirits rather than depresses them. A mist was lying on the lake and it stretched upwards to an ocean of coppery clouds where fragments of broken rainbows made brief appearances. It is a beautiful road of a mile or so with only the occasional small grey stone house nestled into the near-wilderness of Wansfell and allowing constant glimpses of the dull mirror of Windermere.

'He is a very singular sort of person. I am sure you will like Mr Green. He wanders through the district in all weathers sketching and painting,' said Mrs Pedder brightly. 'He works very hard, I am told, with his paints and acids and copper plates.'

'I have not seen him at church then?' I asked.

'I shouldn't think so. But he does speak a good deal about his notions of God in a grand, inflated style. And he is guilty of the most preposterous compliments – sometimes bestowing them lavishly upon himself! Yet he is so likeable, he shocks no one and is welcomed as a friend to visit or to shelter at any house in the district whether they be poor or gentle.'

★

Reaching the market square of Ambleside, we opened Mr Green's iron gate on the main street opposite the White Lion and then hesitated at the door of his exhibition rooms as we shook and closed our umbrellas. The privilege of entering them usually costs a visitor to the Lakes a shilling piece. The walls were covered with pictures, others were on tables, and portfolios of different sizes were all around the rooms. The man I took to be Mr Green was large and tall, with flashing black eyes and a ruddy complexion. He had obviously been engrossed in earnest conversation with another man, who could have been as young as forty or as old as sixty. His dark hair was thinning above thought-worn temples and heavy eyebrows. He gave a general impression of roughness. He was dressed in a rough brown fustian jacket and his face, too, was rough looking, strong with a cleft chin and cheeks that were lined and pitted. He may have spent some time at sea.

Mr Green saw us at once, and came towards us smiling smoothly.

'Ah! Good morning ladies,' he said, bowing formally. 'Kind of you indeed to brighten this rather dull day.'

His companion did not appear overtly enthusiastic about our arrival and was not drawn into conversation, but merely gave a reserved nod in our direction. His attention was taken by two little girls bent studiously over a bench at the end of the room. The older may have been twelve and was busily mixing pigments for colours with a quiet, professional air while keeping an eye on the younger girl who was about six, slight and worryingly frail. She was hunched over a pencil with a frown of concentration, which was broken by a sudden rattling cough.

'Come along, Dora, the rain has eased and we had better be off,' he said.

'She progresses well,' said Mr Green expansively, looking at her efforts.

'Yes, she is sharp enough,' said her father kindly, helping to draw her coat over her thin shoulders and fussing with a shawl in protective concern. 'She does well at drawing, not so well at Latin, I'm afraid, for she does not have the same pride in it.' He lifted her chin tenderly and smiled for the first time. 'Good morning to you all, and thank you, Elizabeth,' he said, nodding to the fair-haired girl seated with Prussian blue, viridian green, and burnt umber before her.

'Goodbye,' said Mr Green warmly, 'and remember for my part at least, I would rather live on bread and water here than on the fat of the land in London. Art! Art is the only true index of civilised life. The city holds no attractions for me.'

When they had left, Mr Green continued in a voice full of admiration, 'An extraordinary, a wonderful man, and a generous one is our Lakeland poet!'

'He is a poet? I would not have guessed from his appearance,' I said.

'There is more to that man than meets the eye I can assure you. What a riotous treasury of a mind!' He sighed audibly. 'But I will leave you in peace.' Saying this he waved vaguely at the walls and joined his daughter still silently at work in what constituted their makeshift studio.

My eyes had been drawn to the paintings around me.

The room fell silent. The creak of Mrs Pedder's shoes on the floor and the slight bustling sounds from the artist only served to emphasise the quietness. It was raining again. I looked at the watercolours. My first impression was of an absence of light, as if they had been painted on a sunless day, but a sharp pleasure had been taken in capturing the nuances of changing misty light dappling the surface of lakes and staining refulgent clouds. The shadowed foreground drew the eye at first, but was then lifted above to be lost in lambent, limitless space. The apparent simplicity of his etchings was also deceptive. His rocks and boulders were objective, particular, solid. They had been sketched in meticulous detail by one who has walked among them, handled them – loved them. Each painstakingly built on each until the pack bridge, or twisted elm, or cataract rested on a solidity, which exerted a palpable gravity. I had thought Mr Green a little affected. I was now humbled before the man who had been so humbled before his god. After I don't know how long, I became aware that he was smiling at me beside a fair woman, much younger than himself, with bright blue eyes and carrying a tray.

'My wife, Anne, would not hear of your leaving without some tea.'

22nd February 1810

My eyes are pouched, my face flabby with grief. Tonight I held the palm of my left hand over the open flame of a candle. It is blistered and cracked and weeping. I left it there for as long as I could endure it. It wasn't for long – it wasn't enough. I can hardly bring myself to write what I feel I must. Gertrude is dead – burnt to death!

★

The morning was bleak with a dull, raw cold. It was Friday, Friday the sixteenth, and there had been an angry scene outside the house between Mr Pedder and Old Solomon.

'There is no doubt whatsoever about it.' Mr Pedder was irate and his voice was raised discordantly to a near shout. He stood with his feet apart – short, staid, serious. 'Jonas Crossely was here himself last night. His fell shepherds clearly saw your blasted dogs after them – and it is not the first time. There is talk of compensation, man! I can't afford to be paying for my neighbour's sheep. The damned things must be put down. Patrick will do it this morning.'

The heavy old man's features were reduced to the bare rudiments of a face. His mouth was pursed, his eyes embittered. He kneeled on one knee and tenderly patted one of the culprits, which had been grinning up at him through its wet mauve mouth. Its thick winter coat was dusty with life. Another was gnawing at a raw spot above one of its paws.

'No. Patrick wad goa and be messing it up,' he said stonily, reverting to a blurred, rustic accent. He was suddenly no longer argumentative but quietly resigned. 'Ye kna I am a verra careful man. I will do it myself.' His old wrinkled face jerked in a spasm of painful struggle and he mumbled on like a deaf man. 'I will take em up the fell. That maistly be where they wad like, ye kna.'

He stood, moved his gun on his arm and walked off, his boots scrunching on the gravel. The dogs padded after him in the heavy light, their noses close to the ground and their plumed tails dragging behind them.

Mr Pedder, still angry, was now striding towards the house, and Mrs Pedder and I escaped with Gertrude to the parlour, which we use as a schoolroom. But it was impossible to settle to routine tasks. Mrs Pedder was agitated and ill at ease and Gertrude, too, was distant and petulant. The room was close and hot. Moving Gertrude further away from the blazing fire, I opened the window a little. Solomon by now was nowhere to be seen. The land was in heavy shade – dark and forbidding – the woods leafless, spectral. He would take them into the exquisitely cold shadows cast by boulders high up in the icy air of the fell. With the wild sob of the gun's report, the first would fall easily on its side to the cold earth, its paws drawn up in simple death. Would he tie up the others first? Would they look up at him through clear eyes and understand?

Then I remembered the cook. She would still be waiting for instructions about dinner. She would not, of course, bother herself to remind me about it. 'I likes to keep me place,' she would say with a sardonic half-smile in mock deference to my station. Her expansive arms would be folded or perhaps be busy drawing a bird's entrails or worrying a slab of red beef with a mallet.

'I am sorry Mrs Pedder. I have forgotten to see Mrs Morley. She will be waiting for me.'

'I saw her just now in the larder. I will come with you.'

It eased the tension we felt to be actively engaged even on so trivial an errand. We left Gertrude in the parlour window where I had put her. She was fond of fire to the point of obsession, and I had, only the day before tried to impress upon her the importance of keeping a safe distance from the fire screen. The thought crossed my mind as rapidly as a swallow flitting across the empty space of sky and was gone. We can never be quite sure how important anything is. The moment is unreadable, as we are not privileged to interpret it in the light of what it may lead to, and the moment cannot be recovered. The poor unfortunate child must have taken the opportunity to indulge her fascination the moment we left the room.

I firmly believe we had not been absent more than a minute – I have sworn so before the coroner – when I heard a scream. I ran instantly. I heard her scream again, and, opening the parlour door, met her running towards it. A whirl of fire higher than her head blazed around her clutching and tearing at her hair. For an instant, I could do nothing. I stood appalled before the crucible of lurid light. Time itself seemed to slow in that terrible moment when the event and its meaning coalesced. A child was in flames. A child was the plaything of fire. Her limbs seemed heavy; her movements slow and laboured as she writhed in the lonely and obscene ballet of feasting flame.

An awful scream from Mrs Pedder brought the servants. Galvanised, I rushed into the servants' hall for the heavy ironing blanket – it was washing week, and I remembered seeing it there. I may have been blubbering incoherently or the screams in my ears may have been mine – I don't remember. I threw the blanket to the nurse who was trying desperately to put out the flames with her apron, injuring her own hands as she did so. While she rolled her in the blanket, I ran into the butler's pantry to find some water or any cool liquid to throw on her burning, melting flesh. I could find nothing. I returned and begged someone to find some water. The blanket lay on the floor beside the suffering child. I grabbed it again to extinguish a glow on what remained of her clothes.

'Patrick! Go for the surgeon in Ambleside. Take the best horse. Go like the wind, for God's sake!'

The voice came from the twisted face of Mr Pedder. His mouth was an ugly red slash in his pale face.

The child was led into the hall, and to our relief, she did not seem badly burnt. We began cutting and tearing off the seared rags that had once been her clothes.

'Will she be marked?' Mr Pedder asked of no one in particular.

Gertrude did not scream again. Nor did she cry or moan, she only whimpered softly between smothered dry sobs. A sudden shuddering fear gripped me that perhaps she was beyond any feeling.

'Dear God!' I groaned, 'will no one bring some water?'

Mrs Pedder jumped to her feet, her eyes wide and staring. 'There is a phial of hair oil,' she said, her voice choking, and ran to her room for it.

I smeared the makeshift unguent as far as it would go on the dry black skin above her knees. Her lower legs were wet and bubbled. Someone had brought a heavy wooden pail from the dairy and we busied ourselves pouring the milk on the poor girl who stood naked and patiently before us on the wet floor. Her legs must have caused her the most pain. She also took up a piece of torn linen and dipped it into the cold milk, and wrung it out over her damaged legs. I grew a little calmer and was going to touch her face to give her some comfort, when the change that came over her clear eyes as she looked at me shocked me to the soul.

'Let her sit down,' begged Mrs Morley.

'No, no, keep her standing,' I said, my voice was no more than a harsh whisper. I could now see that her legs and thighs were shockingly burnt. The skin hung from her trembling limbs like shreds of waxed paper. In places her skin was blistered cruelly and she began to shrink from the gentle dabs of milk-soaked linen.

'Keep her standing until the surgeon arrives,' I said again. I was afraid that her skin might stick to those who held her or to the wool of the rough blanket if we allowed her to sit on it.

Every minute seemed like ten, but at last Patrick returned – without the surgeon. He was attending a difficult birth, and would come later, but his apprentice had brought a bottle of something with which to bathe her. She took my hand. Tears pricked my eyes, blinding me as I led her to her bed. Her firm little hands had been untouched. What was left of the pieces of linen sheet was soaked in the lotion the apprentice had brought and gently placed on the parts seared by the flames. Enveloped in oil, she then began to shiver uncontrollably and we covered her with a fresh sheet and a blanket. She recovered for a time, but was then seized by fits. She had three in quick succession. Mr Pedder retreated from the bed as if in fear and as white as vellum. The thought occurred to me that perhaps he had come to Dove's Nest not only to shield his dairymaid wife, but also to hide his little girl from the prying eyes of the world. I had seen him show little affection towards the child, marooned as she was on her distant silent island. I had to hold her hands to prevent her from plucking at her already tattered skin, which was now the colour of lungs. I discovered her feet were as cold as stones and began rubbing them. Mrs Morley brought some water heated in a bottle and held it to them. At last the surgeon, Mr Scrambler, arrived. Mary was again uncovered, again anointed and bound in long oily strips of linen.

'You are known for a good clever man, Scrambler, but should I send for a physician?' asked Mr Pedder, now in greater command of himself.

'I believe there is no great danger, but if it will relieve your mind, I could certainly recommend Doctor Cassels in Windermere,' he said quietly, leaning over the now sleeping child muffled up in the bed.

Between five and six o'clock in the evening, I was called down to make tea for Mr Langford, the clergyman, who sat talking kindly to Mrs Pedder on the ottoman, and for Mr Scrambler, who was drumming the arm of a ponderous armchair, which he had drawn up close to the fire. When Doctor Cassels arrived, Gertrude had a convulsive fit. Mustard plasters were applied to her feet and Doctor Cassels administered frequent drafts of ether, brandy and water, and wine. They were to no avail. She remained unconscious – she merely breathed. The nurse and I sat with her all night. The two doctors sat in the parlour below, coming up occasionally. Mr and Mrs Pedder were prevailed on to retire but I went every hour to tell them how she was. About five in the morning, she was breathing audibly, but each breath was shorter and shallower than the last. I became frightened and fetched the doctors and at their request called up Mr and Mrs Pedder. We stood helplessly around the bed in complete silence listening to every breath. I prayed for her. I prayed desperately to the God of stone chapels and vast cathedrals. I prayed to the God who had loved little children, but she was gently torn from us in the cold darkness just before dawn. Mr Pedder left the room immediately without uttering a sound. Mrs Pedder crumpled onto the edge of the bed, her slight figure bent in reverent, terrible grief.

★

I helped to lay her out. Mrs Pedder suffered greatly and could not do it. From the time she caught fire to the time it was put out could not have been five minutes. Her body was very little damaged; she was scarcely touched on the breast or stomach. Her legs and arms were the worst. Her little tucked-in chin was scorched and eaten; her ear and the left side of her face were a good deal burnt. She was washed and I clothed her in her white nightdress and stockings and laid her on a clean sheet on the hard mattress. Mercifully, her eyes were already closed and needed no weights. I fastened her feet together with a white satin ribbon and tied it in a bow. We raised the head of the bed by putting blocks of wood under the casters. The fire was allowed to go out; the window closed; and a single candle lit. I was reluctant to leave her. The house was still infested with rats. Although they remained unseen, we often heard them gnawing and scuffling in the walls and ceiling. It was agreed that we could not leave her alone and that someone should sit with her, night and day, to ensure that they did not injure the body.

★

I took my turn on the last evening, which was Tuesday. The coffin had arrived that morning and the funeral procession was to leave Dove's Nest at noon the following day, and it should have arrived in Preston today, Thursday. Mrs Pedder was almost distraught at the idea of going to Preston, but Mr Pedder was confident that their sad circumstances would reconcile them to his father. I was passing the kitchen on my way to begin my gloomy vigil, when I was shocked to hear loud laughter. Mr Pedder was sitting in front of a small coal fire with his footmen and the maid and drinking with them. Mrs Morley was sifting flour over some dough or other mixture on a bench and was ruddy with warmth and apparent good humour. What a strange man! While the body of his only child lay in the house he was listening to Dawes, his servant and drinking companion, regale the company with a story about Old Solomon. The day before, he had quarrelled openly with Mrs Pedder about the expense of mourning clothes for the household. He had declared in the vilest language that he could not afford so much as a few yards of black bombazine – not even for the nurse who had injured her hands trying to help Gertrude. But there he was, his feet on the fender drinking Burton ale with his servants in the kitchen. Not once since his daughter's death had he visited the body in the upper room.

'"There will be another death as sure as rain," he says,' mimicked Dawes, exaggerating Solomon's ancient voice and widening his eyes deliberately. 'You know how he carries on. "Mark my words young man," he says, bringing his old stone face and watery eyes close to mine. "On the day of the fire, I was coming down from the fell and saw an eagle. It screamed until the hills answered it."'

Leaning against the mantelshelf, Dawes looked askance and saw me standing in the doorway, but was not in the least disconcerted. He wrinkled his forehead and offered no more than a peremptory tightening of his lips at me. Lounging whenever he was not formally a footman, he was physically a fine man with his dark, sulky good looks. Idle and sensual, he was committed to nothing in life but himself. I felt his restless eyes linger on my mouth before he turned to his audience with a smile of self-congratulation. Almost against my will I continued to stand on the threshold, feeling as if I had transgressed some private boundary or had been caught listening at a keyhole.

The maid, who was little more than eighteen, her lank hair loose and disordered, gave an affected frightened little pout with her wet lips, 'Oh. I wonder who it will be?'

There was a drunken gleam of audacity in her eyes as she looked at Dawes and yawned without the slightest diffidence. She would be capable of any backstairs lust. Dawes hesitated, raised his eyebrows and said no more. A cold unpleasantness had entered the room, although Mr Pedder seemed oblivious to it. He laughed again – a bitter, strange laugh – his lips curling sardonically.

'I shouldn't worry too much about it,' he said, his voice burred from drink. 'If the superstitious old coot found the nest he would be down in Windermere next week selling the eggs for five shillings apiece and telling the world how he fought off the parent birds with a hand pike.'

His pasty face was puffy and ugly from days of

dissipation. His misty eyes met mine momentarily before I turned and walked up the cold staircase to the even colder room of Gertrude. I chaffed angrily at the bridle rein of restraint that had forced me to stand there and endure such impertinences and petty treacheries without challenging them. No matter where I go, I suppose, I can expect some unpleasantness. I must remember that I came here with a price tag – thirty guineas a year – and so I must hold my tongue.

I knocked gently on the open door and the nurse raised her finely lined depressed face and gave a wan smile. She quietly gathered some sewing together with which she had been occupied and left with a 'Thank you'. The soft brevity of her thanks showed her relief to leave the sad, silent room. The open coffin had been placed on the bed. Shadows from the small fire danced over the walls. The flames licking the coals were blood red. I sat and stared at the lighted candle on the small table beside my chair, and thought of Solomon trudging home alone that night, the winter deepening around him, gazing up at the eagle screeching death, the grating wind riffling its brown plumage. A coal in the fire moved or a floorboard creaked. Startled, I looked up into the mirror in the corner of the room. It was angled in such a way that I did not see myself but Mr Pedder framed in the doorway behind me.

He staggered towards the bed completely drunk, knocking over a little brass bowl of hairpins off a side table. It clattered noisily onto the floor. He was on the bed with the coffin and worked himself into a frenzy of maudlin violence, lying down beside the coffin, getting astride it, pulling at and mauling the body. Dawes appeared at the doorway, but stood there transfixed by the disturbing grotesqueness of the scene.

'She's not dead!' he declared gaspingly. 'She has been this way before – many times! Look! She will wake – she will wake!'

I stood in an agony of dread that at any moment he would have her out of the coffin. He opened the mouth repeatedly, kissing it and calling her to speak to him. It was as if he were playing a part in an opera or some lugubrious comedy and he was called upon to grossly exaggerate his role. He stopped, as if suddenly ashamed, groaned in animal misery and sat on the hard waxy floor beside the bed, his knees drawn up in a paroxysm of rage and mewling grief.

He lifted his haggard face to Dawes who had come forward at last. 'This is what I get for leaving a dairymaid in charge of my daughter,' he ranted accusingly.

Dawes, his own face pale and sickly, bent over him and took him firmly behind the elbows. 'Come, sir! Let me help you up.'

Mr Pedder responded with a violent laugh. Spit flew from his discoloured lips. 'A dairymaid! My God, a poor silly dairymaid!' He was now on his feet, massaging his forehead with the fingers of both hands as Dawes supported him and tried to lead him out of the room. He began to mutter obscenely in another growing wave of agitation. Shaking Dawes from him, he stood swaying unsteadily and looked about the room with unseeing eyes, knifing the air with half intelligible words and phrases, before stabbing home a final, damning statement, which was as lucid as glinting steel. 'If it had not been for Miss Weeton and Mrs Pedder, the child would still be alive.'

He continued to stand there for a moment, as if searching the burgled bank of his mind for some essential fact that he could not remember then passed through the doorway into the hall with Dawes in respectful pursuit. I could not be sure if, at any time, he had been aware of my presence in the room. But he had rent the very fabric of my being and I collapsed into the chair as if I had been physically struck. There was some truth in what he said and I will carry that knowledge to my own grave.

★

The night slowly wore itself away and in the morning the sombre procession left. Several gentlemen attended as far as Kendal. Mrs Pedder, the nurse, the footmen, too, are gone. In the early morning half-light, Mr Pedder himself, his face mottled and unhealthy, had relieved me from my duty in Gertrude's room. My courage almost failed me when his gaunt form again appeared at the door, but he is inconsistency itself. He had regained his self-possession and civilly asked me if in their absence I would assume responsibility for the running of the household and that he earnestly wished me to continue on at Dove's Nest as Mrs Pedder's companion and teacher.

25th February 1810
Mr Pedder, like many of the wealthy has a fine oak library. He reads but little, but his books are numerous, well selected and valuable. How rich in books I would be if I owned all the volumes he has never opened! In the candlelight they glow with colour: some a striking green, others with warm hues of bright red and rich brown. I like the leathery scent of them. Surrounded by millions of words, I write my poor offerings to Ann Winkley and to Tom. I see little of Mrs Morley and the maid. I am interred in silence in someone else's empty house. At best it can only be a temporary sanctuary. I have no home. There is no one anywhere waiting for my return. Tonight, my pages are lonely even when they are filled with

words. My audience is distant – half real, half imaginary. I open the window and breathe in the snow-cold night. The expanse of night sky is starry above a bank of cloud as dark as boredom. I listen to the soft, ancient sounds of the night. An elemental loneliness settles over the house like mist or sleep. I feel the tender new skin on the palm of my damaged hand.

30th March 1810
Mr Pedder frowned.

He sat at the end of the large dining table – saturnine, sullen, sybaritic. The room was hot and the smell from the roast pheasant and bread sauce lingered unpleasantly. There had been little of the meal that I could eat.

'Sit down, for God's sake. I am married, damn it! Surely you can spend some time with your husband. At least have a game of cards and stop carping about money for an hour.' His small soft lips became taut and cruel. 'You don't have to get up early tomorrow morning to milk the cows you know,' he said, ending with a soundless laugh.

Mrs Pedder had dressed for dinner. She was slim and elegant. Her tawny hair was pulled back into a simple knot leaving the lower part of her ears exposed. She sat slightly round-shouldered and her fingers nervously turned a simple jewelled bracelet on her wrist.

In a quiet low tone without turning to look at him, she spoke to Dawes who was standing formally behind her near the wall, white gloved. 'Thank you, that will be all, Dawes, you may leave us.'

'Thank you, Dawes, you may leave us,' mocked Pedder in a high simpering voice, then added with brutal emphasis, 'and bring some more claret – there is hardly enough here.' His delicate hands, sensitive as a girl's, tilted the near empty decanter. I noticed his cambric shirtfront was stained and flecked with wine.

Dawes nodded and left, his boots creaking like a ship at sea in the now silent, oppressive room.

Mrs Pedder looked as if she had a racking headache. Her usually eloquent eyes were silent; her voice was soft and hollow. 'You speak to the servants with more respect than you do to me.' There was a hiatus in which she met her husband's chill grey eyes. 'You humiliate me.' The words obviously cost her a great deal to say.

'A servant must not be spoken to harshly, for they can quit you when they please. A wife may be treated in any way according to the whim of the moment, because she is tied by the law and cannot quit you when she pleases,' he replied dryly and emptied his glass with an expression of bemused satisfaction.

She seemed to sink further under a weary sadness, but she did not keep silent. 'And I was not carping about money, although I could mention that the washerwoman has now waited for weeks, almost months for her payment, and that tradesmen's bills must be paid some time. Why not pay them as soon as they are due rather than keep honest men waiting so ungraciously?' A brittleness had entered her voice. 'It is, of course, your money dear, as you so often point out to me. I also fail to understand why you want yet another boat when we have only had one outing on the lake and that only to Bowness.'

'It's a light rowing boat, not a blasted yacht I'm talking about!' he shouted, his voice husky with anger. 'Dawes, where the hell are you? I notice that there was no complaint from you when I bought those paintings from your friend, Mr Green. Ah, no, of course not! Even when in my humble opinion his sheep look like hide bound rocks in spite of the jackass braying so solemnly about the grandeur of art.'

She gazed appealingly at me. 'My husband acquired his refined speech at university – or was it in the army?'

'We do so little,' I ventured, 'perhaps an excursion somewhere?'

'And you, Miss Weeton,' he stormed, rising to his feet, 'take a good deal too much upon yourself! If I were you I would be a little more cautious in what I said, or you and I will be parting company as easily as that!' He rudely flourished his arm in front of my face and gave a little thwack with his thumb and middle finger. My self-possession nearly left me, but I said nothing. He gave a bitter laugh. 'No, no, you could be right,' he sneered cruelly his mouth wet and purpled from the wine. 'We should perhaps make another visit to Preston!'

Mrs Pedder bowed her head – at last submissive and silent. Her face paled with her shame and anger. Gertrude's funeral had been held at Preston in the hope the sad event would soften the heart of Mr Pedder's father and hasten a reconciliation. He had attended the funeral and had been cordial enough to his son, even offering a room at his own house. But when the old gentleman learned that his son had brought his wife, he didn't utter another word nor did he take the slightest notice of her.

Mr Pedder stumbled towards the doorway, clutching the crystal decanter in one hand. Reeling slightly, he had to steady himself by holding onto a wall sconce and knocked the candle to the floor in a splash of wax. He gave vent to a volley of oaths before making his way to the kitchen to join the company he no doubt found more congenial than ours.

Mrs Pedder continued to sit in her splendid misery for several moments, her soft luminous eyes swimming in repressed tears. Unconsciously, she tugged at her bracelet, so violently at times that she could have been trying to rid herself of a rusted circlet of iron that was biting into her tender blue-white wrist. But it was a lovely thing of gold and diamonds, alive with points of firelight as she turned and twisted it.

I reached out and took her hand.

'I think it best not to antagonise him. Try to bear with him more patiently and quietly. A man likes to be master in his own house, I am sure.'

It was glib, naïve, even hypocritical. There is no pleasing him. He knows no medium between the tyrant and the slave and I was still trembling from the effort of maintaining the pretence of my own passive character.

She was silent, then exclaimed, 'He is master, mistress and housekeeper! He may do as he pleases.'

★

I steal from sleep to write this in the welcome sanctuary of my room. I am no longer needed in this house – perhaps unwanted. When little Gertrude was living my days were fully occupied with the care of her and the instruction of Mrs Pedder. Since we lost the poor child, I am of little service. My days are idle and exhausting! A little household sewing in the morning until Mrs Pedder comes down. She is now seldom early. Some days she will reluctantly take lessons, and some days not. She has lost all enthusiasm for them since the funeral. I expect there will be a terrible row one day when Mr Pedder discovers she has abandoned her learning completely, and then the consequence will be my dismissal. He will think it too great an expense to keep me solely as a companion to his wife. We have an afternoon walk if it is fine, tea time arrives and the evenings are spent enduring the niggling, monotonous hours playing cards – if an ugly quarrel does not erupt as they do more and more frequently. I have little time for reading; less for writing – even a letter; none for my music.

His treatment of me until tonight has been, at worst, grudgingly respectful. My turn has now come. I am kept here for ostentation, not out of kindness to his wife. Like his passing interest in sailing or his momentary lapse into art, I was a sort of hobby for a while. Perhaps he is disappointed that I did not prove to be a permanent and convenient hobbyhorse for him under his own roof. I would not care to look too closely into such a soul. But I must hide my resentment and steel myself to at least an apparent calm and be content to weep in private. I cannot let all go for nothing in a fit of vexation. No! No! I will persevere. I will be humble, patient, submissive, anything but vicious! I must remember – thirty guineas a year. Tomorrow, if he is true to form, wine-scarred and capricious, he will insist on a ride in the curricle with Mrs Pedder. He will be all charming good humour. The sadness of Dove's Nest must not be noised about in the neighbourhood.

7th April 1810

It is an afternoon of clouds contesting with thin sunshine and I am writing this in my favourite place at Dove's Nest, in the old-fashioned arbour that affords a view down the length of Windermere. A letter from Tom, his first to Dove's Nest, lies unopened as yet beside me. Somewhere nearby, but out of sight, Solomon – staunch, durable, guileless – is still working. I can hear the sodden clump of his hoe. He was in the small, walled garden near the kitchen when I met him on my way here. He is confident that we have had the last frost and was planting out some herbs. He stood, crushed some leaves in his gnarled, heavy hands, raised them as if to hide his sagging dewlaps, and breathed in the clean pungency of fennel, land cress, marjoram and mint, before greeting me pleasantly.

'Early spring this year Miss. I never recollect a warmer winter. Last year now, the lake was frozen over so that carts could pass upon it.'

'If my life were my own, I should like to have some lonely farm house near here, with a wish to live and die there,' I said abruptly. I am still a little shaken and surprised at the intensity of feeling that had arisen with my reply. 'For six months out of twelve, I would be content to ramble the country over and run up the hills like a mountain sheep and scarce heave a sigh for society. I must confess the colder months would draw me to my own kind a little more perhaps.'

He knelt and turned the rich spring earth splashed with buttery light. He looked as thoughtful as a chess piece. He then paused at his work, gently scratched his forehead on the hairline, cleared his throat as if he were going to speak, but he only gave me a puzzled look of what could have been troubled entreaty or even embarrassment.

★

The arbour is almost strangled by a climbing rose tree, which, in spite of its appearance, lives and will soon reveal its simple beauty. My eye is drawn from habit to the ambiguously worded message pencilled on the inside of the time-stained wall: *Adam Walker was delighted here, 24th June 1807*. Underneath, to explain who Adam Walker was, but not how, or with whom, he was delighted is written almost certainly by the same hand – *The celebrated experimental philosopher*. It is but a small celebration of vanity, I suppose! I must open Tom's letter.

What a letter! I transcribe it here for posterity!

Dear Ellen,

Forgive me for not writing sooner. The children have been ill – two, dangerously. The fatigue of attending on them brought Mrs Weeton into a pleurisy. You may have some idea of the state of the house when I inform you that two Miss Scotts are here, two nurses and two servants. In my distress I sent for Doctor Caunce from Wigan and now Doctor Guest of Leigh refuses to attend any longer. May he go to the Devil!

Ellen, for God's sake write to your aunt. She talks much of her uneasiness in not knowing your whereabouts. Why must you be so close and independent? She has heard from someone in Up Holland a curious if laughable account of you having gone off with a young gentleman in a coach from Liverpool! I see no reason why I should be forced into the role of mediator on your behalf, and I certainly cannot afford to upset her given my present circumstances.

Yours,

Tom

Adam Walker, I wish I were enough of the philosopher to believe that in a few weeks I will be ready to laugh at the tattling, meddlesome district of Up Holland and my malicious relatives, but a milder temper than mine would burn with resentment at such injustice. I know my aunt so well! No doubt she is still suffering from her last illness and still fastidiously sniffing out sin with an acid pessimism. Why did she not ask Tom immediately? She could have found out long ago if she were not blinkered like a saintly workhorse. It matters so much to her to have something to tell and the sour little tale would have suffered nothing in the telling and re-telling. And *she* is hurt at the noise being made! What a poor wounded name, things standing thus unknown, shall live behind me! And there is nothing from Tom, no consolation, no interest in me, only acrimonious nagging. You are no Horatio, Tom! When I was last in Leigh, you reproved me for being too open and humble, now – too close. Whatever I do or whatever I say is wrong.

Should I write to the Braithwaites? Surely they would not listen to the rumourmongers? I informed Tom of every particular before I left Liverpool, but I wanted to keep the motive of my departure a secret in case I was obliged to return. If I failed why should the world know?

★

The light is beginning to slowly seep away from the soft, changeable sky much to the noisy chagrin of some diminutive birds darting about in the hazel bushes. A large striped bee searches the intricate calligraphy of the rose's leafless branches, impatient for its flowers. The shadows lengthen. The cold is coming up. No. Let the report die away unnoticed. Let it be like its propagators, unworthy of notice. I rejoice at having left Up Holland. I will make little effort to see it again.

2nd May 1810

I enjoy the solitary freedom of being on the lake in early morning when the mist is rising from the cold water. I like the dip and hiss of the oars, the wooden rumble of the rowlocks, the tension across my shoulders, the smell of new wood and new rope. Intended only to convey passengers from land to Mr Pedder's yacht, the little boat is no more than seven or eight feet long, but it skims across the water like a swallow. Simple as the art of rowing is, he will not venture out on the lake alone and has given me the free use of it. I would like to row as far as Low Wood Inn or around one of the smaller islands. It is still early in the season and there are as yet few visitors. Seen from a great height, I must appear to be no more than a mere speck crawling slowly over the surface of the earth's eye. Yet this morning, I was not entirely alone. I shared the lake with other living things. Swans – salt white – glided in the thinning mist like creatures of myth; a grey heron stabbed the stippled shallows; the first of the sedge warblers whirred in the reeds; insects clicked and flicked in the warming air around me. There is so much variety, so much more beauty than we need. Wet light on tree trunks; silver grey clouds in the sky; old willows, skeins of mist. I stopped rowing and drifted into stillness – into an immensity that is surely not blind, but alive and somehow connected with our minds.

8th July 1810

Miss Rhodes, from Walton, is staying with us for a fortnight and Mr Pedder has been civil even if his amiability is always premeditated and never spontaneous. A party was made up to climb to the summit of Fairfield, a high mountain a few miles from here. We were twelve in number, not including the four men who attended and carried provisions. Mrs Pedder, Miss Rhodes and myself left Dove's Nest shortly before five in the morning in a cart. Mr Pedder was on a pony and Dawes rode a sad looking donkey. We stopped for breakfast in Ambleside at the White Lion Inn. Here the Partridges of Troutbeck, Miss Russell, the two Travis girls and Mr Green joined us. Mrs Green, whom I now consider to be a firm friend, is expecting another child in November and was unable to accompany us on such an expedition. The silent early morning light made the most ordinary of nature's objects beautiful as we made our way up an astonishingly steep and rocky road – the ladies in carts, the gentlemen on foot, with the exception of Mr Pedder and Mr Partridge senior. More than once there was a stifled scream when we expected to be overturned or roll backwards out of control, but no accident occurred.

High stone walls made entirely of loose stones of every shape and size ran up the steepest hills at odd angles to the very summits through the gorse and heather. One could easily convince a child that they were the work of some forgotten mountain giant still to be found high up in the mountains with a map of the land spread across his bare angular knees. But no, human hands – generations of rough, work-worn hands have built those miles of stone. On the heath-covered hill, a few mouldy cottages made in the same manner with stones untouched by the chisel sullenly turned their blank faces to us. One only was alive with hollyhocks, their showy pink flowers reaching almost to the narrow peaked roof. Such houses are completely without mortar of any kind, and although they are plastered on the inside, how the people bear in winter I don't know. Even at this time of year, the weather side was damp and mossy.

When we arrived at the extremity of Scandale, the provisions were taken out of the carts and placed on the donkey, which had been brought for that purpose. Just as we were about to continue our ascent on foot, Dawes announced our presence on the mountain by blowing a small hunting horn. The donkey perhaps mistaking the graceless sound for one of its own kind commenced a loud braying, which was only slightly more discordant than our laughter at the poor beast. Setting off, scree slopes rose high on our left and a cold wind tugged at our clothing. Our shoes were soon glazed with heath and moss and we slipped amongst wet smells as fecund and musty as mildewed bread. Bright, gaudy toadstools lifted themselves out of the shadows of rocks. We laboured for an hour or two before reaching the summit. There we found a convenient resting place partially protected from the wind, sat on the ground and enjoyed a meal of veal, ham and hung leg of mutton. There were also gooseberry pies, bread, cheese and butter, so I did not starve. The men drank brandy while the ladies had wine or bitters.

Our hunger appeased, the conversation became desultory until attention focussed upon Dawes. He was totally at his ease with a tumbler of Mr Pedder's brandy in his hand and his back securely up against the flat of a stone.

'Talk to them, you will soon discover that the Borrowdale shepherds are ignorant and superstitious to a proverb,' he said to Mr Pedder, but clearly aware that his audience had grown.

Miss Rhodes, who sat beside me, turned her willowy figure to face him directly. I continued to keep my back to him and looked at the surrounding roll and fall of the earth and the far hills made almost invisible by distance despite the clear air. Dawes as feckless and selfish as I know him to be will survive the challenges of life. His flagrant charm alone ensures that. Miss Rhodes' well-shaped face was instantly attentive. Her slender fingers unconsciously caressed her lower lip.

'They are convinced that all the witches have been smoked out of the manufacturing towns of Lancashire and have flown north to these hills and valleys,' continued Dawes. 'It is said of one of them that as he was returning from driving sheep into Borrowdale, he saw something on the ground, which glinted in the sun. He approached it as near as he dared. It was about the size and shape of a small turnip, perfectly smooth and bright, but oddly spotted. To his horror he discovered it had a long tail and concluded it was alive. Imagine his terror when he heard it speak, clearly pronouncing the words, "Tick him, tack him, trick him, take him!" He took to his heels, returning some time later with several cottagers having told them his amazing tale. They too heard the witch's plaything or her minion cry, "Trick him, take him!" Expecting the creature to fly at them at any moment, they began pelting it with stones and when they durst approach near enough, completed its destruction with sticks. The story was told by many a hearth that week, but none knew that they had taken such pains to demolish a handsome silver watch!'

It was a wonder that the resulting laughter did not start the donkey braying again. Miss Rhodes actually applauded him. I rose, determined to explore more of the summit alone. Turning my head, I saw Dawes. His hands did not shake; no more colour had crept into his healthy face. He was as self-possessed as if he had been in the kitchen at Dove's Nest. My own feelings were full and confused. The cold wind began to water and sting my eyes as I ventured to the edge of tremendous rocks and cliffs before me in several directions. My blunt boots scuffed and tore at velvet-soft mats of moss. For all its harshness and its apparent hardness, the place was soft and vulnerable. I could, if I had chosen to, easily have stooped and uprooted a fragile fern without the least effort.

I sat down on a projecting lip of rock. Empty space opened before me as suddenly as a fan snapping open. A perpendicular drop yawned around me on every side but one. Wind rushed upwards at me. My head swam. I would fall. I was falling! I lay full length on the hard ground and shut my eyes. I have never felt more frightened or helpless. Motionless I lay there, my head resting on the back of my hand and my hip bruising against hard stone, powerless and utterly unable to move. I tried to tell myself that I was in no real danger. I was not far from the others, they would easily hear me if I called for help. But I could not bear the thought of being rescued by *him* – *his* hand reaching out for mine, touching it – seeing my hopeless face.

Opening my eyes at last, but without looking to left or right, I stared at the rock an inch or two from my face, my whole body quaking as I tried to blot out the thought of where I was. What was below me! I am not sure how long I was there – perhaps no more than a few minutes. Finally, I steeled myself to crouch, then, half blind with fear, to crawl, and then to run to safety – headlong into Mr Green!

'Ellen! Are you all right?' he asked, his dark eyes alive with immediate concern. 'You quite startled me. Has something happened?'

'I drew too near the edge,' I said haltingly. 'I am growing calm again. I only wish… I wish that… I am sorry if…'

He offered his strong, honest arm, which I gratefully accepted.

'To wish is often to lose,' he said, with a mirthless smile.

'Have you come looking for me?' I asked, suddenly horrified that I may be the centre of attention.

'No. No. But they are readying for departure. No. I came to see God's grandeur spread beneath me. A rugged, noble mountain like this gives me greater pleasure than the most formal garden in England.' He patted my arm reassuringly. 'Yes, you are looking a little better, Miss Weeton. You are quite safe now.' He laughed quietly. 'I hope you will always fly as swiftly to the Greens of Ambleside if you are ever in need of help. You know you are always welcome and the children are so fond of you,' he said kindly. 'We had better join the others.'

11th July 1810

I have not been entirely honest. Dove's Nest has had another visitor and although Miss Rhodes has returned to Walton, he remains with us until Friday. There was someone else on the summit of Fairfield who upset me almost as much as the dizzying heights of that place. He has the gentleness of Mr Price, but not his bantering smile. Life is serious for Reverend Thomas Saul of Lancaster. He is a good man, and unusual in that he wants to do some good. I am frightened to look at him in case the intensity of my longing will be all too obvious in my eyes. Frightened, too, that he will haunt and soothe my dreams, that I will not be able to overcome what I already know is a sense of loss. He is kind and courteous to me, but nothing more. How can he be? There is a fixed gulf between a clergyman of rank and fortune and an insignificant governess who is unable to share even a fragment of herself. I wish he were gone. He is too much for me.

★

Dressed in clothes of deep black, tall, strong in mind and body, he makes a striking contrast with Mr Pedder at the table. The meal is over. Mrs Pedder and I have said little.

'This is a comfortable room, Edward. You are fortunate indeed to be away from the fret of industry.'

'Away from the fortunes generated from the genius of industry as well, I can assure you,' replied Mr Pedder acerbically.

'Men and women who see their livelihood taken away from them can hardly be expected to wax enthusiastic about inventive genius,' responded Reverend Saul with genial tact.

'The mills provide employment surely?' queried Mr Pedder, offering Reverend Saul more wine.

'No thank you, I have had quite enough, excellent though it is,' he said, raising his open hands before him. 'The handloom weavers are quickly becoming wretched and miserable, and I predict the recent prosperity of the factory workers will be short-lived. Their wages are already in serious decline. No, this is a new world Edward. We need a strong church, especially in the growing towns. The distress of the people is palpable. There is hardly a home that can be kept going unless children, some as young as five and six, go to the mill.

I tell you the working man is not so ignorant that he cannot remember a time when he could dig in his own garden and smoke when he liked, when he was as much a farmer as he was a weaver or spinner and could tap the occasional barrel of ale in his own cottage.'

'I can't believe this,' said Mr Pedder in mock seriousness, 'we have a radical preacher amongst us! I fear you will be quoting our local poets next!'

'No. Not at all, but I am afraid, Edward. Take a man's pride, his space, his simple pleasures away from him and how can his spirit be nourished? He will be rendered dangerous and capable of tearing English society in two.'

'If he has the power,' shrugged Mr Pedder, and having offered this neat aphorism he smugly raised his glass again to his soft lips. 'Surely the Bible itself shrewdly prepared the world for the poverty of the poor.' He then added indifferently, 'Things are as they are. We must take the world as we find it.'

Reverend Saul looked directly at me for some moments. A hint of sadness, perhaps wistfulness, lay in the depths of his eyes. His face was kind and enquiring. My heart lurched; my mind grew numb – but his gaze returned to Mr Pedder. He had not really seen me at all.

'In some parts of Lancashire it is now the custom to forbid music in the public houses. Parsons can be found, and no doubt magistrates, who think that the worker will be demoralised if he hears a few chords from an organ in church on a Sunday. Such recreation is deemed a waste. The man playing a fiddle might be more profitably wielding a hammer or tending a loom.'

'Surely you exaggerate,' interjected Mrs Pedder.

'I do not, Mrs Pedder,' he said sadly. 'I do not.'

'Ah, Dawes with the port! Come Thomas, don't be so

serious man! Have a glass of port with me. You are not amongst your poor tribes here.'

13th July 1810
He is gone. I avoided the moment of his departure. He did not ask about me. Mr Pedder is right. Things are as they are. We must take the world as we find it. I will not write of Reverend Saul again. David, we are told, was the man after God's own heart, but I will always like Saul better, which is wicked of me.

21st November 1810
He has taken to prowling the house at all hours of the night. His boots on the creaking boards of the hallway cause a quick wrestling scuffle of rats in the walls. He stops outside my door – perhaps he tries the handle. I lie in my bed, tense and silent, wondering what I would do if he came in. Foul-mouthed with wine, he mutters the crudest of obscenities about me – quietly, but slowly, deliberately. I would rather face Benson's ghost than the soft, fleshy presence of that man, his mind raddled and vindictive with drink.

The days are wearisome to him. Incapable of dedicating himself to any serious purpose or even to a rational amusement, he is becoming sullen and morose. If he is in a cheerful frame of mind for a day, the household is as much surprised as pleased. He bluntly finds fault with everyone and everything. When he is in one of his ill-humours, if Mrs Pedder and I so much as look at each other, he flies into a rage saying we are laughing at him. And since the days have become shorter and colder, his drinking has been more thorough. We no longer attend church. The servants are given a choice and so spend the day in idle drunkenness with their master. Mrs Pedder is thin and pale. She often clutches her left side, which troubles her. Her one pleasure is to ride, which he will no longer allow, and consequently she rarely leaves the house. If she buys a few yards of cloth, a little ribbon or thread, he breaks out into a rage swearing horribly that she will ruin him. She will not; she has neither the power nor the will. Whenever he ridicules her, or rages at her, he always takes care to do so in the presence of Dawes – why, I cannot understand, but it must be grating to one of her sensibility.

I am no longer required to do much. I scarcely stir from my seat from morning till night, sewing, writing or reading. I do my utmost to avoid him, shunning even the garden where I might run the risk of a meeting. Once again my life is reduced to a blank, listless solitude. Sometimes I imagine a letter from Tom, inviting me to live in a cottage near him – but our silence has remained unbroken. Not a single relative has written to me for months.

★

But there was no avoiding him after supper last night.

'Well, can a man never have a moment to himself?' he blurted out petulantly.

There were tiny veins of broken purple in his cheeks, which were the colour of dirty tallow and his dull grey eyes were red rimmed. He would be old before his time. We were more than happy to be granted a reprieve and quietly left the room and went to another. Fewer than ten minutes had passed, when we heard the bell ringing violently and Dawes appeared stating that the master was asking for Mrs Pedder. Although his face was duly impassive, there was a supercilious tone in his voice that galled me.

'What the devil have you left the room for?' Mr Pedder demanded of her. 'Do you think I should allow fire and candles in two rooms? I am hardly surprised that Miss Weeton would give herself such airs and graces, but you should not!'

I shook with the vehemence of my feeling, but said nothing. Mrs Pedder was so pale she looked ill. In a further show of contempt he then proceeded to read the newspaper in silence, ostentatiously turning the pages and completely ignoring us. For a full five minutes, the only sounds in the room were the cold wet squalls sweeping over the house from the northwest, the creak of his chair as he shifted his weight and the occasional splutter and crackle from the fire.

Mrs Pedder rose from the settle. 'Good night, Edward,' she said calmly, 'I am going to bed now.'

'You are not, you slut!' he blazed. The word hit like a slap. 'I have had enough of your damned tempers. Sit down!'

She did not – and had nearly reached the door when he lunged towards it himself, slammed it forcefully and turned the lock.

'We are to be your prisoners then?' she said, a little colour rising to her face, as she looked directly at him with her lips a little apart and almost white.

Something moved in his face. His sullen temper spilled out into dangerous rage.

'No, by God!' he raved, completely out of control. 'If you want to get out, you can get right out!'

He violently grabbed her arm above the elbow with his left hand, opened the door with his right and dragged her towards the main door cursing her like a lunatic. Instinctively I went to her aid and tried to take hold of her hand, but he wrenched her away from me so violently that her head jolted solidly against the oak of the door making a dull heavy sound like a hoe hitting grassed earth.

'Keep your filthy sow's snout out of my affairs!' he almost shrieked.

Mrs Pedder, her eye already swelling, looked at him as if she did not recognise him, this man shouting at her as if in a storm, his mouth twisted and flecked with spit. Something stirred in the dead fire of her heart – her husband! His hand was raised as if of its own accord to strike her. He was a small man; debased, cowardly and so full of self-loathing that he did not know how quickly fear can congeal into anger.

He dropped his arm. Her eyes – elegiac, truthful – had unnerved him. She was not cowed and would not cringe.

'If you put me out, I will walk home,' she said flatly.

'To Holms Head? You fool! In this weather and at eleven o'clock at night?'

But he said no more.

★

Today they left intending to spend a month in and around Allonby near Maryport. I will not be here when they return. I have been paid my last quarter's salary and have received my half-year's rent from Up Holland, which I have asked Mr Price to put out to interest for me. Mrs Pedder cannot escape, the laws of the land prevent that, but I can, and must. This afternoon I visited the Greens. There I was reminded that there are people of purpose and humour in the neighbourhood of Ambleside. For so long I have scarcely been permitted to speak or even to stir in Mr Pedder's presence and yet Mr and Mrs Green have seen it fit for me to be godmother to their new baby William on Thursday next. I was deeply flattered and tears came to my eyes. Perhaps to quell my rising emotion, Mr Green amused me with a story about how a nearby landowner protects the trees he has planted near Keswick. 'His fairytale woods are not guarded by a dragon amidst the trees, but by fierce bulls, one of which recently drove from his labours a celebrated local artist, who, with difficulty, narrowly managed to escape over the wall and into the lower park.' Our laughter filled the room. Poor Mrs Pedder – what a life awaits her. My plans are not fixed as yet, but I hope to board with a respectable family in Ambleside, or near it, for some time to enjoy the countryside and to recruit my health and spirits. I must, of course, look for new employment.

4

Highroyd House near Huddersfield
2nd July 1812

I arrive at Highroyd.

'And please, no modern literature, novels are a dangerous, fascinating kind of amusement, but they destroy all relish for useful instruction – or looking at pictures of great art. It only encourages daydreaming and will make them dissatisfied with their lot in life.'

A new place, new employers, the depressing business of new routines and learning to fit in again.

'As you wish, of course,' I replied.

My head swam with fatigue, in truth, with sickness from my long journey. It had been wet, obliging me to travel inside the coach, which I hate. Had I been able to walk the whole way in two days, I am sure I would not have been so ill.

A window close to my right was heavy with stone tracery, and full of a shadowed, almost treeless landscape of gold and green hills. The light began to change colour with the waning of the evening. Patches of vulnerable blue in the heavy sky leaked sunlight and distinctly marked a row of distant poplar trees that lined a stone bridge on the way down to the tiny village of Honley. Immediately below me in the garden overgrown with nettles and ragged weeds, the branches of an old, unpruned plum tree were alive with a small swarm of sparrows. Blackbirds clacked quietly from the high stone wall, which surrounded the house. I could see Mrs Sudlow. I had met her briefly when I had alighted from the cart that had jolted me over ruts and stones for the last four miles from Huddersfield. She was struggling to shut the heavy iron gates on the short gravel drive. Heavy keys on a metal ring clinked at her ample waist as she tested her strength against the stubborn rusty hinges. It struck me as being a little odd that this would be one of her duties. Highroyd is a country house, not grand but substantial, weighted onto its bleak and isolated hilltop by its squat stone towers and solid oak – and its money and traditions – like the old Armitage documents I had glimpsed in the hall with their little bags of *Heighroyd* soil attached to them, attesting to the ancient roots the family had put down in this their mother earth.

The present Mrs Armitage could not yet be thirty. Pale and tired, her eyes were a little hollowed under her short sparrow-brown hair and they held a hint of bewilderment, sulkiness, or resigned patience – perhaps, it suddenly struck me, even of fear. She darted a quick glance at the long case clock that ticked soberly in the large room.

Her thin-lipped mouth smiled weakly. 'You will be welcome to dine with the family, Miss Weeton, and to take tea with Mr Armitage and myself in the parlour while the children have their supper in the nursery.'

She did not want to make me feel my inferiority at least, but there was something in her nature, which made me feel, if not wary, reserved in her presence. Mrs Armitage would not be one to seek out my company or need my friendship.

'Thank you,' I replied as warmly as I could, conscious that my smile was stiff and forced.

'The children are of course most anxious to meet you, but I insisted that they wait until tomorrow morning when you have rested.' She turned to the door. 'Come in Mrs Sudlow.'

There was another swift glance at the clock.

Breathing noisily, Mrs Sudlow walked purposely to the

windows and drew the heavily brocaded drapes against the dull evening light, plunging the room into sudden gloom. She lit a single candle, which cast a meagre yellow glow over the plain wood of the table.

'You must be desperately tired after so long a journey, so I will bid you good night, Miss Weeton. Mrs Sudlow will show you to your room.' This was said in a noticeably more relaxed tone, and, seemingly content in the half-light of the room, she sat down on a low ottoman.

My battered portmanteau and inelegant green umbrella were still in the hallway. My slight hesitation before picking them up elicited a ready response from the garrulous Mrs Sudlow.

'They keep no carriage and no man-servant; there are but four women servants in the house,' she announced forthrightly, selecting a key from her iron ring, which would presumably give entrance to my room. 'This way please,' she said abruptly. Without the assistance of a candle, I followed her sturdy frame up an ancient staircase. Its balustrade was unpleasantly sticky under my fingers. 'Mr Armitage has but lately come to Highroyd. His father has long wanted him here, but Mrs Armitage objected to such a retired situation. Mr Armitage is engaged in the woollen trade, as you may know. A bad harvest last year brought misery enough, but now our croppers, through no fault of their own, mind, are begging for bread because of them new machines. Mr Armitage's house at Lockwood was one of the first to be attacked by the Luddites as they call 'emselves. It was the same day that old Mr Cartwright was shot at last April.' Her voice continued comfortably without a trace of irony or sympathy. 'They threw stones at the house to draw Mr Armitage to the window and then shot at him. He will not keep a man on the place now for fear he will be betrayed to their so-called

General Snipshears. Mrs Armitage is that worried all the time, she be expectin' and all – and the master is late home tonight.' Reaching the top of the stairs, she paused, heaved a wheezy sigh from the exertion and met my eyes for the first time. 'None of us has forgotten Mr Horsfall, murdered he was on a public road on Crossland Moor. Though there be hardly a man, or a woman neither, in the West Riding who would hesitate to protect the breakers from the gallows – not even for the two thousand pounds on offer I'll be bound.'

She turned the heavy rusting lock in a door at the end of a narrow uneven hallway and then stolidly stood aside holding the large key out to me. Again I hesitated.

'I don't open no doors for them that takes wages same as me,' she said bluntly.

'Then goodnight Mrs Sudlow,' I said with frigid politeness, taking the key.

'Mind, you be about by six now. Mrs Armitage is a great one for looking at the clock and you will be expected in the nursery at seven sharp.'

'I am sure Mrs Armitage will fully inform me of my duties tomorrow, Mrs Sudlow.'

★

I settled into the pillow, which had an odd smell about it – the linen had been poorly aired – when I heard distinctly enough, although it was little more than a whisper, a young voice outside my door: 'Ugly face!' A scurrying of bare feet and a high-pitched giggle followed. Childish thoughtlessness; childish cruelty – it was nothing more – but I sank under a complexity of feelings: anger, self-pity, loneliness. Leaving my bed, tears flooded my eyes. I went to the window and looked out. A melancholy wind moaned, distressing the silence of the night and a grey, misted moon struggled through dark scuds of cloud. The cold would be relentless in its search through such bare hills in the winter. I found a poor stub of a candle, lit it and placed it on a small table near the window. I have no fear of these Luddites. What does it matter if my life is long or short? My future is a blank grey fear.

The one small event of my brother marrying has brought me to this place. How long will grim necessity keep me here, bound, gagged, confined, defined? The great crime, which has cut me off so completely from my brother and my aunt, still remains unknown to me; and that I can be so easily forgotten by them is a constant astonishment to me. They are hard people. They neither know nor care what roof shelters me. And how they represent me to the world God alone knows! It probably does little harm if you tell the occasional lie to others, if you have a good memory, but surely they will suffer for the lies they have told themselves! I know the unfeeling will accuse me of weakness. It is easy to do so if you have a family to cling to and friends nearby, people who sympathise with your disappointments and rejoice with you in your happiness, but let them be deprived of all, let them have no one to whom they can confide and then hear what they say. I dwell upon one depressing subject after another, having nothing and no one to divert my attention. Mr Braithwaite is dead. How I will answer Mrs Braithwaite's sad letter, which I have carried from Ambleside, I don't know, but she is one of very few links I have forged with my past – she, and Ann Winkley who is now Mrs Price – and the Greens. Never in my life have I passed so many happy weeks in succession as those with Mr and Mrs Green when I left the Pedders. For once, I felt at home in the world, alive in the present moment. I was content, and would often think, *now, in this place, I am happy*. Such happiness is as evanescent as the colours of sunset. Even as I revelled in it, I felt it slipping away, day by day, amongst the laughter, the laneways dappled with leaf shadow and the moss-covered trees.

The candle has gone out. I am left in the silver-blue light of the moon listening to the sob of the wind outside.

22nd July 1812

I usually enjoy my time with the children but this morning was wet and plaintive.

'Why did God make lions,' asked five-year-old George, 'when they do nothing but kill and eat us?'

He left the coloured globe we had been studying, grazing its shabby wooden pedestal lightly with his shoe and stood near the window.

'If flies could speak, George,' I answered, more to myself than to George, 'they would say, why does God make little children, who do nothing else but kill us for their sport?'

'Have you been to Africa, Miss Weeton?' asked Miss Sarah Armitage, lifting her small sharp face and self-willed eyes to mine.

'No, child, I have been to no such place as Africa.'

'When I grow up, I think I will go… there!' she exclaimed, jabbing her forefinger somewhere in the vicinity of the Atlas Mountains.

'Well right now Miss Armitage, you can return to your sewing,' I retorted.

She met my gaze before returning to her work. She is a girl of strange temper and will often purposely do the very thing that she knows will most annoy me, but her desire to learn is real enough. She has a quick and hungry mind, which has been sadly neglected by her parents.

'George please stop that immediately and come here! Why that thing is in here I don't know!'

I have been unrelenting in my severity towards them. My mandates, if not my requests, are now reluctantly obeyed.

'Mrs Sudlow says there is no room for it in the nursery because of Emma and Joseph and that it must stay here,' he piped bravely. But he did stop pushing the smooth varnished side of the rocking horse, putting an end to the loud creaking, which had so irritated me. He rested his forehead on the moist pane of the window and looked out, large eyed, at the sodden landscape waving and rippling through runnels of water on the glass.

'We won't be able to go outside again today,' he said sullenly.

'Never mind, there will be other days,' I said cheerfully.

He turned and rubbed his hands together in front of the fire. Although it was July, the gaunt schoolroom had been cold before Mrs Sudlow had grudgingly and noisily brought in wood and paper. The schoolroom bell is often left unanswered. She had left wiping her hands on a stiff grey rag without a word to me. George edged closer to the fireplace. Flame light danced over him; red glints were in the fine nimbus of his hair. Hot sap from the logs popped and spat. Powdered white ash fell from the grate. Three rapid strides brought me to him. I scooped him up into my arms and hugged him tightly to my shoulder. Turning away from the fire, I vaguely registered amazement in Sarah's sharp, cold eyes.

21st August 1812
I hear echoes from the world outside.

I have been invited with Mr and Mrs Armitage to tea and supper at nearby Parkriding, the residence of Mr Armitage senior and his wife. The old gentleman's household consists of two women servants and a boy in livery. Attired in the flowered vest, silk stockings, knee breeches and diamond buckles of a former generation, he is Justice of the Peace, and is as bluff and straightforward as a mill foreman.

'It is not like the old days, Joseph,' he said irascibly, 'when the lawless were dragged to the entrance hall of Highroyd – hardly one could not boast of a lost finger, or a nose severed in some squabble or other – and there receive due punishment. I tell you an iron fist is needed to remind these people of their place in the world. The least we should be able to expect from them is a little deference.' He drew in a long breath through his prominent nose and sighed. 'Rumours! Nothing but rumours everywhere!' His voice grew louder and more commanding. 'This man Barrowclough now, we had pinned some high hopes on his arrest. He would have us believe that French officers on parole are drilling the Luddites on the moors at night, that there are secret depots of arms near Holmfirth, that our very roads are being mined with powder! There seems no limit to his inventive powers.'

'I doubt very much if what John Hinchcliffe had to say was mere rumour,' said Mr Armitage the younger woodenly and leaned back into his chair.

The older man's eyes narrowed behind his thin glasses.

'They intended to take his life, as they did yours! I am sure of that. He was tied hand and foot in his own bed. The shot took out his left eye! And now Schofield has made off God knows where!'

A sober silence ensued for some moments.

'Still nothing on Horsfall's murderers?' asked my master. There was something disconcerting in his tone in spite of his attempt at casualness.

His father's mouth tightened and he shook his grey head slowly.

'Radcliffe is a good man, even if he does talk too much.' He bowed towards his son and said in a quieter voice, 'But the people are not for the likes of us, Joseph. You mark my words and take care.'

★

Fragments of conversation; events randomly prised from the reality of hard-lived lives; names which were meaningless to me. I might as well be blind and deaf for all I see and hear.

★

Highroyd looked ponderous and solemn on its grim sweep of hill as we walked quickly home in the silent light of dusk. Wispy fair-weather clouds moved over the rough immensity of the darkening hills. Silence. No one spoke. Our footsteps were almost soundless in the dewy grass still intoxicated from sunshine. Anxious footsteps. Climbing up to shut out the world.

2nd November 1812

Sometimes I think I must lead the dullest life ever dragged on by mortal. Mill workers are at least able to return to their homes at night; servants gather around the table in warm kitchens; my only refuge after a grinding day of monotony is the empty grey rectangle of the schoolroom made ghostly by the flickering light of the single candle I am allowed. My eyes are inflamed and ache – from hemming yards of cambric. My neck is surely growing longer with trying to get near enough to the light to thread my needles. However, what I gain by length of neck, I suspect I lose in a stoop of the shoulders, which is just as well for I am tall enough! My only entertainment is the oddity of my thoughts. I have little to read. The single book so obligingly lent to me by my employer is Volume II of the *Edinburgh Encyclopedia*. I go to it now remembering some nameless wild flower little George had chosen and we had put it in its pages to press. Caught between life and death, it is faded but it still retains some of its colour if not its lost living beauty.

If only it were *my* room, *my* chairs, *my* books, *my* home. I am thirty-five – an old maid. If love is one's destiny, what grudging charity can I look forward to? I kiss the rod wielded by dull routine and embrace the ordinary. I know my mood will pass, but tonight it seems my life will go on like this forever.

The hollow globe mocks me – and the rocking horse – its peeling canvas saddle and dead glass eyes; its tattered hempen mane. It is an ugly parody of horse. Like some sad, defeated god I turn the sphere of coloured maps and look impotently upon the cities, the vast distances of heat and cold, whole continents that I will never see – the beating heart of the world. I long for the calm and disturbance, the pull and pleasure of travel. To see ostlers in busy inn yards; to hear the clink of harness and to feel the lurch and thud of a coach with four-in-hand or the heaving deck of a ship at sea. But why should fate be kind and partial to me? There must be thousands like me in like situations – and worse.

★

The long days are gone, the winter hardens and the roads are rough and nearly impassable. Walking here is, even to me, almost as much of a labour as it is a pleasure. I see little of Mr and Mrs Armitage. They are a plodding, money-getting, good kind of people. There is no quarrelling or drunkenness here, no conversation after dinner, no cards – all is efficiency. I generally hurry from the table before I have finished the last mouthful. Trade is my master's learning; trade is his life; money is his reward. One suspects that he believes men and women *ought* to spend their lives in hard toil without relief or distraction. They have not once visited the schoolroom or acknowledged the children's rapid progress. Certainly I have never been thanked for my efforts. Nor do they have the least idea what I teach them.

The world turns. Tomorrow will come with another round of petty servitude – and so will the day after that – and the day after that. I cannot lie any longer than six o'clock of a morning, and if I have anything to do for myself I must rise sooner. At seven, I go to the nursery to hear the children's prayers and must remain with them until they have had their breakfast. I am then let out with the children for their exercise. I must be in attendance even though they only play in the grounds. I am often so cold I join in their games to warm myself. I suppose the fresh air is good for me, but I resent it. The nursery maid could well spare me that task. At half past eight, I join Mr and Mrs Armitage for breakfast and return to the children by nine, when we go into the schoolroom until twelve. Cloaks and bonnets and gloves are donned for a short walk or for play until one, when off they come again to dress for dinner at a quarter past. The children always dine with their parents. Dinner is over by two o'clock and we again return to the schoolroom until five. While I have tea in the parlour, the children have their supper in the nursery. I go to them immediately I have finished and remain with them until seven. I then hear their prayers and see them washed. At half past seven they are usually in bed.

The routine is unchanging. We are as punctual as the clock.

27th November 1812
From my aunt and brother I have not heard a word, but they begin to stir a little on my account. I know they have gone to some trouble to obtain my address from Mrs Braithwaite.

5th January 1813

Yesterday, Mrs Armitage's waters broke about three o'clock in the afternoon. Her pains came slowly at first, but inexorably.

Outside was frost bright and piercingly cold. The thin limpid air hung in perfect stillness and in perfect silence above ice-crusted snow. The boughs of the few garden trees were black in the white light. There was ice in the water barrel. Mr Armitage has little faith in the local midwife and set off immediately, shoulders hunched against the cold, for his friend and surgeon Mr Gwinn in Huddersfield. Then at Mrs Armitage's request, he went to Parkriding for his tea. He returned about eight o'clock and waited anxiously downstairs.

Unsure whether I would be expected to perform a part, I was a tangle of shifting emotions as I led Mr Gwinn, still muffled and overcoated, to Mrs Armitage's room. Her face was drawn and already tired, but she gave a weak smile when we came into the room and thanked him for coming out in such weather. She was not afraid. How little we really know about the people around us. This woman who cannot bring herself to stand before an open window at night now lay in a bed sodden and stained with her own fluids ready to face her ordeal, if not with philosophic calm, then with a quiet resignation. She would not call out in her pain, but merely groan softly.

Gwinn stood with his back to the fire holding the palms of his now ungloved hands behind him to the flames. 'Well we had better do something about having this baby, Mrs Armitage,' he said amiably as he removed his thick scarf and coat. He made a cursory but gentle examination with confident, reassuring hands, looked at me with serious eyes and a slight frown and said, 'Miss Weeton, we will need some fresh linen for the bed, a jug of water and a log of wood about this long if you can manage it.' He held up his hands, perhaps a yard apart. 'Later tonight I will require about half a pound of butter that I can warm before the fire.'

Before I could leave the room and set about these, what I considered in my ignorance, unusual requests, Mrs Armitage was gripped by intense pain. She shut her eyes tightly and her face was suffused with colour from the strain on her body. Her shoulders lifted from the pillows and she hunched forward, then, given a brief respite, she eased herself back on the bed again. The room suddenly felt oppressively close and I briefly had to shut my eyes against a darkening faintness. Willing myself not to fall, I hurried from the room to get what was required. Sweat – cold and clammy – beaded on my forehead. Mrs Sudlow, white-aproned, her face ruddy from the kitchen fire, betrayed a slight impatience when I entered the kitchen, but she listened attentively enough to my instructions with her hands on her hips. She raised her eyebrows higher, rubbed the side of her nose with the back of her hand and instantly began to bustle about for a pat of butter while instructing the kitchen maid to keep a cauldron of water near to boiling and the house maid to fetch fresh linen. There was a clatter of pots and a sharp hiss as the stumpy little kitchen maid slopped some water into the fire in her haste or nervousness. I turned and opened the kitchen door to the night. I stood there for some moments gulping the cold reviving air and breathing whitely. The night was diamond hard. My eye strayed to the high garden wall stark and sombre in the snow-light. 'There is no escape for Mrs Armitage,' I thought. 'She must endure or die.'

There was little I could do. The small bottles of smelling salts were at the ready if she fainted. But I held her shoulders and encouraged her to manage her breath during what Mr Gwinn termed her 'throes'. He had set a smooth log across the foot of the bed and Mrs Armitage braced her feet against it. I rubbed the small of her back where she was convinced bone was rubbing against bone. Mr Gwinn remained cheerful and matter-of-fact. Mr Armitage waited and waited.

The butter was not needed to smooth the baby's passage. He was able to grasp the baby's head to help it along. When he saw the cord around the child's neck – thick, like a noose – he was all deft seriousness and urgency. Mrs Armitage, her brow pale and her face exhausted, helplessly sensed his momentary dismay. Perhaps she thought all might yet be ruined by some unfair power beyond her influence. Her lips moved but no sound escaped her. Moments later a baby girl lay on the sheets. Her head was wet and waxy; her tiny chin quivered as if from cold – her thin neck was now miraculously free. Mrs Armitage craned to see her newborn as Gwinn expertly cut the cord for the second time. He tied it and wrapped the child tightly and warmly before placing her in her arms.

'Thank you, Matthew,' she said simply, her eyes brightening with a rush of tenderness. She began to partially unwrap the child to inspect her for herself, breathing in the fresh new scent of her soapy skin.

'All is well, Mrs Armitage. She is a fine healthy girl.' His smile was slight and became ironic when she again grimaced in pain. 'But as you know we haven't quite finished with you yet.'

He cleared his throat and again leaned forward to peer closely at his work. His expression became one of pleased satisfaction. The after-birth came away without strain.

A moment of completeness. I found myself trembling, in the way one does in the presence of the extraordinary or the beautifully fragile – or something much longed for.

Mr Gwinn stood, stepped back from the bed and briefly worked his shoulders backwards and forwards.

'Miss Weeton, if you could organise a thick, hot linen cloth, it would be very soothing for Mrs Armitage.'

'And if you could ask Mr Armitage to come up please?' she said. Her tone was one of quiet humility mingled with elation. Her eyes had not left the child she was fondling gently.

Mr Armitage must have heard the baby's cry of outrage a little after midnight, but still he waited.

I was on the point of leaving when Mrs Armitage looked up at me.

'Thank you, Ellen.'

Mr Armitage met me before I reached the middle landing of the staircase. Gazing intently into my face, his own grim countenance broke into an exultant smile and he took the remaining steps two at a time.

★

Little spurts of snow were shocked free from the mossy twigs of the plum tree by darting sparrows. Their noise could be heard faintly from the window where I was standing. The sky had greyed; the day was unshadowed but still frosty. Earlier, the Armitage children had inspected their new sister with suitable gravity and hushed voices. She now slept, warm and snug in her wicker and wood swing cradle, the weight of the big house protecting her.

'A little warmer this morning, Joseph,' said Gwinn, including me in his glance.

He was readying himself to leave. His small leather bag containing the mysterious paraphernalia of his craft was on the table.

'Perhaps, but if there is a slight thaw later, the roads will be as slippery as oiled glass. 'Tis a fearful day for travellers and horses' legs alike.'

A brief, brittle silence settled in the large room. Outside another clod of white dropped lifelessly from the thin black fingers of the plum tree. The chirping from the little dun birds continued undiminished.

Gwinn struggled into his overcoat, drew out a watch from the hidden folds of his waistcoat and looked at it with a reflective air. 'They'll be hanged by now,' he said. 'May God have mercy on them.'

Mr Armitage frowned and tensed. 'A terrible justice for a terrible crime, sir.' He was suddenly defensive and emphatic. 'These Luddites are murderers, blood-stained murderers! And what was Horsfall's crime? He employed four hundred people in his mill, used the latest machinery and publicly vowed to protect it.'

'Indeed,' Gwinn sighed.

The master of Highroyd's face had paled with the intensity of his feelings. 'This brave George Mellor and his men fired from behind a wall. Horsfall's hip was smashed to splinters. It took the man thirty-eight hours to die. Let God's mercy be on him!'

Gwinn, now at the open door, met his gaze. 'Amen to that Armitage, amen I say. Don't mistake my meaning. And rest assured York will witness more such justice before this week is out.' He stepped outside, grimaced as the cold bit him, then turned and raised his hand in salute, 'Goodbye, Joseph.'

★

I sank down onto a wooden settle, my mind bruised by the hardness of the words. *They'll be hanged by now.* A moment of ugliness, like a moment of beauty, often takes us unawares – suddenly, when we least expect it. Unbidden, it lodges in the folds of the mind and there it resonates achingly. *They'll be hanged by now*. Perhaps, I thought, at this very moment while I sit in this warm clean room, a drunkard near some stinking ditch was raising his heavy stick to a snarling, cringing cur. Perhaps a butcher humming at his work had just released the heavy grey and purple guts of a large animal with his knife. A horse may have fallen heavily, its blue-white shinbone broken on the ice as if by a heavy mallet. And in York, moist-eyed, slack-jawed, trembling in their lust, eager crowds may be swaying forward as they have always done in their malignant curiosity to see the law cut, burn, brand or hang – their wet slippery mouths raised; their nostrils filled with the filthy smell of pressing excited bodies – and with the deeper bowel stench of fear. *They'll be hanged by now*. The hierarchies must be restored. The public houses will be busy in York today – and the brothels. Obscene old hags would soon be selling the rope by the inch in the streets and what they swear is the grease from the noose itself, much prized among the ignorant and superstitious for its obscure powers to cure and charm.

★

I became aware that George Armitage was standing in front of me. Under his rope-coloured hair, his face was raised to mine – earnest, puzzled, his lips slightly parted. Perhaps he had spoken to me.

I could hear that the sparrows were still in the garden.

20th January 1813
It is late at night. In my little cell of a room, on an old chest of drawers splashed with cold candle wax, there is a week old copy of the *Leeds Mercury* that I have been reading. Condemned, the three murderers of William Horsfall had, to the last, refused to acknowledge their guilt. 'They were

young men,' it was reported, 'on whose countenances nature had not imprinted the features of assassins.'

25th January 1813

I sit with my face resting on my hands in front of an old gilt mirror, all blotched from sunlight and moisture. It has a small crack in one corner. Dark, deeply discouraged eyes etched in lines cobweb-fine stare back at me puzzled by the mystery of the self. Face, body, bone, nerves – living, yearning, pulsing blood – intimately known and yet strangely unknowable. Those who think they know me so thoroughly as to judge me confidently are ignorant of this person I hardly know myself. What have I done to you, my aunt, to be condemned by such silence? What have I done to you, mean-spirited and selfish brother, to merit such neglect without so much as a shadow of an error laid to my charge?

28th March 1813

A muddy morning after a night of thin rain. Light leaks weakly through the narrow windows of coloured glass set in the stone walls of the village church.

The new curate climbs the stairs to the pulpit above the heavy pews and stands between candles. Clean-shaven and correct, he has prominent eyes and wears glasses. His name is Winterson. Everything about him is neat, clean, polished. A literary man, his conversation is quite out of the way of the Yorkshire gentry here, but his unassuming manner when he is away from the pulpit gains him friends. He has been to Highroyd once, but I had no opportunity to speak with him. His truths are neatly arranged, hard and proclaimed severely from numbered verses:

'Wherefore if thy hand or thy foot offend thee, cut them off, and cast them from thee: it is better for thee to enter into life halt or maimed, rather than having two hands or two feet to be cast into everlasting fire.'

Everlasting fire. Gertrude. His voice has a slight quaver. 'For the Son of man is come to save that which was lost.' It continues. Comes to an end. There is a cough from somewhere in the gallery, a shuffling of feet on the stone floor. Communal waiting. Public silence. His sermon begins. How I envy him his clarity, the cold fire of his words, his certainty. Perhaps I shouldn't. Such self-assurance must have its limits, be limiting. *Everlasting fire. Poor single thing tossed and swirled in flames, lost to empty darkness and the black scars of pain. She was coming to meet me, burning, suffocating, drowning in flames.* Would his self-mastery, withstand awful suffering or deep loss, or deep desire, or an outburst of violence of the sort that leaves the perpetrator gasping, confused, humiliated? Perhaps, in spite of his good intentions – and good actions – his mind has narrowed into self-deception, a false simplicity, and he is now unaware and no longer receptive to the mystery underlying even the most unheroic and ordinary aspects of life? There is no way of knowing.

I like to come to church. I feel it puts me in touch with something old and good. But my mind at times runs kilter to its formulas. I cannot believe in eternal punishment, in a God who would dispense everlasting fire – the hell fire of isolation and terrible loneliness. A God of fire? Surely the prison, the lash and the hangman, the loneliness and pain of this life are enough. Perhaps my own ignorance and the narrowness of my life's experiences have made me arrogant? There is no way of knowing. But what a shallow victory was God's if he could only save a few and not all? Guiltily, my thoughts drift to the font; to the complexities of a marble tomb in the floor of the nave, the epitaph has been worn by countless feet and is no longer legible; to old John Scholfield, who, I discovered, had been looking directly at me. He turns away quickly. His hands move indecisively – the mottled hands of the old. I like old John. A kind, chatty old man, he tells me his grievances and I try to console him.

★

He is standing by the lychgate when the service is over, a red Sunday-scrubbed look about him, and a simple bunch of misty white flowers in his hand. His gaze wanders to the heathery hills where the snow has melted into slush.

'For your wife, John?' I ask.

'Tha'rt right, Miss Weeton,' his glance now took in the nearby gravestones. 'I did aught without her for near two score years, but I mun live on alone now. If I could find one such as the last, I would go forty miles to fetch her. Aye, I would. Or if summat could render me thirty years younger and grant me a thousand pounds a year, I would bestow it all on you, Miss Weeton.' He bows slightly in mock graciousness.

Such extravagant compliments from him are not uncommon. I respond with a laugh. Given my circumstances and his loneliness, perhaps I should give him a hint to make me an offer! But he is not an old gentleman only an old man, upwards of seventy, a kind sociable farmer subsisting on thirty pounds a year. One Sunday he gave me the precious gift of three mogul plums!

'Where are your charges this morning?' he asks, looking at the people milling around the now smiling Reverend Winterson.

'It is a sad house just now. All but the baby have the whooping cough. I am as much nurse as governess at present,' I say, giving what would no doubt be a wan smile. 'And what did you make of the sermon, John?'

He smiles and says affably, 'A trifle puzzlin', Miss, a trifle puzzlin'. But I not be one to gainsay him, mind.'

I watch him for a moment as he makes his way slowly through the cold shade of a single ancient yew tree to the churchyard, and then I turn to the pleasant walk, which will return me to my own solitude at Highroyd.

8th May 1813
A section of overgrown garden has become the scene of daily hard labour when I go out with the children. We began by cutting some walks through the nettles, but now we have finished cutting blackberry vines, bracken and broom, and are planting flowers. It has been enjoyable work. Mr Armitage, always aloof but pleasant, had an arbour of latticework built in it last week. The children will have something to remember me by. The spot commands a fine view and at the moment there is the scent of freshly cut grass, but the confined life I lead, makes me almost hate the countryside in which I am imprisoned. There are days and weeks at a time when I writhe in angry dissatisfaction and long to escape, even by way of books or through the deceit of deep night dreams, to a realm beyond the glum silences and the petty jarring tasks of the classroom. Am I to renounce the world? Am I to learn to envy the likes of Mrs Sudlow who cares for nothing beyond her work and the bread it earns? Whose subtlest pleasure is to doze in the stale familiar surroundings of her kitchen with the door shut so the servants will not see the mug of porter at her side? Whose greatest ambition is to see her son married and settled on his father's small farm? For her, ten miles the other side of Huddersfield is the edge of the world.

22nd October 1813
I have determined to quit Highroyd.

I had not received Tom's letter, the first for more than two years, above an hour when Mrs Armitage called me to help her seal some jars of preserves. I complied but I could barely restrain myself from flinging the saucepan of hot wax at her. The poor woman was oblivious to my feelings but I was so angry I could see my hands trembling as I poured the hot liquid, scalding myself slightly. I did not care. I tied the linen around the jars with a violent pleasure. My throat was tight and my voice sounded as if it were a stranger's when I informed her that as I looked upon my departure as next to certain she might be preparing for a successor. Her eyes registered no great surprise.

My Aunt Barton is dead – has been dead for nearly a month.

Ellen,

No doubt, you have been informed of the death of our aunt who passed away on the 25th of September. I find our uncle very dull and it has occurred to me that you would be wise to accept the position of housekeeper for him. You will not be expected to pay for your board.

I have in my keeping a parcel, directed in your aunt's own hand to you. If you advise me to send it, I will do so by any conveyance you think best.

Yours,

T R Weeton

The abrupt beginning – but for the direction, I would hardly know for whom the letter was intended – and the terse signature argue no returning affection. Ah, Tom, would it not be a masterstroke to have me draw our kind uncle more closely to the interests of our family, to have me as agent on the spot to render him malleable and sentimentally inclined towards his nearest relatives? And I am to throw over a well-paid post and gladly undertake the duty for you? Even Mrs T R Weeton must approve of such a policy!

★

I have begun my letter with 'Dear Brother' and ended it with 'Yours affectionately'. I have written to my uncle as 'affectionate and respectful niece' accepting the offer. Where else could I find a home if I needed one? I do not want my aunt's parcel.

9th December 1813
I wish my brother had not written without knowing my uncle's sentiments. It has placed me in a very awkward situation. For nearly two months I have been in daily expectation of a summons. A young lady, well known to the family, has expressed a keen interest in my position at Highroyd. Mrs Armitage has kindly delayed her reply. I have written to Tom again, but have received no answer. What can be the reason?

12th December 1813
It has been agreed that I may take a month's leave in order to visit my baffling relatives in Up Holland.

'Well, there will be those who will miss you, Miss Weeton,' said Mrs Sudlow.

The kitchen was perhaps the most pleasant room in the house at this time of year. Copper utensils hanging on the wall glinted with soft lights from the flapping flames in the large hearth. The door was shut firmly against the cold of the outside world and the air was filled with the fresh warm smells of baking. Mrs Sudlow shut the oven door with a bang, turned and sifted flour over a mixture of dough. Her large elbows dimpled as she cut the next batch of biscuits with a heavy hand. Each was an exact copy of its neighbour as she placed them in tidy rows on a baking tray. She did not pause in her work. It would be one of the many recipes of her mother's she had committed to memory from which she would not make the slightest deviation. Her lips were pursed and there was something elusive in her tone making her straightforward words difficult to interpret.

'I would like to think the children will,' I said.

'Aye, that's to be expected, especially little George.'

'It is only for a month after all, Mrs Sudlow.'

'That it is, but a month can be a considerable time dependin'.'

Again there was a hint of sarcasm. She cast a knowing look and the beginnings of a smile at the kitchen maid, who was noisily scouring a pot over a frothy copper. Her hands were red and raw from the soda. Mrs Sudlow as cook and *de facto* housekeeper was a hard taskmaster to those beneath her.

I could feel my chest tightening and my voice now had a hard edge to it. 'Mrs Sudlow, is there something you wish to tell me? If so, please do.'

She stood upright, wiped her floury hands on her apron and lifted her prominent chin higher. 'It is hardly my place to instruct me betters, Miss,' her tone giving lie to the statement. 'But I have heard some talk that your going away may forestall the intentions of your beau, John Scholfield.'

'My beau! John Scholfield! Don't be ridiculous, Mrs Sudlow,' I retorted venomously.

'You needn't be so high and mighty with me. It's only what I hear,' she said peevishly, her flaccid cheeks reddening.

Turning on my heel, I left without another word. I heard

163

her angrily fling a ladle or suchlike at the table and bark an instruction at her assistant. But why should I justify myself to the likes of her! To them! Why should I entertain such a ludicrous suggestion for one moment!

★

I now recollect some of the old man's speeches. How once he said he would visit Highroyd one evening when the Armitages were out and pay court to me. I had laughed and joked with him imagining the difference in age, manners and rank were a sufficient licence and protection. Have I flattered myself a little in receiving John's attentions? If so, I have not done it deliberately. I felt for his loneliness. But now I have reason to believe he is foolish enough to think seriously of it. This morning at church several people stared at me in a most unpleasant way and then looked at old John and laughed. I know now that I did not imagine it. After the service, he was by the lychgate as usual. I could but nod curtly and pretend to give my full attention to the children. I have secretly packed all of my belongings in the hope that I may permanently escape from the heartless laughter of the pious, from those good church people who enjoy another's discomfort.

7th February 1814
On the morning of my departure from Highroyd, I woke early, slept again, dreamed.

I was standing on something submerged; perhaps it was the deck of a ship. I then felt myself being lifted up and carried in the swell of the sea. I did not struggle for breath, nor did I feel the chill wetness of the water. I became aware of rocks and tensed against their sharpness, but people were reaching down to me; their hands were beckoning just above the water. I clasped none, but found myself on the sands of a beach – safe and enveloped in warmth, but overwhelmed by a terrible feeling of desolation.

★

I passed through the iron gates on the gravel drive, stopped and looked back at the silent house; its heavy stonework was grey and grim in the early morning light. The older children had risen at five and walked with me part of the way towards Huddersfield under a rushing winter sky. They parted from me with a cheerfulness that made me inwardly wince and I continued on alone, the wind tugging at my clothing.

I went to the Prices in Liverpool. They were as friendly and welcoming as on the day they asked me to join their picnic at Eastham. The streets were all grey light and wet pavements. My head had begun to swim with fatigue and from the occasional hard whiffs of sewage. Blanched, unknowable faces hurried along dim byways or disappeared down narrow abortive streets. But there was a cheerful fire in the Prices' drawing room, the comfort of tawny leather chairs, and the pastel blues of poplin reflected in the bright light of mirrors. Life again held possibilities.

On Mr Price's advice, I wrote a note to my uncle asking him to collect my aunt's parcel from Tom and to send it by William Hindley, the local carrier, on the following Saturday. I grew hopeful that it might contain some explanation of her conduct towards me and of my brother's mysterious silence. No parcel arrived. But there was a letter from my uncle, in which he said several things – a black and grey sarsenet, a muff and tippet, two gowns and a maroon velvet bonnet – had been left to me by my aunt, that to my brother, she had given a purse containing forty guineas in gold and ten pounds in bank notes. The parcel and a purse for me were still with Tom. The next morning, Sunday, I set off for Up Holland in William Hindley's wagonette. His worsted figure and his two aged ponies have been a familiar sight to me since childhood. I was going home!

When the dark squat tower of St Thomas's came into view, I stared hard (as poor Miss Dannett used to say) but the windows of my pretty cottage did not serve to frame a single face. The flowerbeds were empty; the only movement was the agitation of the trees in a slight breeze. The Sunday silence was broken by no more than the twittering of linnets. I drank thin tea out of thick cups with Mrs Braithwaite who begged me to be her guest while I stayed in Up Holland, and I very gladly consented knowing full well it would hardly be necessary. Her house, now that the master is dead, is much altered. The boys who used to fill it are now gone for want of a teacher and it seems, like Mrs Braithwaite herself, to be a little smaller, a little quieter, a little neglected. It was afternoon when I called on my uncle.

He opened the door himself with a faint, 'How do ye?' His eyes looked blank under his thinning iron-grey hair before his face lit up with recognition, 'Ellen! Come in. You are very welcome.' I felt a thin hand press my arm lightly as he led me into the parlour. 'Are you for stopping here or going to Mrs Braithwaite's?' he asked.

Such a question set my lip trembling and coldness spread over my face. 'If I am not welcome here and as I cannot get back tonight I am sure Mrs Braithwaite will take me in.'

I was close to tears.

My uncle looked down at me and in a softened tone said, 'Ellen, you are most welcome but as you can see things are at sixes and sevens with me at the moment.'

For the first time I consciously saw that much of the

furniture was draped with sheets and that my uncle was obviously on the point of leaving. The house already had a melancholy hollowness about it. I could feel my hopes curdle into lumpy fear and sudden disappointment. 'But why are you leaving, Uncle? I thought I was to keep house for you?' The words were sour now – suffocating – almost gagging me. 'No one told me of this.'

'I miss your aunt so much,' he said abstractedly. His face was pale. My eye was drawn to a tiny crescent of grey bristles high on his cheek, which had escaped his morning razor. 'The house has been in such confusion and the servants have behaved so badly that Tom thought it best that I go into lodgings – for a few months at least. I will keep the house and furniture as they are now, but I think I will be happier away from this house.' He sank apologetically into an armchair without bothering to remove the grey-white sheet covering it.

★

'Ellen, your brother is in the front parlour and wishes to see you,' said Mrs Braithwaite a little breathlessly. I could not rise from the chair and could say nothing. 'Shall I show him in here?' she asked, her forehead drawing into a concerned frown.

'No. Yes. Stop a little – well – yes, do,' I managed to say. I felt ill – confused – unprepared.

He was shown in and he held out his hand in a composed, affectionate manner. I feebly offered mine and he squeezed it. He sat down keeping a parcel tied with string across his knees and took out of his pocket a silver spoon, which he presented to me. He then settled back with his elbow on the back of the chair. On the spoon a family crest had been neatly engraved.

'The positive arms of Weeton of Weeton, Lancashire,' he

declared emphatically. 'I have been looking a little into our family history. The claim is still before the Heralds, but in the meantime your worthy tenant, Mr Winstanley, as well as looking over watch-wheels is a fine engraver.'

I became a little more composed, but even more confused. I still could not bring myself to speak although words rose and vied with each other to be free.

'I was in Preston yesterday,' he continued, 'spent the night there, and I am late for home. I must go, but I thought I would come through Up Holland to call on Winstanley – and on Uncle, of course. He wrote to me about this,' he said, indicating the parcel.

I mutely handed the spoon back to him. A short silence ensued before I quietly broke it with a question about his children.

'They are well thank you.' He rose and placed the parcel on the table. 'Now I must go.'

'Goodbye,' I answered, barely above a whisper. I tried to rise, but my knees failed me. I rested my head on my hands and leaned over the table to support myself as he left the room.

Why had he called if he had no intention of vindicating himself? I could easily imagine how he will report the interview. 'She hardly spoke a word to me. She couldn't even bring herself to rise from the chair. Not a scrap of interest in *my* affairs of course!' And what a sympathetic ear I would receive from Mrs Weeton!

It was some time before I could rouse myself enough to open the parcel with trembling fingers. The purse contained five, one pound notes and a child's double-hearted signet ring, not worth seven shillings. It was only then with a sickening lurch that I realised that the seal on the purse had already been broken.

9th March 1814

A morning of dense fog and dank smells of decay. Water dripped audibly from leafless willows and dark holly bushes, from iron railings, from mossy eaves, onto cobbles slippery with rotting leaves and manure. I could see nothing of the distance below Up Holland. The street was chill after Mrs Braithwaite's warm kitchen and I was pleased to hear the 'cling-cling' of the blacksmith at his forge where I could shelter while I waited for the Liverpool coach. At work on the links of a large chain amidst red fire, dark coals and hissing steam, he took little notice of me after a brief salute. I was left for a time looking blindly through a grubby window at the smoking white air and at a spider on the sill busily fashioning its snare in the warm glow of the shop.

There was a clatter and clip of hooves on stones, a dog barked from somewhere and the blacksmith came forward wiping his hands on his leather apron to help me with my bag. I began to make my way gingerly over the treacherous cobbles towards the blinkered horses steaming in the cold wet air. The door of the coach opened and a large fleshy man in a sage-green frock coat reached down to me with his hand. As I clasped it I found myself looking full in the eyes of this handsome man. No, not exactly handsome. He was past the first flush of youth and was too soft and heavy for perfection, and his mouth had a hardness about it despite its smile. But his eyes were arresting. They were not unduly large, but their calm gaze was naked – penetrating. Such an exposed look brought the blood to my face as quick as flame. A second passenger half raised himself from his seat, pocketing a small leather book as he did so and gave me a thin public smile.

'Thank you,' I muttered weakly.

He nodded and again I was briefly captured by dark restive eyes and fullish lips. I felt the pressure of his thigh on mine as he spread a warm, travelling rug over our knees. The intimacy was as sudden as the lick from a puppy. Vaguely troubled, I felt the need to draw away – but did not. The journey began. Ensnared in the softness of the rug, his close warm masculinity gave me a feeling of slight suffocation. Breathing slowly through parted lips, I turned my head and looked unseeingly at the grey desolation swirling outside the coach. He, with an authoritative, almost theatrical gesture, seemed intent only on continuing his conversation with the passenger sitting opposite.

'Sixteen shillings and sixpence a week! Going to weavers, some of whom are too old to wipe their noses. Mark my words, this will long be remembered by the weavers as a year of plenty, my friend.' Here he produced a brown paper bag of walnuts and accompanied by the occasional click and snap of strong teeth he continued with a touch of bitterness. 'With a little capital a man could easily be a factory owner and not a buyer compelled to travel the length and breadth of the country in weather such as this.'

'You are no doubt right, Mr Stock. I know little of such things.'

He then crossed his thin legs and smiling indifferently, waved a polite refusal at the proffered paper bag. Straight and dignified, he preferred to argue gently about religion. He was all cool and subtle reasoning, until the large, comfortable man beside me, his lips glistening from the walnuts, leaned forward and with a satirical note in his voice declared that he was a strict Calvinist at heart.

'I draw pleasure from it as I draw pleasure from a glass of brandy before the fire or from these walnuts.'

A hint of self-consciousness, perhaps annoyance, appeared in the greyish-golden eyes of his opponent and the conversation became more desultory. Outside I could see nothing but the dark shapes of trees, drenched fields and the grey, fog-blind road. The rug was soft – soft. I took sides with the Calvinist.

★

At Liverpool we were emptied into broken clouds, the ceaseless movement of mud and the low throbbing rumble of frustrated thunder.

'You have no one to meet you, Miss – um?'

'Weeton.'

'Of Leigh?' he said, arresting his movements and regarding me carefully.

'I have a brother in Leigh,' I said dryly.

'And a good man he is!' he declared. 'A legal man, is he not, and of growing reputation? A fact I was recently very grateful for when he quite rightfully demonstrated before a magistrate that a blow dealt to one Robert Balshaw, cotton rover, coxcomb and braggart recently of the parish of Leigh, was thoroughly justified given the circumstances.'

Thin rain seeped across the old, dun-bricked buildings darkening the dimly lit street to a gloom. He turned up the collar of his well-cut coat now flecked with dark spots of wetness and drew blue-black gloves over his large dimpled hands. They were the movements of a city man – with city-secrets in him.

'Well, I am for the Crossways hard by here,' he said, glancing quickly skywards. 'You do have safe lodgings, Miss Weeton? I would not like to leave Mr Tom Weeton's sister to walk the streets in the rain.'

'Oh, yes, I have friends expecting me in Seymour Street.'

'Seymour Street – I see. That's some way off.' He pursed his lips and looked thoughtful for a moment before his face brightened. 'Would you care to join me for a light meal at the Crossways before you go? They serve a wonderful Julienne.

Or something warm to drink? A drop of mulled wine would do us no harm on a day like this.'

My luggage was now off the coach.

'No thank you,' I said glibly. 'I am hardly at liberty to accept such an offer from a man about whom all I know is that he has struck another and has a fondness for walnuts.' I smiled to make light of the situation.

'Humph! Then at least let me find a suitable conveyance for you,' he said laughing as he hailed a passing hackney, which clattered to a halt in the wet street. 'This lady is for Seymour Street, driver, number…'

'Thirty-five. Thirty-five, Seymour Street,' I said, lifting my bag into the vehicle.

10th March 1814
I met Ann in the hallway; her effulgent blue eyes were alive with curiosity.

'Ellen, there is a Mr Aaron Stock downstairs to see you. He says he is an old family friend of yours.'

16th March 1814
Night fears. He is a widower with a daughter. But weigh the odds. Weigh the odds. Should I return to Highroyd? And after Highroyd, what then? My life is grave-lonely. Where do people like me end their story? I can find no fault in him – perhaps a little gruffness, but I would have a home of my own. And he is pressing in his suit, overwhelming in his need to undam his emotions.

15th April 1814
I have written to my brother. It is so uniquely short a letter and considering its importance, I transcribe it here in full.

Liverpool
April 15th 1814

Dear Brother,

In the midst of bustle and preparation, you must not expect that I can say much to you. It is enough for the present to inform you, that on the day you receive this, I shall most probably have resigned my prospects of future happiness or misery for this life, into the hands of another.

My best love to your little ones.

Yours affectionately,

Ellen Weeton

5

Standishgate, Wigan
8th November 1816
This morning I bullied open a drawer and took out my journal – poor, blankfaced friend – I have neglected you woefully. Life has piled up and left you behind. How wincingly sad to read those last few hopeful pages! I am, as usual, alone. The beech trees and sycamores are without their leaves and I hear branches scratching against the outside wall in gusts of wind already winter-sharp. I settle in a wedge of sunlight near the window in church-like quiet.

★

I married Mr Aaron Stock at Holy Trinity parish church in Liverpool. I had known him for a matter of weeks. The Prices were the only people who witnessed our little ceremony. We left immediately for Wigan and the few rooms at the back of my husband's cotton factory which he rented from Tom's mother-in-law. The uncurtained windows were dark, sightless, soulless and the drearily persistent clattering of machines came from behind its walls. Yet, I considered myself content in our little home in Chapel Lane. My husband was all kind attention and bolstered by my savings his tottering cotton-spinning concerns began to prosper. He soon talked of moving to a grander house in Standishgate. Little Mary was born exactly nine months and nine days after we married! I recovered rapidly from my confinement and my little one was healthy. For above a month we went on very well, but then we both fell ill. Mary was too weak to be weaned, and

I was no longer able to nurse her. A wet-nurse was procured and I went to Southport where it was hoped I would regain my strength. There, without Mary, the mordant scrape and squeal of gulls and kitty-wakes did nothing to lift my spirits. Walking along the sad sweep of windy beach under a grey wash of cloud, I felt as stranded as the strings of brown seaweed and bladderwrack abandoned by the dun sea-foam. After a week, I decided to return to Wigan and our narrow rooms in Chapel Lane.

★

Aaron and I were still at the table. Kitty Barker, the wet-nurse, sat raven-haired and grey-eyed beside the fire with Mary in her arms. She was no more than twenty. The fate of her own child is unknown to me. She would not be drawn on any aspect of her life. Sullen and withdrawn, she behaved well to the child but showed an almost haughty indifference to me. I may have been a thing of rags and straw for all she cared. Mary was as restless as an eel and squirmed fretfully and lifted her mobile little face. Wordlessly, Kitty slipped her shoulder free from her pale, dingy dress fully exposing her naked breast to Mary. Warmth mantled my cheeks at the sudden sight of her firm young body lambent with health and vigour which she had so casually revealed. Kitty lifted her eyes strangely in a speaking glance but did not meet *my* gaze.

A few weeks later, I suddenly came upon her in my own room! Weeks of accumulated, inchoate anger were released.

'What are you doing in here?' I demanded shrilly.

She laughed briefly on a false note, but was otherwise perfectly under control which provoked me even more.

'You have no right to be in this room,' I continued, struggling to breathe.

She lifted her brows slightly, almost questioningly.

'I was looking for something I may have left here,' she said, giving a used-up smile.

'Left here! Yes, it is time you left here. You are dismissed. You are no longer wanted. Go! Now!'

My rage was less to her than a broken shoelace.

'I am to go now? You are dismissing me without a word to your husband? What of Mary?'

I grew confused, desperate. 'As soon as it is possible to wean Mary you will go.'

★

No one used to living in another person's house as long as I have, can be said to have much their own way. It breaks the spirit to be a private teacher under the authority of others. But I was determined that Kitty Barker should leave us. And leave us she did. But from that time forward I have received nothing from Aaron except deep-seated antipathy.

5th January 1817
I wake to another day. When and how will this end? I will never live to educate Mary unless I leave this place. Oh, if I could get away! Perhaps I could start a little school near here or work in a private house, which takes boarders in the summer at Crosby or at Bootle. I think I would be happy as an under-gardener. I wish I could go to Liverpool for a day or two. I wish I could go, never to return here again! But it is vain to wish. My efforts to live are the weak struggles of a drowning insect and there is no one to rescue me, so I must sink. He is determined to be quit of me. His campaign is protracted, unreasonable, unrelenting. It is not drunkenness; it is more settled, more calculated. He never speaks to me unless in anger and he claims that his daughter Jane refuses to

come home from Liverpool because of me. He forbids me to leave the house – I do, even if it is only to the Hawardens. I cannot ask them here. We receive no visitors. He refuses to sit at the table with me; mocks my looks, my thin face. And in truth I am but a poor caricature of the governess I once was in the Pedders' household when Reverend Thomas Saul... but no matter. He gives me no money. I have no authority, no dignity, not even the servant Alice will acknowledge me in his presence. I am locked in and I am locked out.

4th April 1817
A letter from Ann Price! I happened to meet the post. I grow braver. He spends so much time away that I begin to venture from the house more often.

> *35 Seymour Street,*
> *Liverpool*
> *Dear Ellen,*
>
> *At present, my dear friend, I have plenty of time and much inclination for writing to you. I forgive you for not replying to my previous letters. My uncle allays my growing concern and speaks warmly of you. Let me assure you, you have a friend in Doctor Hawarden.*
>
> *How is little Mary? But come and tell me with your own mouth, and I will not now ask you any more questions. I wish you would come and see me. The coach fares are so very low, that now is the time for travelling. We are very comfortably fixed here and I think you might spend a few weeks without being very unhappy.*
>
> *The steamboats will amuse you; they go puffing and blowing, and beating their sides, and labouring along with all their might. Please come.*
> *Yours most sincerely,*
> *Ann Price*

It is not right that he should take my letters. Would he have the world forget that I exist? I wonder if he is a little mad. But I must hide this. He is no Miss Chorley. A struggle for its possession is not likely to be attended with polite protests on my part and ineffectual, hysterical efforts on his. I should not write at all, but it is a need, a compulsion. Perhaps I imagine that in recording the mundane, the meaning and the mystery lying at the edges of things will eventually emerge. Words are not reality; all testimony is equivocal. But I find a comfort in naming, in taming the chaotic. It allows me some control. It is only when I am writing that I am free. When I am writing, I have no master – none.

12th September 1817
Ten o'clock at night. I cannot sleep. I have discovered something and everything is changed.

Today was fair day in Wigan. Large caravans entered the town with wild beasts, monsters, and jugglers who walked on high stilts. Buoyed up by the pleasure of release, I joined the anonymous visitors; the hordes of beggars, the barefooted Irish and the lounging discharged soldiers to show Mary the wooden horses and whirligigs, the barrel organs and fiddlers. To add to these novelties, the new Cloth Hall was to be opened and crowds had gathered in the square to see it. The richer inhabitants of Wigan were seated under fluttering pennants for the opening ceremony, waiting for the Mayor to arrive, when a snare drum and fife sounded discordantly and a phalanx of noisy, angry men entered the square hooting and hissing.

One of them yelled, 'Damn the Mayor! We may wait forever if we wait for him. He will order us carrion soup!'

There were angry shouts – confused and excited – dangerous because they were confused. The beginnings of a chant arose: 'Work not charity! Wages not alms!' A half-starved mongrel dog barked in mindless excitement and ran and leapt amongst the men until it yelped in sudden pain and cowered away. Some were bedraggled in dirty tattered military coats; others were sleeveless and collarless. Their faces were grim, grey, hard-lined from savage want. Their eyes gleamed with intoxication, one different from that with which the Eagle Inn or a poorer pothouse could provide them. Their individual hurts and indignities, the grey monotony of their wretched lives had turned them into a desperate mob hooting and hissing and pelting insults. Some were little more than boys, thin-legged, goblin-like with pale pinched faces and shaven hair. The clothes of some were falling almost to rags, some had bits of shoes tied on their feet and rags tied around their ankles, and others wore heavy clogs, which I knew could be a ready weapon if needed. A woman, too, was amongst them, her matted black hair streamed down her back like wet seaweed over her filthy rust-black coat. Her face was twisted and ugly as she shouted. They carried a man of straw, an old worn-out soldier dressed in the faded remains of a uniform. In one hand was tied a large soup kettle, in the other a halter; at his knees was a placard: *The Calls of Hunger.* He jerked obscenely above them on a pole as they jostled and elbowed their way towards the Cloth Hall. I learned later that the procession had ended with the drowning of the effigy.

I tightened my grip on Mary sheltering her in both arms and made my way as well as I could towards a lane-way and away from the square, which was now awash with distorted shouting faces and pale-cheeked fear. A large man in front of me suddenly grunted, stopped – cursed.

'Christ!' he muttered. 'Christ!'

He stooped forward; his face was the colour of buttermilk

and his nose was leaking blood. His lips were already purpling into a pulpy plum red.

Frightened now, I darted into the alcove of the nearest doorway to escape the press of trampling, hurrying bodies. The crowd quickly thinned; the noise became more distant. My breathing eased. Mary was safe. Opposite my refuge others had also withdrawn from the sudden tumult to the shadows of a protective shop front. There was no mistaking the heavy shapeless form of my husband and clinging to him, looking up at him with her chin uplifted, was Kitty Barker, her face moistly alive with excitement.

29th October 1817

Even a walk was an act of rebellion and my soul shrank at every step. I am not to stir anywhere; I am to be content at home. My chest tightened with shuddering dread at the thought of returning, but Mary was tired and we had had no more on our walk than a penny cake each. He allows me no money. Mary raised her arms in mute appeal and I stooped and picked her up. Her face was soft and velvety against my neck. I will not give way for her sake; for her alone have I any wish to live. All else is despair. I feel as low as I did at Southport. *Kitty Barker. To win the heart of such a person!* No doubt he was tired of his first wife long before she died. Now it is my turn. He will torment me to death; I see no escape. He will never mend; he grows worse and worse. It is over. But when is anything really finished? The past refuses to die and my future will be the present endlessly repeated. I cannot leave him free and he hates me for it. Even after my death my life will be recreated in the mouths of others. Such easy judgements! But I am powerless. I am a thing. Mary was squirming to be put down again. There had been few children on the streets and she made her way with uncertain balance towards a little boy who was playing with a wooden top on the shadowed cobbles. His head was large and bony; gaps of vulnerable white scalp showed under his close-cropped hair. He extended a grimy hand and gave her the simple toy.

We had walked as far as our late 'house' in Chapel Lane. Dull shop fronts and ancient buildings heaved up against it. The rooms were abandoned, left to rot in dank silence. House of secrets and deceit! It was there that I had so loved the idea of a home – the idea of Aaron Stock – that I had given him full possession of all my property, twenty-three pounds excepted and that was grudged me. Nor can Tom complain. The week after my marriage, he duly received the hundred pounds I had promised our mother to give him. It was there behind those oozing walls of dark brick that I had loved an idea for a few short months. In a blind quivering of desire I learned what the edge of lips and fingertips were capable of achieving. For a few months only, we tried to press our lives together – loving in blindness. Then, we could go no further and we were left frightened at the sudden collapse of our lives – the lack of mystery – the inescapable ordinariness. Our love, if it was love, died. Who we are is largely a matter of sophisticated charades. It was as if we had stumbled upon an object in the dark and then had to discover its qualities in some grotesque game of blind-man's-buff. But what action is entirely our own given the unforeseen and the tangled skein of blind circumstance? We cannot will the future and so we must be gamblers whether we want to be or not. And I have lost – am lost.

★

I became aware of a gaunt woman standing on the worn steps of the house opposite. The little boy ran towards her. Mary, suddenly bereft of her companion, looked to me. She still held the wooden top.

'She's a sharp one that one,' the gaunt woman said. She made a tired movement with her hand against her eyes before bending down and gently taking the proffered toy. She hoisted Mary up and clucked and cooed maternally over her. 'Careful ye don't slip.' She nodded at the foul green slime in the clotted gutter and beckoned me to enter the darkly shaded doorway.

It was a narrow damp room, dim as a cellar. There was no fire. Her husband was at work at a clacking loom near the window. It seemed as if he were somehow fixed to the machine, which jerked his arms forward and lifted and moved his legs. He looked ill; his forehead was beaded with warm moisture. His chest was pressed against the board and the muscles in his neck bulged and relaxed above the coarse flannel of his shirt with each throw of the shuttle. *Kitty Barker – her mouth on my husband's neck.* Standing beside the weaver was a girl of perhaps ten holding a cop of yarn. Her dark, deep-set eyes watched for faults in the cloth with the concentration of a scholar perusing a manuscript. Her feet were bare; her face was pinched and sharp. The man's purple-white throat jumped and pulsed. *Her own throat exposed, she was reaching up to mouth the blue veins of his neck. They saw me looking. And didn't care.*

The gaunt woman tapped the back of a plain wooden chair. 'Rest a moment or two with the little one.' *Rest. You need rest.* Her voice was tinged with a tenderness that comes from sadness. 'A little tea and treacle?' I shook my head. *Why don't you go to Southport for a few weeks? I have organised a wet nurse, Kitty Barker. The child is too weak to be weaned.* She rocked Mary expertly on her hip. She was not as old as I had first thought. A vague prettiness still haunted her face. There was the stagnant smell of tripe boiling, or perhaps it was the feet of pigs. I thought of black beetles – the risk of fever. The smell was awful.

Still abstracted, I replied quickly – too quickly, 'No. No. I must go. Thank you.' I wanted to be outside again. I wanted Mary in my own arms. I was close to panic. And I was ashamed.

★

I had to go home to my own fireplace in stylish Standishgate. There was a stink of rotting vegetable matter. I was walking too quickly and nearly stood on a dead bird amongst the muck on the greasy cobbles. A pigeon, its eyes were gone, white bones broke through its purple-grey and iridescent feathers. Ugliness.

'Damn your blood then! You can do nought for me, hey! You durst na! Thou mun not tarry here you say!'

He was shouting at me. I stood staring at him. But no, his watery-blue eyes reddened by tiredness and pipe smoke were looking beyond me, through me, to a soot-blackened building of old gritstone. His young fist was raised. A soldier or sailor no longer in uniform, the war with Napoleon over, he was now steeped in misery – jobless, hopeless. He looked down at the rotting bird between us, touched it apathetically with his boot, and then kicked malignantly at it in savage distress. There was a sickly reek of oil on his clothes and cotton flue stuck to his greasy black hair. He noticed me for the first time, propped and stared at Mary, as if surprised at something, and then wheeled into a narrow melancholy alley blotched and sore with shadows. I had to go home. Home? My throat tightened. My head ached. My shoulders ached. Mary was sleepy and was a dead weight in my arms.

★

The warm, intensely still twilight was thickening into purple darkness. The handsome chimneys of the house were silhouetted against the blue-clouded sky. Not a single light could be seen in the front windows even though the last of the sun was dying blood red like the last of a smoking fire. A thin watery moon swam low in the east between the roofs of houses. Mary was fast asleep and I wrapped my shawl around her to ward off the falling moisture in the unmoving air. Lapwings cried out a distant protest against despair somewhere behind the house. The street was eerily quiet. Like some furtive thing of myth or nightmare, I passed through the gate in the low stone wall and avoiding the front door under its small triangular portico, I followed the brick path to the rear of the house. There were no garden scents from honeysuckle or lilac bushes, no tracery of ivy on the raw brickwork of the walls; there were no clusters of purple-white violets or the mauve flowers of creeping thyme beside the path. Dank weeds brushed my ankles. The dark grey of the sky was scratched and marked by the black branches above me. There was a coppery, metallic taste in my mouth and I struggled against a suffocating queasy soul sickness. I knew I would have to be defiant. He delights in abject submission. It gratifies his pride to see me tremble.

Thank God the door was not locked! Alice, our only servant, stood at the scrubbed deal table and looked up sharply as I entered, but then studiously ignored me and continued to rasp away at a loaf of thick-crusted bread with a long, black-handled knife. There was a sweet smell of baking fruit. Cored apples filled with rum-soaked raisins. The fresh spice crimped my nose – cloves perhaps, or cinnamon. I was hungry. I could hear him in the dining room. I hesitated.

'I have a headache, man, that only leeches can cure! Enough of business for today,' he whined petulantly.

'They are tired of soup. The Rector's committee sitting to consider how best to administer relief to the poor was stoned yesterday. Windows were smashed. Most are earning a third of the wages they were getting this time last year, but they are openly refusing charity.'

My heart sank. Kearsley was with him.

'Man, they are dangerous!' he exclaimed. 'You are aware that Rushton and one Mr J Smith are in town and have been honoured with the presence of hundreds of vagabonds?'

There was the sharp clink of glasses, a heavy sigh, and then the dull, self-satisfied voice of my husband.

'Kearsley, they are too disorganised and even if there are riots next winter, for as long as exports remain unrestricted, *we* will not be reduced to five shillings a week.' He gave a high, empty laugh, which was almost a giggle.

I walked quickly past the doorway without looking in. My footsteps sounded loud and hollow on the bare wooden floor of the hallway. I settled Mary in my room. I knew she would not sleep for long – she too was hungry. Then, hardly able to breathe, I returned. Kearsley was an opportunity. I might be able to eat.

'Ah, the mistress of the house has returned.' He leaned his loose, fleshy body back in his chair and allowed himself an indulgent, sarcastic smile. Kearsley did not stand. I hate that room. I hate its great dead fireplace, its dark mahogany chairs, and its viewless window. Things have been burned out of me in that room. 'And where has the mistress of the house been today, pray tell?'

'I walked to Chapel Lane.'

There was a bowl of red-gold apples on the table. Like a cat, I sat by and watched them. Waiting.

Again he gave a startling, odd little laugh.

'And what sort of time did you have in Chapel Lane?'

The sarcastic tone was gone from his voice. There was now a barely suppressed anger, which almost choked him.

I tried to hide my fear. 'Oh, a fine time. It brought back such happy memories.'

Nettled, he abruptly stood, picked up the bowl of apples, locked them in a cupboard in the sideboard and put the little silver key in his pocket.

He turned and said callously, wanting to hurt me, 'Well, I suppose you would be safe enough there. No one would look twice at your skinny face.'

Kearsley, looking every inch the overseer of his master's spinning factory, pursed his lips and smirked in amusement. To please Mr Stock he must set himself against me. My cheeks grew hot.

'If you don't like my face, why do you put up with it?' I replied. 'You have a grown daughter, let Jane be mistress, and let me go. Surely you would think me bought off cheaply for seventy pounds a year?'

Kearsley slouched to his feet. 'Well, as you said, enough of business for one day. I'll be off.'

He did not so much as nod in my direction. My husband scraped his chair heavily across the floor as he stood and followed Kearsley from the room. There was mirthless laughter, a bang as the front door came to. I trembled with fear and anger. Two empty wine glasses were on the table and a white china plate with the remains of a cone of jellied brawn on it. In the stale light of the candles it looked like a jagged wound in white skin.

I heard his heavy tread in the hallway coming to claim me. He shut the door behind him, looked at me, but not at my face, and slumped into a great, balding armchair, raising a fat leg across his knee. His broad, podgy hands rested uselessly on the worn arms of the chair. Two thick fingers tapped silently.

'Am I to fare as the servant does, or go without?' I said, indicating the plate with a shrinking movement. Beside it was a sharp two-pronged fork. The handle was white.

'You can starve until your meatless gut cracks for all I care.'

Dry, emotionless words, they cut and stung like primitive flints.

'I do not like that man. Why do you have him in the house?'

'He is profitable. He has the right temperament for his job,' he said sneeringly in a hard voice.

'He is not a good man.'

'He is not a good man,' he scoffed in a false high voice imitating me. 'You simpleton! Not a good man? And what is a good man?'

I looked fully at him, noting the blackness under his puffy eyes, the greasy pallor of his neck. 'Someone who makes me wish I were a better person.'

He laughed a dead, bitter laugh through a wet, open mouth. His head was raised. I saw the blue veins in his neck and the bands of soft flesh that Kitty Barker had found so attractive. They swelled and moved. I felt dizzy with a churning sickness. *They saw me looking. And didn't care.* I imagined reaching out and picking up the ugly little fork. I imagined him thrashing in his own blood on the gritty wooden floor – screaming through the red hole, which was his mouth. The curved prongs of the fork were in his neck, which was white – like cheese. The handle of the fork resisted as I tried to pull it out, lifting and drawing the flesh of his neck with it.

The corner of his upper lip twitched into a half snarl. 'I don't care what you think.'

My clenched hands had not left the table. I was crying uncontrollably. Deep shuddering sobs were wrenched from me. My face was offered to him. He did not move from his chair. Physical contact would have been as revolting as mud in the mouth – a violation.

'I am sorry,' I gasped wretchedly. At last I was able to shut my eyes, move my hands, smear the tears across my face. 'I am so sorry.'

His eyes widened in horror or amazement, like a butcher who looks at his fingerless hand, which he himself has ruined with the cleaver he still holds. 'You're mad – mad!' It was little more than a hoarse whisper. He stood – stared at me – I realised he was deeply afraid. 'I must make inquiries,' he muttered. 'Perhaps that brother of yours can help.'

★

The next morning was full of a soft greyness. Mary was a huddle of sleeping warmth in the bed. One dimpled hand rested on her cheek. Her hair was tussled and lay spread across the white pillow. Miraculously, she had not stirred all night. I was safe for the present; in my room – my prison – I was calm again. The madness had subsided. I had to search for food – some milk at least. Alice is no match for me when we are alone and he leaves in darkness for the factory in Chapel Lane. But he is given to returning home at any time. I had to act immediately.

The door of his room was ajar. On impulse I entered it. I don't know why. He had not drawn the curtains to let the grey-brown light in. It was a room of shadows, of dark hidden corners, of secret empty niches. A heavy chest of drawers from a previous generation brooded in the melancholy grey light. The bed was unmade, chaotic, violent. The musky pink coverlet was rucked up with the sheets and blankets. In the half-light it looked as if a thin corpse lay there, its arms spread out in grotesque crucifixion. Never has he kissed me with quiet selfless joy. There was a sour, intimate odour mingled with the empty smell of the room; it was the smell of mortality. The silent room was lifeless and dull and final. This, I thought, is how it will be from now on – forever. An armchair, uncongenial, flaccid, soft, had its back to the light of the window. Its greasy arms were strewn with clothes. On the washstand, a basin of soapy water was cooling into grey scum. Beside it was a brush matted with dark hair and his shaving case. I lifted the clasp and took out the razor. I opened the blade and gingerly felt its edge with my thumb. There is something sinister in the daily repetitions of life, something deathly in their weary banality. I can imagine real despair – the sadness of a wasted life. My hand did not tremble when I replaced the razor. The muffled call of a cuckoo came from outside in the shifting light. The last of the warm weather is dying. The call came again, dull, repetitive, insistent. I looked at my tired, lucid face in the mirror. I have become gaunt, grim, creased. I idly opened one of two small drawers under the mirror and my fingers found a small squat bottle of thick glass. I had seen one like it before! My eyes widened behind the dusty mirror. He constantly complains of insomnia and headaches. I decided to take a few drops. Surely he would not miss a few drops. My fingers trembled and I had trouble prising the little stopper from the throat of the bottle but at last it came free. I raised it to my lips. No. It was not the same. The smell was different – deathly. Surely he wouldn't? I was tempted to take it to Doctor Hawarden. He would know, but I could not risk discovery. I replaced the ugly little bottle and closed the drawer carefully. I did not look at the mirror again.

1st March 1818
Doctor Hawarden's, Wigan

Aaron had journeyed to Liverpool determined to bring his daughter Jane, from whom he had heard nothing for months, home with him. He had returned – without her – and sat before the fire eating a late meal of beef and giblet fry, which Alice had prepared for him. Beside him was a mug of beer. I could smell the frothy yeasty odour of it. He preserved a bitter silence for awhile and then said with schooled inattentive sarcasm, 'Would you like some of this?' He held a piece of rusty brown meat caught on his fork above his plate. He looked directly at me and gave a slight, canine smile. His face was pale, fleshy. He could not conceal the sneering hostility he felt for me.

'No. Thank you,' I replied, annoyed as I heard the tremble in my voice.

Silence again, but I waited, I wanted to know. There were sounds of him eating. A newspaper lay discarded beside him. I eyed it hungrily, and then forced myself to look away from it into the fire in case he noticed my sudden want. The flames licked and enfolded the dry wood forming tiny caves of molten gold edged with blue heat, of beauty and dead white ash.

He finished eating. There was a cold silence – irksome, awful. I squirmed in my mulish determination to stay.

'She's married some fellow called Peck,' he stated flatly.

He looked at me fixedly. Perhaps I smiled. I don't remember. But it was as if I had dashed raw vinegar in his face. His anger suddenly uncoiled and with a snarling grunt he struck me across the ear with a heavy open hand. He would have hit me again but I reeled back in pain and in quick shuddering anger. My vision misted and blurred. There was the salt taste of blood in my mouth. He had me by the upper arms. His stale breath came in huge rasping sobs. A fleck of spit hit my face as he raved.

'Because of you! You ugly, pettifogging, sad lackwit!'

Still gripping my left arm he savagely dragged me down the hallway wheezing with the effort. I cannot recall what protests I made or whether I spoke at all. A scream came from somewhere, from someone. I don't think it was from me. He became inarticulate in his rage.

'The street… at home there… you slut!'

He managed to open the door and almost howling he flung me from him. I stumbled down the two stone steps and fell heavily. I vaguely registered that I had hurt my knee. He stood there a moment cursing and writhing before slamming the door heavily. The night was cold with misty showers brought on gusts of wind. Huddling against the door afforded me some shelter but my head was bare, I had no shawl, no cloak. I struck the door viciously with my open hands but he refused to open it. I sank to the step gasping, breathing out white warmth into the cold air. I did not cry. Crouching there, I became aware of the silence, the dripping hedges, and the damp odour of old stone. My hair was beaded with moisture and my head ached from the cold and from the blow he had given me. I began to shiver uncontrollably. Still the door was shut. Mary would be safe, I thought. Even in the depths of his extraordinary rage I knew he would not hurt her. I rose stiffly to my feet. The path was black with wet leaves. A lean cat entwined itself through the railings before vanishing. The rain stopped. Clouds moved across a veiled moon. My own street was eerily unfamiliar in the dark silence. It had become a frightening place, a small part of a larger maze of empty laneways and quiet side-alleys that ended in confused darkness and where danger lurked. I walked tentatively as far as the Hawardens. Parts of the road were frozen hard and I glanced nervously, childishly, behind me more than once. They had been painting the outside of their house and that adjoining, which was let to a straw bonnet-maker. How willingly I would have changed my life for hers! Inside were warmth and comfort and hope. But such things cannot be changed at a single stroke. I did not disturb them. My knee was bleeding and I felt light-headed and a little dizzy. The cold seeped through my thin shoes. I tried desperately to stop my teeth from chattering. A fine sleet began to fall as I limped back to my own door. Yes! It opened at my touch. Alice! It would have been Alice who had quietly shifted the bolts after he had gone to bed.

*

The next day, Mary and I walked the four miles to Up Holland. If great exertions were necessary, I had great exertions in mind, and I knew Mrs Braithwaite would not shut her door to me. My husband's crude insults still smarted and stung. I have been as faithful to that man as the tides to the moon. And what have I received in return! It was unjust. Unjust! And now I was to be blamed for his daughter's way of life? And in such a vile, unreasonable way!

*

Seated in her battered armchair, Mrs Braithwaite turned to me without moving her outstretched hands or her splayed fingers, which were cobwebbed with wool. She was amusing Mary with the mysteries of cat's cradle. I had been ill for some days and I was still a little feverish. My arms were blotched with bruises faded to a yellowish purple.

'Why don't you apply to your brother?' she asked. The concerned little frown she has worn all week returned. 'He lives so near; surely he would take it as his duty to protect his only sister from ill usage.' She directed Mary's small white hand. 'Through there pet, now...' She opened her arms wider.

It was Mary's turn to frown when she discovered that her wrist, which had been entrapped in the wool, was free from the tangle as if by magic.

'Will you show me how to do that? Please!' she said.

Mrs Braithwaite shuffled a little to make room in the ample armchair and Mary snuggled in beside her.

'You will need your own thread of wool, I think,' she said and began rummaging through her sewing box, which she balanced on her knees.

'What can my brother do? And if he cannot do anything effectual, why bother him?'

'As the Clerk to the Leigh magistrates I would have thought he would be able to do something for you.' She snipped a length of wool and tied it into a loop. Glancing down at Mary, she said cheerfully, 'Now Miss Ariadne, watch carefully.'

'Who? That's not my name. Why did you call me that?'

'Well, there is an old story,' began Mrs Braithwaite.

I smiled sadly and looked enviously at the coloured clew of wool.

★

I received a letter by the morning post. I did not expect him to be so prompt.

Avenue Place,
Leigh

Dear Ellen,

What an unhappy state you find yourself in!

I have visited your husband and found him to be an eminently reasonable man in all matters except money! While he is very willing to accede to your request of either a separation by which you may leave in peace or for you to live in his house merely as a boarder and be free to devote your time to Mary's education, he adamantly refuses to grant you the sum of seventy pounds per year as a condition of your leaving him. In his words: 'You may bestir yourself and starve as you please!'

As for your demand that on no occasion of quarrel are you to be deprived of money for housekeeping and that you would prefer a regular weekly sum, it received no more than laughter of some considerable mirth.

I have done my best for you on these matters. However, my position is a decidedly awkward one at this juncture. Mr Aaron Stock is not unknown to me in the way of business and Leigh is not many miles from Wigan. Any unpleasant gossip being connected with my name locally could be detrimental to one in my position. Mrs Weeton has suggested to me as delicately as possible that while you are of course welcome to visit, perhaps, all things considered, it would be wise of you not to stay with us for any length of time.

Yours,

Tom Weeton Esq.

Ah, brother Tom! Even *you* felt it! He overawes all who come near him. But I had to go back to him. To be subject to the arbitrary will of another means you are a slave. I was a slave. I had no will. And what a reception awaited me!

★

Alice had worn a troubled, unreadable expression on her face when I entered the kitchen.

'Now young lady, I have been given strict instructions that the moment you arrived I was to take you straight to your room. Say goodnight to your mother. You will see her in the morning.' She held out her hand to Mary who took it readily enough. Alice paused a moment and there again passed a look of anxiety, or perhaps of knowing sympathy directed at me. 'They are in the dining room quite expecting you,' she said with a strained hollowness.

They had been feasting on boiled hake and shellfish and were drinking wine, a straw yellow colour. The empty grey shells gave off a sharp hot stink. Kitty Barker's eyes were brisk and showed her fear, but she drew her throat up in expressive triumph. There would be no compromise from Kitty Barker! She knew her power. I wanted to rake her face! I wanted to feel her skin under my nails. I could look at nothing else except her lips, which had a moist slightly bruised look about them; at her rudely handsome hard face that held the story of her past – and she would have a lot of past! My blood surged, my reason clouded in a mist of hopeless rage.

'I will not have that thing from the stews in this house! I will not… will not!' I screamed or whimpered. I don't know which. 'Painted and patched and perfumed like a sweet-bag! I will not!'

He rose, his face tumid with suppressed anger. She laughed stupidly. I burned and shuddered. My heart was like a mallet striking on dumb wood and I sank to the floor under the blows, my arms around my knees. I rocked backwards and forwards. 'I wish harm to come to you!' My voice was wrenched from deep sobs. My anger frightened me; my words disgusted me.

'Can you see?' he nearly screamed, pointing at me and glancing at her. 'The woman is mad! Who knows what maggots squirm in the dratchell's brain! Tonight, now – as you are, you will go with me to Chapel Lane. And if you so much as speak a word, I will clap you into the nearest Bedlam house! Do you understand?'

'And leave Mary here with that thing? I will not. I...'

His voice cut through my ravings. 'Tomorrow Mary will be leaving for Parr Hall Boarding School. It has all been arranged. It is high time she was weaned from your mad, blighting influence.'

'Aaron, she is still a child. How can you do this to her?'

'I have every assurance from the school authorities that it is quite in order. Now get up before I lose all control. I can't stand the sight of you! You mad thing! Now!'

I was not permitted to see Mary. I did not say goodbye to her. I had no time to try to explain or even to hold her in my arms by way of explanation. She should be delighting in a bright world. How will she remember her mother who did not say goodbye to her, who did not come when she called her in the morning? What will they tell her about me?

A closed chaise was waiting. The driver leaned forward as I was bundled inside. It was Kearsley. There was no mistaking his sleering manner. We were soon outside our old, ruined rooms in Chapel Lane and the stale reek of neglect and poverty caught in my throat. I was reduced to degrading childish terror. It was the darkness. I clutched at his arm, but he violently shrugged me off.

'Please, please don't do this to me!' I begged imploringly, urgently. I cowered back in revulsion. 'Don't lock me in there, please!'

He rattled some keys on a wire ring. The door opened. A mixture of odours met me as we entered what had once been our home: unsunned rotten wood, wet hessian bags – I would discover in the morning that they swarmed with black beetles and other vermin – dust, sour acrid waste. There was the hiss and the orange spurt of a match as he lit a candle. Black shadows leapt up the walls and flickered. It was as if we had entered the confines of some primitive, savage cave. I felt weak and giddy.

'The door is locked from the outside only. You are free to leave at any time. Please do!' he spat out venomously, his voice high-pitched and piercing with anger. He rummaged in his pocket, found some coins and slammed them down in the light of the candle. 'But do not set foot in my house again or I will not answer for it!'

The door closed and I was left alone. I started to shudder uncontrollably. My eyes began to adjust to the half-light. I could see a bed with rough grey blankets – they were dry, clean – a large earthen chamber pot, feathers, debris, cotton reels, remnants of bones. Brown paper had been glued to the inside of some of the windowpanes. The floor was rough and as uneven as an old barn. I lifted the candle higher. A rat! Ink-black vicious little eyes, a long naked tail, indecent, it bunched in a squirm of excitement and slid from the light – an ugly noise. I was close to panic, perhaps gibbering hysteria. The cold drove me to the blankets. Their coarse furry texture was a comfort. I tried to take long, full breaths. I had become a nameless thing of nightmare, a mad witch in her garret. I thought of vagrants, loiterers. What would I do if a window shattered and an arm came through to loosen the sneck? The damp smell made me sick. I was almost delirious from tiredness and fear. I imagined a rat tearing at my cheek if I fell asleep – lifting its sharp snout, scenting the strangeness of the air. I wrapped a blanket tightly around my face, and lay on my left side with my legs drawn up tightly, looking at the candle. Its golden glow misted and moved like yellow fog. I drifted out into its light before sinking into blackness. Mary!

She was some distance in front of me, laughing, and I tried to call out to her. Mary! I could only manage a groan, a grunting noise. She did not see me. She did not look back. My limbs were weighted and I could not run after her. I tried to wave goodbye, but I could not move my arm. I stumbled. I had the physical sensation of falling, descending into a sunless cell, from which it was hopeless ever to escape. Putrid straw was scattered on the floor reeking of wet human waste. A wave of terror gathered and broke over me. There were others! I could sense their presence. I breathed in the sour smell of them. I would not look at them! My arm! My arm was dying, rotting. I was biting on the chain, which bound it. Someone was holding a filthy rag to my nostrils. Struggling against it, I awoke to the brown raw light of morning, to brown-shrouded windows, and to a smell like that of decaying shellfish. I massaged my arm, which was heavy and useless. It was numbed and tingling from my own weight.

★

I endured three nights and had ventured out only once. I was a prisoner in Chapel Lane and my own husband was the turnkey. The next day was Sunday. The sky was snow-grey – all shades of grey: silver, pewter, lead. Church bells from St Paul's in Standishgate pealed, faded, died into silence. The faithful gathered. I sat in silence, my eyes shut, and saw Mr Aaron Stock nodding familiarly to Reverend Steill, heard the shuffling of feet and hymnbooks, and voices raised in worship. I felt a little dizzy and leant my forehead against the ice-cold window and looked into the laneway. The soft knock at the door jolted me from reverie and sent my heart racing. Had he come for me at last? Or was it Kearsley? 'Let it not be Kearsley,' I whispered. It was Alice; I could hear her calling my name anxiously.

'He is with Reverend Steill,' she said by way of greeting, 'so I took the opportunity to bring you some things.'

'He's probably discussing theology in Reverend Steill's fine library and making a great show of borrowing another book from him,' I scoffed. 'But surely he doesn't intend to leave me here any longer. How can he?'

'I'm sure I don't know,' she said tensely, unpacking a basket. She had risked dismissal to bring me soap, my sewing box, my writing materials, some food wrapped in paper – and my diary.

I thanked her. 'Is that woman still with him?' I asked hoarsely, struggling to control a surge of anger.

She nodded silently and looked about the room. It was filthy and a pervading odour of damp and desperation was mixed with the smell of burnt tallow and rotten wood. The room made her nervous. She moved towards the wavering fire.

'He must allow me some more coals or he will be guilty of murder as well,' I murmured bitterly. 'Alice if I write a letter could you post it to Mary and send her doll for me? Assuming she is in fact at Parr Hall,' I added. 'He may have put her somewhere where I will never be able to find her.'

'But she is there. Your mind may be at peace on that score.'

I grimaced. My love was possessive, impotent. What could I do? *If my mother loves me why am I in this place? Why didn't she say goodbye? Why did she leave me?* Outside the callous lane laughed and tramped with heavy boots.

'The carrier, old Hindley, says it is a solemn place right enough, very exposed it is.'

Her words were directed at my makeshift bed; the blankets were uncreased, guiltless, defeated. My misery and shame lay naked in its narrowness. My pride smothered.

'The living rooms are below, and above is a series of attic rooms for the pupils and servants. The dormitories hold four to six beds, each shared by two girls. Saturday is bath-night, church on Sundays, he says.' She busied her fingers, which fidgeted and plucked at the grey coil of hair pulled back behind her ears.

'And who are these Grundys?'

'Husband and wife. According to Hindley, she is steadily drinking herself to death, an event eagerly awaited by the employer of a staff of young lady teachers.' She squeezed the fingers of her gloves, looked behind her with a gathering frown. 'The child should not suffer any positive harm at their hands.'

She settled by the struggling fire. I drew a blanket about my shoulders and reached out wearily for my quill.

Wigan
31st December 1817

My dear little Mary,
(At Parr Hall, nr. St Helens)

I am writing this letter in a large hand in the hope that you will be able to read some of it yourself. I trust that there will be an older student or a teacher who can read it for you and who will be kind enough to write back to me to tell me how you are circumstanced, if you are well or ill. It would make such a difference to me to hear from you — just a few lines would be a great comfort.

I know what your fears must be, but you must be content and do all you can to improve yourself while you are at Parr Hall. You are in my thoughts by day; you live in my dreams at night.

I have sent Miss Watts to you. She will be a good little companion for you, but remember she will be new to the school as well and a little lonely.

I promise you that I will come to see you as soon as it is humanly possible for me to do so.
With all my love,
Your affectionate Mother

I faced another night in my hovel; my one consolation was that Alice had promised to visit again when the opportunity presented itself. Outside it began to snow. Encased in brown silence, I peered through a partly papered, frosted window with the clarity of solitude. Snow was falling. Quickly. Great feathery flakes of it blanched the ugly lane, the ugly walls, and the ugly cobbles stained green with the slippery filth of decay and waste. The ugliness of the mud-black lane sank – or appeared to sink under the white fullness of the snow. The sharp ugliness of black, slate roofs was snow-moulded into round, white, misting smoothness. The silence was absolute. Snow-silence. Old houses, hunched with snow across their shoulders, listened, shivered. Snow. Cold. Beautiful. Inexorable. *Why doesn't she come? Where is she?* It was at least seven miles to Parr Hall. And the snow was falling. Large flakes sailed silently through the air, others wheeled around to fly back up into the darkness of the empty night. I recalled some lines of William Cowper's poem and whispered them into the darkness: 'I, fed with judgement, in a fleshy tomb, am buried above the ground.' Seven miles was now an impossible journey. I turned from the snow-flecked window towards the fire.

I remembered Alice's parcel – paper and string – plum cake. Its winey smell swam to the surface of my mind. Memory had become another level of dream consciousness. Raisins, lemon peels – rum-soaked – clean calico rubbed with icing sugar and flour – whiskery string. Plum cake.

★

I was in the kitchen. It must have been early November. Wood smoke, the clatter of cast iron, and my mother was at the stove. To forget is to betray, but I could not remember her face. I was a child. I saw sunlight on her arms, a falling lock of hair; I heard a voice; I felt the texture of her clothes. Words as soft as sifted flour fell from her hands. The brown kernels of three almonds were clenched in my left hand. I was carrying a large pannikin outside to the rain barrel. *Christmas. It will be Christmas soon, the anniversary of my birthday. Tom will be home.* I struggled with the lid; its wet woody smell competed with the sharp-scented mint growing near my feet. I filled the pannikin with cold water. My mouth was sweet almond whiteness. I looked at the shiny watery sunshine, the milky horizon clean as boiled bed sheets. I slowly breathed in the drenched grass – the sky-washed morning.

★

I started at a half-heard sound. There was a handful of fire in the rusty grate. The smoky tallow candle had an unpleasant smell in the poorly ventilated room. I was frightened at night and I dreaded the darkness, its silence and its noises.

★

I shivered from cold and fear. I tore the blanket from my bed, wrapped it around my shoulders and began to pace to and fro on the uneven floorboards. I was shaking uncontrollably. I had been out to buy a few simple things, when I came back Kearsley had been standing in the alley with his stupid grin. I moved to the window. He was still there despite the cold. What was he waiting for? He stamped his feet and moved away, hunched and shadowy against the white of the snow. Poor minion, he must be off to report to his master.

I continued to march up and down my cell until I felt weak and ill. Snow was falling again. I wept – inwardly, silently – not only for myself, but also for everything that must sink into nothingness – to be lost and forgotten. I wept with Miss Watts who was beside me with her limp kid-leather arms and china face. Her glass blue eyes stared tearlessly. The Wigan postmaster! It must be. Alice found her amongst my husband's boots!

Was I mad? Would I know if I were insane? Did I need to be watched? I knew I would soon sicken and perhaps die if I did not escape my prison. I had to reach the Hawardens and get word to Tom.

★

It was a little warmer; the snow was melting. The street dripped and ran with water. I craved the warmth of the sun. Liverpool! I remembered the sea at Liverpool; the excitement I felt when I left Up Holland for the first time, the Chorleys – the Chorleys of Liverpool! – Mile-End House, Ann Winkley, as she then was, but most of all I remembered the sea – the freedom of the sea – and the sun warm on my back. Memories crowded my waking hours. Colours, sounds – the smell of cut hay drying in the sun. Lakes and sun-filled showers of rain.

I no longer believed in myself. That was why I was lost. My faith, my confidence had worn thin. I could no longer rely on credit. My appearance was too much against me. Thin to the point of being emaciated; my hair was unbrushed, unclean. I had written to the Grundys of Parr Hall but had received no answer. No doubt they were well aware of the conditions attaching to Mary's attendance. And Alice had stopped coming.

★

Kearsley must have been watching, waiting. I am sure of that now. He must have seen me leave. He knew the door was left ajar – he knew – and he had waited.

I expected to be turned out again, to be driven out destitute. So I had been keeping myself locked up day and night, going out by stealth only in the late evening to try to find some simple provisions. My body was no longer my own. My gums were swollen and my teeth were loose. I could move them with my tongue and taste the black, salt-sick taste of blood. When I returned something terrible happened.

He was there – waiting for me. I felt as if I were already inhaling raw smoke. I coughed, almost gagged, as I struggled to control my sudden, lurching fear. My hands fumbled. The door was shut, locked. He leaned forward in the twist of the narrow lane. He did not come closer – not then. The window. I could reach the latch through the window. I punched it lightly with my thinly gloved hand. Nothing. I tried again – this time harder. I expected a loud shattering of glass, but there was only a dull, sickening crack. I plucked at the glass sticky with old glue and brown paper. I could not look at him again. The sense of his presence overwhelmed me; it suffocated me. I had to get inside. I put my arm through the bared teeth of broken glass and across to the lock. Yes! The door was open. Now he came forward. I panicked, slammed the door. Laughter – hollow, cruel.

Smoke, thick, black, sluggish, was uncoiling from its foul orange nest, and was burning a widening circle across the ruin of my bed. The wooden pail poured a sodden stench on it. I buried the mess under what remained of the ruined grey blankets. The room was still tense, sinister, violated. I found it hard to breathe. I didn't want to breathe. I stood rock still in the darkness, helplessly staring at the gaping broken mouth in the window. Fear twisted inside me. Nothing. Was he still out there – waiting? I edged closer to my bag. I knew I was close to collapse of some kind – would it take the form of bodily exhaustion or would it be a screaming rending of the mind? My diary was in my bag, that I knew, and Miss Watts, but I could not force myself to remember what else it contained. My head started to swim, nausea, and the taste of blood was there again. The floor creaked under my foot – silence. Tea-coloured light trickled through the broken window. I half-imagined his arm coming through the broken glass. The thread that held me snapped. I lunged at the door, opened it, and stumbled into the laneway. He was not there.

The night air was as still as stagnant water, not cold but damp. There were few lights. I rested for a moment against a dark wet wall. Above, the sky was an impenetrable vault of blackness. I could have been underground or in an ancient gravesite, a sepulchre. The familiar misted streets had taken on a strange alien quality in the darkness, which intensified their haunting confusion. I knew I had to make my way to the Hawardens. My life depended on it. I moved on into the slimy maw of the labyrinth as powerless as if I were in the contingent world of heightened dream.

Voices and laughter spilled out from the straw and the sopped tables of a squalid public house. Saturday night. A square of lurid light opened on the cobbles before me and a perfect stranger stood there swaying slightly. He threw back his heavy shaggy head, and then moved it from side to side as if to give some relief to his thick neck. He shook himself; shivered, beast-like; perhaps he shuddered. I had a fleeting impression of blotched white skin and gingery russet hair. I dared not shrink back into the shadows, but stood as if weighted to the spot. His eyes, slowed by casual drunkenness, crawled over me like flies – mutton at a market. He lifted his brows in mock surprise. His crude unspoken question hung in the air between us, vibrating. His pale left hand snaked towards the buttons of his trousers. Shaking my head I hurried forwards past him, but not before he spat a single word, bluntly, obscenely, into my soul.

'Whore!'

The streets widened; the sky grew lighter – not far now, not far.

★

What an awful mess I was in. But I knew I should sleep, sleep. I wanted to sink into oblivion under the warm soft snow of clean sheets. They smelled of lavender. I was safe. The slivers of dirty, sticky glass were gone. The oily black smoke and orange flames were gone. The dark figure in the laneway was gone. I no longer choked with sick fear.

★

There followed days of lassitude. Days of sleep and hot steam baths, of starched-white surfaces, crisp white pages, big brass taps, and the clean shock of brandy. I had yearned for such days without really believing they would ever be granted to me. I looked up at the great beams of the ceiling. My room seemed unnaturally large. The floor was stained with a slab of clean yellow sunshine. There was a clatter of fire irons at the hearth. Muffled, friendly voices were outside my door. Clever eyes, the colour of the steely sea – searching, professional – looked down at me, expressed concern.

★

This morning, I was able to venture into the Hawardens' garden. The sunlight fell full on my face. Swallows swooped amongst spiralling clouds of tiny insects. I walked to a wild little corner where a crumbling dry-stone wall covered in stonecrop trailed blackberry vines and where elder flourished. I saw a robin. The roses were beginning to bud. They smelt like wine.

16th March 1818

Tom, when he came, refused the offer to sit and remained standing. Bearded, refined, Doctor Hawarden sat at the large desk in the room he uses as his surgery and tapped his chin with the thumb of his right hand. Mrs Hawarden was beside me on the sofa. She took my arm reassuringly. Outside beyond the window behind him the sun was shining white in a mackerel sky. The small clouds were luminous and silvery. Doctor Hawarden was the kindest man I have ever met, but his customary calm had deserted him. Affronted, he looked steadily at Tom, his grey eyes narrowed. His deep, sonorous voice when it came was measured, steely, it did not allow for doubt.

'Well you can tell your friend, Mr Aaron Stock, that I am prepared to match purses with him. And kindly inform him that I will also be demanding payment for the expenses I have incurred in this matter. If we are to have recourse to the law so be it.'

'He is not my friend as you so nicely put it. He has sought my legal advice on some points and I have answered him to the best of my ability.'

'You astonish me sir! You act as attorney on behalf of Mr Stock against your own sister's interests! You will be the talk of Wigan! Would you remain quiet if the poor woman were in a murdering?'

Tom was visibly struggling to keep his voice neutral. His mouth jerked charmlessly.

'Again sir, you misjudge me. Mr Gaskell is acting for Mr

Stock. It is he who has drawn up a deed of separation. I simply want to be left out of the affair. I fear the expenses. You may or may not know that Mr Stock rents a factory in Wigan belonging to my wife's mother. If I were to give him offence he could well throw it upon our hands.'

'Tom.' My voice was little more than a whisper. 'Tom, have you read the deed? I must know if there are any restrictions or conditions placed on me regarding Mary.'

'He is prepared to grant you seventy pounds a year, to be paid quarterly through an agent you yourself can name. I would persuade you to sign it, Ellen.'

He looked older, softer, more driven. Time's awful changes – mysterious, baffling – had torn at the tough sinews of memory and made even the past vulnerable. We were playfellows once. We shared our time of innocence when it was easy to be good. Now a cold chasm had opened up between us. I would never be able to cross it; the wound was too deep. His words filled it with despair. With a deep shuddering obscure emotion, I realised I never wanted to hear from him or see him again.

Frowning, Doctor Hawarden placed his hands neatly in front of him and spoke quietly but measuredly to them. 'And in that eventuality, would you be prepared to be bound with your sister and act as bondsman?'

'No, I would not!'

'I am compelled to say that I am astounded!'

'I have been reliably informed that my sister cannot be trusted. Be careful she does not take you in, sir!'

'Tom!'

Tom, or the remnant of Tom, faced me, his eyes glaring.

'A witness will attest, if necessary, to the fact that you broke into a residence in Chapel Lane and started a fire on the premises. No, I will not stand bondsman for you! No, I will not stand as attorney for you! I am not entirely bereft of family feeling, but a man's right to chastise his wife is enshrined in common law. If you are determined to pursue this matter I suggest you enlist the services of Mr Battersby of Battersby and Banks and proceed on the plea of adultery only.'

Doctor Hawarden stood to his full height and marched with heavy steps to the door, opened it and said brusquely, 'How very scrupulous of you! I trust you can find your own way out, sir!'

'Tom, have you seen the deed?'

'Sign it, Ellen. Have you no pride? Have you no thought for those in your family who have made something of their lives?'

Without waiting for a reply, he turned on his heel and left.

Mrs Hawarden's arm encircled my shoulders. 'What a very disappointed man your brother must be!' she said, her eyes large behind her rimless glasses.

★

I was to receive another setback. Mr Battersby who at first gave me great hopes of rescuing my child withdrew from the case. His partner, Mr Banks, was an intimate of Mr Stock... the inference was easily drawn.

I signed the deed. I had no alternative but to sign it. I was dependent for my very bread on the charity of the Hawardens. I signed it in the presence of Doctor Hawarden's attorney, Mr Stopforth, through whom I was soon given my first quarterly payment, and Mr Ackerly, Mr Gaskell's clerk. I was not allowed to read the document, nor was I given a copy of it, only to hear it read by the clerk.

I returned to Up Holland, not to my own cottage, but to

Garnett Lees, an old farmhouse that sits without compromise below the windy summit of the village. Here, Doctor Hawarden assured me, I would soon regain my health under the watchful eyes of Mrs Ball.

6

19th April 1818
Garnett Lees
I awoke suddenly from a troubled sleep with a sense of awful helplessness. For a confused moment, I was once again in my room at Dove's Nest. I thought of Gertrude – then of Mary. The moon was shining silver through my tiny window – a hopeful portent perhaps after blank grey days of rain and wind. The house creaked its protest when my bare feet touched the floor and it determinedly resisted my first efforts to open the window. Then the cold night air reached in and held my face in its pale hands. Out in the blue-black dimness the few wind-torn trees were standing silently in pools of deep brooding shadows, at peace at last in the stillness. Somewhere a cow coughed. The long field sloping down to woodland was glassed with brittle frost. A star, like chipped ice, was near the white-grey moon.

I returned to bed but not to sleep.

It would be morning soon, and the mornings were the worst. My health had improved and I should have had the pleasure of rising and retiring with no employment other than that of attending and amusing myself, but I was tormented. I felt it as a physical force in the pit of my stomach, a profound emptiness, a sense of loss and futility. It weakened me into a state of despairing inaction. Mary was my life and she had vanished from it. I had become dull – absolutely dull. My whole life seemed little more than a series of beginnings – a tragedy of unfinished things. The day ahead, I knew, would bring endless thoughts of Mary tugging and tugging at the fabric of my mind.

I must have slept again. Noises made by Mr and Mrs Ball in the kitchen below entered and confused my dreams, which I could not recollect on wakening but they left me feeling strained and anxious. Mr Ball whistled for the dog. My money was not unwelcome to them, but it was not enough to stave off the spectre of enclosure and the fear of rick-burning hands. They were up by candlelight and bustled about on dark mornings to live their unglamorous lives according to the changing rhythms and seasonal rituals demanded of them by the farm. I heard Mrs Ball rake out the ashes from the stove, the heavy clank of the kettle as she put it on top of the range, the scrape of the wood box across the slate flagstones. Every morning before she left for the dairy, she brought me sweet creamy porridge, brown sugar and strong tea. They were pleasant, hardworking and kind. They had a determination that I had lost, a stoic refusal to accept the limitations of life. There was much I could learn from them.

*

That afternoon, I walked alone to the small woodland that lies on the edge of the farm. I left by the back door into the barton with its sharp scents of hay and hens and cows. I carried my flageolet. I wanted to play it out of doors away from the gloom and damp of the poky little parlour. The season had turned and my spirits lifted a little. It was good to be walking in the soft light of early spring. Starlings lifted and settled on the clods of a fallow field. Blackbirds and thrushes called. A crow flapped black against the pallid blue of the sky, which was cloudless except for a thin scarf of swirling white. Wrens darted in winter-brown bracken near the old moss-grown field gate. I liked the feel of its ancient white wood, smooth and cracked under my ungloved hand.

A breeze came up as I entered the wood and I drew my shawl more closely around me. Perhaps wood is not the right word, it is little more than a copse, really. There was a soft moan as a heavy branch rubbed and wounded another with its weight. The soft spongy moss underfoot muffled my steps. When I stopped walking I became aware of a vast silence, ancient and frightening. The trees were watchful, suspicious. Patterns of dappled light and shade moved across the tangled undergrowth and played lightly over some rocks blotched with lichen. I shivered. There was the rich pungent smell of decay and hidden moisture – last year's leaves – disturbing, fecund, unpleasant. I had not had the foresight to bring something to sit on. Instead, I arched my back a little and pressed my shoulders against the hard green trunk of a tree and self-consciously played a few notes. They sounded thin and alien. My fingers trembled; my breath was shallow. Why was I afraid? I found it suddenly hard to breathe. A few more lonely notes sounded in the tree-shadowed silence. I was panting for breath and could play no more. The empty, yearning moment frightened me. My separateness frightened me. I closed my eyes aware of my dry-mouthed thirst. The cold smell of earth and decaying leaves was overpowering. A dead branch snapped and fell. I started violently. The sound was instantly taken by the silent chaos of the trees and the soft, welcoming earth. A chaos, a silence that was all-powerful, inescapable. Recognising it, I cowered before it. It was easy to imagine in those few fleeting moments that I had never existed. I wanted desperately to be out in the clean open expanse of the fields, away from the listening dark trunks of the trees, the maze of spectral branches and twigs, the sharp green claws of ivy. I heard the distant sound of a sheep-bell, the bark of a dog. The trees could hold me no longer. I moved forward at a half run towards the ragged light.

My dress swished rhythmically through shaggy tufts of dead grass. I saw Mrs Ball. A great piercing warmth welled up in my heart at the sight of her trudging homewards from the dairy with a heavy dogged determination. Her gaze was fixed on the ground a little in front of her feet, in the crook of her arm she carried a large heavy pail, and the scarf she wore when milking was wrapped loosely about her head. I stopped, called out and waved. Her weary face brightened with surprise and friendliness. I had such a desperate need of her presence I could hardly restrain myself from flinging my arms around her. Together, we went into the cold air of the kitchen. A match dropped from her hand and wood-smoke coiled from the fresh pine tinder as she talked animatedly of the holiday she had long promised herself at Southport, but had never taken.

I had left something of myself in those thin woods. I was glad.

19th May 1818

The tiny corpses of gnats that have been attracted to my candle lie on the table. The night is still and warm. A large dark moth was also drawn in from the night. It fluttered near my face and startled me before it disappeared behind a curtain. I shut the window against more. My diary is the only book in the room. I have sat for some time in the smothering peace of my little bedroom at Garnett Lees with my right hand against my forehead. Determined not to succumb to the bitter ironies of my predicament, I have written two letters. And such is the uncertainty of my position in the world I will make a copy of both, despite the lateness of the hour and my tiredness.

Garnett Lees, Up Holland
19th May 1818

My dear little Mary,

I hope you will rejoice to see a letter from me when I have been silent for so long. I had hoped to see you long ago. I long to do so but fear I must see you no more. But surely I may write and tell you how much I love you. I pray that you are well. If Mrs Grundy permits you, let me hear from you soon, or I shall think you want to forget your mother.

I am living at Up Holland with Mr and Mrs Ball. They are busy every day with their cows and their farm and have very little time to sit in their parlour. I have a bedroom to myself, but being very much alone I sometimes feel it dull. Mrs Braithwaite invites me to dine with her one or two days every week. Indeed, since I came to Up Holland, everybody has been very kind to me. The poor people bid me good morning, or goodnight, and the little children smile and call after me if I know their names. I think of you.

My health is much improved and I spend my time most agreeably walking about the farm. I wish so much you could be with me.

Give my respects to Mr and Mrs Grundy. Remember me kindly, Mary.

Your affectionate Mother

The second letter:

Garnett Lees, Up Holland
19th May 1818

My husband,

Please consider calmly what I urge in this letter. A strong sense of duty alone compels me to write to you. Is it not our duty to do considerable violence to our own inclinations and feelings when the welfare of our child is at stake?

If you love our little daughter, please do not deny her a mother's care and affection. Let her have two homes, let her vacation time be divided between us. None but a mother can act a mother's part. Do not deprive Mary of her mother. Grant me the favour of seeing her, even if it is only for a week. Why deny me her company when you would in no way suffer yourself? It is in your power to make us all happier.

If you refuse this most natural of requests, let me beg you to make it up to me by providing those comforts you can well afford. I have no home of my own. I am obliged to live as a tolerated guest in other people's houses. Should I fall ill, what would become of me? My present income is not sufficient to allow me the services of a doctor. Could I not have a small home of my own and a servant's assistance? I have so little. The very paper on which I write is, strictly speaking, yours. I gave you all!

Since I left you, I have shown great patience. Consider carefully what I have written and let me have free access to my child that I may show her a mother's natural love, which she stands in need of. My wishes are so reasonable that surely you cannot deny them. Let me be favoured with as early an answer as possible.

Yours respectfully,

Ellen

My candle guttered and died. Outside a nearly full moon was lifting itself up from the horizon. The large moth, like a black, stippled leaf blown in winter-wind, was beating itself noiselessly against the invisible barrier of my window.

22nd June 1818

When I arrived, the doctor was enjoying a leisurely breakfast. His ample frame was settled before marmalades, clotted cream and fresh bread baked on embers. Bacon garnished with parsley was neatly arranged on a bright silver platter.

'John! John! Ellen is here!' exclaimed Mrs Hawarden. 'She has walked all the way and looks a picture.'

He rose with his habitual professional calm, 'Good Lord,

Ellen, you must have been up at starlight! I am pleased to see you looking so well.' He motioned to a small ottoman. 'Please sit down.'

'Mrs Ball, good woman that she is, would have me as robust and as stout as herself,' I said brightly, trying to mask the nervousness I felt. 'There is no shortage of butter or eggs at Garnett Lees, not to mention the abundance of fresh air.'

I tugged at the fingertips of my gloves, drew them off and placed them on a mosaic table. A teapot of old fashioned Worcester porcelain was brought in and another cup was fetched for me.

Mrs Hawarden's glasses flashed in the brightness of the morning streaming in through the French doors behind her. New wisteria blooms nodded and waved their purple in the breeze beyond the clean glass. 'But is it wise, Ellen, for you to be in Wigan?' She lowered her neat dove-grey head in thoughtful concern.

'Not even Mr Price has been able to discover whether the Deed explicitly and directly prohibits my coming to Wigan or any place within two and a half miles of it, or if the question is really a matter of preventing me from seeing and speaking to my husband. That the Deed expressly forbids my residing in Wigan is very plain, but whether or not I will incur troubles by merely visiting is not. I thought if I can safely visit once, I might as safely do so again.'

'It is infamous that the jumped-up jackanapes could insist on such an injunction in the first place,' rumbled the doctor into his teacup. 'I am sure it would not stand up in open court.'

'But I am hardly in a position to challenge it in open court,' I said flatly. 'Doctor Hawarden what troubles me the most is that I may have to go back to him. I think I must on Mary's account.'

Mrs Hawarden's eyes widened in alarm, 'Oh, Ellen, I don't think you should do that,' she said, her voice quavering slightly. 'Remember what you have been through!'

The agitation I felt probably sounded in my voice. 'Mr Stock insists that I am legally bound not to see Mary more than three times a year, the days to be exactly specified, and only in the presence of Mr or Mrs Grundy. I reject such a proposal but as a consequence I have not seen my child for months. I will have to go back to him! Just think, Mary must have spent her last vacation at home with a kept mistress in her mother's place!'

'Have you written to these Grundys asking for a private interview?' asked Doctor Hawarden kindly. His voice had lost all traces of its earlier gruffness.

'Mr Price advised the same,' I said. 'And I did so. I heard nothing. About a fortnight ago I wrote again to Mrs Grundy asking her if the letter had ever been received. To make quite sure I begged William Hindley, the carrier, to deliver it himself in case Mr Stock may have intercepted the other at the Wigan Post Office. The Hindleys have always behaved kindly towards me. To this I have received no answer. I worry that Mary is no longer at Parr Hall or that the Grundys have received positive orders not to see me.'

Two minutes passed in silence. The case-clock on the wall ticked away indifferently. Doctor Hawarden stirred a second cup of tea meditatively, tapped its delicate rim gently with the little silver spoon, and then said, 'Mr Stopforth shows an interest in your case, but even he cannot see a way forward. He is, however, adamant that the deed you signed is good for nothing. It has no legal standing whatsoever.'

'Are you sure of this?' I said, rising from the sofa in disbelief. 'But this is wonderful! Are you saying I may come and go as I please, that I may at this moment go to Standishgate and brave my husband and demand to see Mary?'

'Certainly, but that is not the point of importance, Ellen,' returned the Doctor, his face full of sadness. 'The law simply does not recognise your legal standing. You and your husband may have both signed a document, which states that a certain allowance will be granted to you; it may also specify that you may visit Mary under certain conditions, but your husband is under no legal compulsion to honour the agreement.'

'I don't understand,' I said, sighing audibly.

'It means that as his wife you have no existence in law. You are not entitled to enter a contract with him. Your husband has complete authority over Mary. He may let you see her or he may not with the full support of the law behind him.'

'But does my husband know this?'

'I believe,' his voice had a sharp edge of sarcasm, 'he has received excellent legal advice from your brother, for which, no doubt, he has been well paid.'

'So, I am utterly at my husband's mercy in this matter?' I groaned. 'He owns me – poor obscure half-thing that I am, neither married nor single. Doctor Hawarden, there are times when I truly think I shall go mad. I had to leave my child without so much as being able to kiss her goodbye. It tears at my very being. It is a grief that will never pass. It will haunt me forever.'

'Of course, *in honour* he is obliged to keep his word,' offered Mrs Hawarden.

Neither Doctor Hawarden nor I answered her.

'My husband lives openly with another woman who is only fit for a fair tent,' I said bitterly breaking the silence. An angry throbbing sadness welled up inside me. I could no longer suppress my feelings. 'He has been cruel and unmanly in keeping Mary from me. I am tortured with the thought that she may be neglected – or worse, that she may be suffering – or that she may be becoming coarsened or weakened because of her treatment and my absence. It clouds my very life. I have nothing. My dresses, my personal belongings – little things of no importance or value to anyone but myself are still in his house – with her!'

During the pause, which followed, Mrs Hawarden came and sat beside me.

'Ellen, you have received your quarterly payment, I trust?' asked Doctor Hawarden. He had stepped to the window and stood with his back towards me.

'Yes. I may rely on Mr Stopforth for that. He was also kind enough to send me a copy of the Deed.'

Turning he regarded me earnestly. 'You must – now I simply insist on this Ellen – you must inform me immediately if for any reason the payments are forfeited.'

He looked directly at me with an index finger raised. His face was as solemn as if he were telling a patient about the critical importance of taking the exact measure of a potent medicine.

Shamed by the man's kindness tears pricked my eyes. I blinked and managed to keep them in their place. 'I will. Thank you. Thank you for everything you have done for me.' My lips tightened into silence and bowing forward I hid them in the palm of my right hand.

'I don't suppose there is any point in appealing directly to Mr Stock to allow you to see Mary?' posed Mrs Hawarden gently.

'I could try. Yes. But I think it far more likely he would remove Mary where I will never be able to find her, if only to harass me as much as possible. He is determined to be free of me.'

There was another awful pause. Then the parlour maid, in crisp white and mottled pink, knocked at the door, entered and began clearing the table.

'At any rate I am convinced I must try a different approach. It seems to me that all my life I have been patient and submissive to no avail. I am now more determined than ever to defy the restrictions of the Deed. I will haunt the streets of Wigan if there is a possibility of snatching so much as a glimpse of Mary. I must see her – even if it means I will never see her again.' My voice dwindled to little more than a disturbed whisper. 'I simply must see her.'

'Ellen, stay with us tonight and come to church with us tomorrow morning,' suggested Doctor Hawarden. 'Sit in our pew. Let the world gape and talk if it must.' He looked at his wife and smiled, 'Our ship can stand the wind of a little gossip.'

'You are very kind,' I said, regaining a little of my composure, 'but I must return today. It is not far and I now teach Sunday school at Farr Moor Chapel. The days drag by so slowly that I look forward to it. I am quite attached to the children.'

2nd August 1818

It was a hot, bright morning. The sun poured yellow on the heightened green of the grass. A few tattered white clouds drifted in a blue sky. The road, little more than a thin white ribbon of dust in places, was empty. The silence unnerved me. No, not the silence, it was the absence of human sounds. Insects whirred. A wood pigeon called. The hedges and thistles hummed and chittered with a life of their own, intent and purposeful. My mouth was dry already, more from anxiety than thirst, I suspected. The peppery smell of the dust crimped my nose. I sneezed, laughed. I had told no one where I was going. Dressed in a simple deep coloured brown habit, I had left home about nine o'clock carrying my simple gifts: Miss Watts; a small ivory case with a ribbon marked for a yard in inches; some gimp, about two yards in length and a little narrow green ribbon; some Spanish juice, which I had sent up from Liverpool. I walked. My body seemed to take on a life of its own, separate in its own independent movement. It allowed me to think – or not to think. Not knowing the road beyond Billinge, I walked near a mile in tracing and retracing my steps before I was compelled to ask the way of a young man scything hay. His face glistened with sweat. I could feel the heat and steam of him as he took off his hat and wiped his brow with a bare forearm – strong, brown, and littered with stalks of yellow straw. I passed no one else.

I was thirsty when I reached the little wooden bridge near Parr Hall gate, but I had brought no cup with me. In the deep shadows under the willows, I dampened the edge of my handkerchief and cooled my face. Dragonflies darted red on veined glass wings. It was months since I had seen Mary – months! I peered into the still pool of water. My reflection was no more than a dark shadow on its surface. I moved into the light. There was the sky in its depths, the willows above me. I was not looking for myself but for Mary. There in the distortions of my own watery face, framed by white clouds and willows, I searched for a younger face in mine, beyond mine – hoping.

Parr Hall, small-bricked and angular, rose starkly from behind a low, roughly trimmed hedge that would offer little protection from the winter winds. Some straggling ivy clawed at its walls below two chimneypieces. A solitary tree struggled for light in its shadow. The last few steps set my heart beating. My resolution was shaken. Would I be refused admittance? For such were the orders I understood Mr Stock to have given.

*

Mr Grundy stood in the entrance hall at the base of a staircase. One hand rested on the moulded baluster on the handrail. His face was without the slightest hint of a smile.

'Mrs Stock, you place me in a very awkward position. I have been given very precise instructions not to let you see your daughter without your husband's written permission. I have received no such thing.'

Suddenly close to tears, I could do nothing to help his discomfort. I stood there and pleaded with him in total silence.

His mouth relaxed a little, 'If you would wait in the parlour with Mrs Grundy, I will see what I can do for you in the present instance. But in future I insist on the established procedure.'

Grim-faced, Mrs Grundy led the way to an old fashioned scrolled sofa, which was almost the only item of furniture in the dismal little room. There she sat, sour and shrivelled, with an air of crumpled hopelessness and said not a word. We waited so long that I began to fear they were taking Mary away somewhere. Perhaps twenty minutes crawled by before Mr Grundy returned, looking grave and solemn. He ushered Mary into the room with unsmiling serious eyes. She was thin-boned and pale and looked frightened. I was surprised at her tallness. I knelt on one knee and opened my arms in wordless supplication. Hoping. She paused, frowned in her puzzlement. Searching. She took one diffident step and stopped. Her soft mouth puckered with anxiety. I reached into my bag and brought out Miss Watts. A wistful little smile and she came forward. 'Thank you', she said, taking the doll and giving herself to my arms. I took her hand. It was cold. I ached with sad joy.

She was very pale, although she said she was well. Silent and self-contained, there was a sense of solitude, a resigned obedience about her that made our conversation forced and clumsy at first, but only at first. She was soon chatting with me quite familiarly as she hugged Miss Watts.

Dinner was brought to me on a single plate and Mary was called away to join her schoolfellows. I ate my dinner, making no observations and asking no questions. Mrs Grundy, unhappy woman, remained with me and kept her stony silence – I suppose it was to comply with some order from Mr Stock. Mary came to me as soon as she had dined carrying a bonnet, and Mr Grundy, evidently wanting me to leave, informed me that the girls were preparing for a walk. I asked if I could walk some of the way with them. He sighed uncomfortably but grudgingly agreed with a tightening of his lips and a reluctant single nod. Not at any time was I left alone with Mary – not for a single moment. Did they think I meant to run away with the child? I had prepared a card with a direction to Doctor Hawarden in Wigan. I had hoped to be able to tell her that if she were ever removed from the school, she must write to tell me and be careful with whom she entrusted the letter. Perhaps she was too young to manage such a secret business even given the opportunity. I said goodbye to her at about half-past three with Mr Grundy standing by my side. It occurred to me that perhaps it was for the last time, that her father, in one of his mad passions, might place her where no one but himself knew. Poor Mary. Poor gentle, quiet Mary. Her feelings must have been in turmoil. What was to become of her? What passed for education at Parr Hall was only preparing her for a life of trifles and silly vanity. *No father is fit to educate a daughter!*

I turned up the road through the wood that Mr Grundy showed me and found my way through some fields. It was a little shorter and I had no fear of losing my way while I had Billinge beacon in view. I dreaded the loneliness of the road, but I met few people on the way and those who passed me greeted me quietly and civilly enough. I have never been robbed – by strangers. I arrived home very little tired and I was determined to see Mary again as soon as possible. Let Mr Grundy treat me as he may. It was about seven miles each way, a journey I knew I would not be able to make in all weathers or at all times of the year.

28th September 1818

From the first of my coming to Garnett Lees, I have taught Sunday school at Farr Moor. No weather deterred me. Often I had to wear pattens to lift my feet out of the mud to stumble the mile or so to the chapel. Not once have I been late. The girls I taught were attentive and attached to me as I to them. I believed I did some good. I felt like a missionary in a little obscure place where most would not give themselves the trouble to bother about. But I found once more that I was out of step with my fellow man.

That morning as usual, I had set off early, before eight, dining on a tuppenny loaf at the chapel. It was from Mr Tunstal, a young man very active in the school, that I learned the congregation of Farr Moor were to form a regulated body for the first time since Mr Holgate, our preacher, came amongst us. The Reverend William Roby, Wigan born and a forceful preacher in Manchester, was himself coming to form them into a church. I had not been invited to join them. I had heard nothing about it. I discovered from Joshua Tunstal that my character had been the subject of discussion at several meetings. What my faults were I could not get from him. I sought out Mr Holgate immediately. I could hardly speak. But it was agreed that I should meet my accusers after evening service.

★

Imagine my feelings. Ten, perhaps twelve coarse and illiterate men and women had gathered in Mr Holgate's parlour and I, an object of suspicion and curiosity, sat before them like a criminal awaiting their judgement. No, not so, for I found that I had already been tried and condemned although my accusers had never confronted me, nor had they told me of what I had been accused. The dull cacophony of rough voices and quick whisperings ceased the moment I entered the room with Mr Holgate who was flushed and uncomfortable. He visibly squirmed in his chair, his head bowed. For a long time no one spoke and I was determined that I would not be the first to do so. I trembled but sat steadily enough and studied my accusers. They were mostly elderly men – colliers, weavers, and labourers – accustomed to dressing in fustian and leather on weekdays. One pulled at the tightness of his collar stud with a raw, scrubbed, work-red hand. His face was the colour of the earth. Their eyes were dull and stolid. They did not look at me, preferring to study the candles or stare vacantly into the corners of the room. The few impassive women sat scraggy-throated and grimly bonneted. Piety pursed their lips. Duty creased their brows. Only Joshua Tunstal looked into my face – his eyes smiling silent encouragement.

A wet cough – someone was wheezing audibly. There was a scrape of heavy work boots. At last, Mr Holgate gave out a hymn and a prayer in a thin tremulous voice – then silence again. My thoughts shouted: *I have been condemned unheard!*

I have been accused and therefore must be guilty! I could remain silent no longer.

'Mr Holgate, I would like to know of what I am accused and why the matter of forming a church has been kept secret from me.' I managed to speak calmly and without vehemence.

'Mrs Stock,' he said a little hesitantly, 'some time ago, I had occasion to speak to Reverend Steill.'

He faltered and another short silence ensued.

'Reverend Steill of St Paul's Standishgate?' I said, feeling my shoulders droop.

'Yes. He was of the opinion that if Mr Roby were to see your name on the list to be presented to him on the occasion, he may judge unfavourably of the whole.' He spoke quickly now. 'There are some amongst us here who share that fear.'

I was vaguely aware of a murmur and looking again at my accusers saw that some nodded.

'Mr Holgate, I have been most faithful to my teaching. I have attended to my own class and interfered with no one else. The number of girls attending has increased. They have shown improvement. I would ask you to speak to their parents about me.'

Despite my determination a long breath turned itself into a half sob.

'Your present conduct enjoys an excellent reputation, Mrs Stock.' He placed a slight emphasis on the word *present*. 'I make no criticism of it, but there are those whose minds are not easy about receiving you.'

'Then please, let me hear what they have to say.'

I looked at my accusers. Not one person spoke.

I rose. 'I bid you all goodnight.'

Mr Holgate is not an unworthy man but he is afraid of the austere and unbending Mr Roby. He followed me noisily into the hallway, his ruddy cheeks glowing in his confusion.

'Mrs Stock! Please! Please wait a moment,' he pleaded earnestly. 'If you would be prepared to be elected by a majority only, and not unanimously – after Mr Roby's visit…' He almost swallowed the last of the words.

My unfair treatment made me reckless. 'You would have me introduced into a Christian church as it were by stealth, Mr Holgate?' I regarded him angrily as I pulled my cloak tighter around me. 'No, Mr Holgate, I would not!' I turned towards him once more at the door. 'I will never come to your church again.'

*

I endured two weeks of blank monotony. I received no mail and no visitors. I had no change of scene. Mr Roby arrived in Farr Moor and formed the congregation into a church. Of course, I did not go.

*

The following day, I left home before nine to go to Parr Hall. I walked by way of Winstanley, the Bear in the Ring, Senela Green and Black Brook. An awful sense of foreboding knotted my stomach almost to the point of nausea. Would I be allowed to see Mary this time? I tried to distract myself with the beauties of my surroundings, the shifting light and cloud; wild flowers – dandelions, white archangel, oxeye daisies; the warm, sweet scents.

*

Once more Mr Grundy stood and reflected for a moment and gave a disdainful pout. I stared fixedly at the floor determined not to antagonise him in any way. At last he broke the awkward, prolonged silence and acquiesced in a hollow tone to my meeting Mary. She was glad to see me and we had a good chatter in the garden. And the dour Mrs Grundy was not in attendance! I gave Mary a present of a little print for patchwork and a score of walnuts, asking her to make sure she offered some of them to her father, as I knew he was fond of them. What he made of the gesture I know not.

But our happiness was short-lived.

When Mary had left me, Mr Grundy insisted on seeing me in his office. There, sitting importantly behind a large mahogany writing table, he made it perfectly clear in his solemn, polite voice that if I again came to Parr Hall unannounced he would flatly refuse to allow me to see Mary.

'Are you fully aware of the consequences of your visits, Mrs Stock?' he asked. His vaguely handsome features were impassive. His voice was brisk, businesslike.

I well understood the purport of his question but thought perhaps there may be something further. 'What consequences?' I enquired with a smile I knew to be false.

'Mary will be removed from this school.'

'Mr Grundy, if I am not to come to Parr Hall, and if I am not to see Mary at all, it hardly matters to me where she is.' I was on the point of adding, '*The only loser will be yourself!*' but I refrained from caution.

He lifted a folded newspaper off the desk and dropped it a little further away from him. 'But it will be such a loss to the child,' he said in a tone that may have been sincere.

And of course there is not such another school in the whole of England, Mr Grundy! His vanity was stunning! I was becoming agitated and felt the tears starting. 'The loss of her mother is the greatest loss she can sustain and it will not be my fault, Mr Grundy, if she is without one.'

He remained adamant. Such was the influence of my husband.

★

My knees trembled so much as I left Parr Hall that I thought I may have been in danger of some sort of collapse, and to add to my misery I was caught in a light, but cold shower of rain. I had no umbrella. My thoughts were dismal and angry. Again I had been forced to leave Mary without giving her an explanation – without my saying goodbye properly. I imagined her wondering why she should devote such fruitless loyalty to me. I crossed the little bridge but was so weak with faintness that I turned into a tidy cottage and knocked on the door.

A neat little woman was in, young and newly married. She ushered me immediately into the kitchen, poked at the fire, and soon had a scalding cup of tea for me on her scrubbed deal table where a wooden bowl of limes gave off a fresh, clean fragrance that I will always associate with her unexpected kindness. I told her of my situation – of my fears that I had seen my child for the last time – of the difficulty of getting even a letter to Mary with any certainty. It was strange that I unburdened my soul in such a way to a total stranger.

She listened patiently to my story, kept a short silence as she reflected a moment, and then said softly, 'Well, you could take care to visit me sometimes at this hour on a Sunday. Miss Mary will be walking with the other young ladies from Parr Hall with Miss Hammond to chapel. I always see them go past on a Sunday, unless the weather's too bad. Surely no one would refuse you entrance to a Sunday service.'

★

I left the little cottage near Parr Hall gate a half an hour later in bright air freshened by the shower of rain. I stepped out with renewed energy. Not only was I hopeful that I would see Mary again, but the kind mistress of the cottage had promised me that she would deliver any letter or parcel to Mary. She would give them to the cook, which she said was the only way, otherwise Mary would not get them. I was gladdened by the thought that in the winter months when it would be impossible for me to walk the distance from Up Holland I would still be able to contact Mary!

I had just left the village behind me when I became aware of a horseman approaching at a slow, uneven gait. The rider was heavy with large fleshy thighs, and was well dressed in a bottle-green coat, nankeen trousers and maroon cravat. There was no mistaking him – he was my husband!

The legs of the fine horse were almost beside me. There was no time to avoid him. Events slowed in the intensity of the moment – into the stillness of dread – became dreamlike, over-vivid. I raised my eyes no higher than the plump white hands that ferociously gripped and tugged at the reins. Perhaps he was a little tipsy or else one of his angry nervous agitations was upon him. He wriggled and twitched and bounced uncomfortably on the saddle, viciously pulled the horse to a stop while whipping it to go! The poor harassed animal ruffled its nostrils. As it lifted its big head, the bit cut at the softness of its mouth. He would be its master. An inarticulate growl came from deep within the rider's throat, whether it was directed at me or at the horse I was not sure. He then kicked at its poor naked sides with his heavy boots until it lunged forward into an awkward trot. And he was gone! Not once had I looked up at his face, and whether he knew me or not was hard to say. I suspected he did. It was the first time I had seen him since we had separated. It was unlucky that it should be so close to Parr Hall. He would learn of my visit – but it couldn't be helped!

When I arrived home clouds moved like smoke in the dusking twilight and there was distant sheet lightning. I was very tired. Fourteen miles! I hoped that Mr Grundy would keep quiet!

Some weeks later I received further confirmation from Mrs Hawarden that my husband's behaviour was becoming quite odd. She had seen him in Wigan. He was carrying a bundle of papers and was flourishing them in the faces of passers-by and calling out like some half-crazed ballad-seller at a street corner.

21st November 1818
I sit beside my little window and look at the lonely colours of night through the glass wet with rain. Half a lifetime lies ahead of me – perhaps. Half a lifetime! I have taken out some clothes in preparation for the morning. I am no longer undecided whether to make for Parr Hall or wait one more week. Winter with its incessant rain and storms of wind will keep me quiet for months at Garnett Lees. I will brave the road once more.

★

The heavy rain over night cleared into a raw, gloomy day and a white ribbon of fog lay below Up Holland. The trees were on fire with autumn under the dull sky and I was again racked with worry that Mary may have been removed from the school. In places the road was little more than a muddy narrow trench between hedges that guarded wet, empty fields and the wind buffeted me full in the face. My eyes stung and reddened; my lips dried and split.

The woman at the cottage near Parr Hall gate proved as true as her word and gladly welcomed me again, but my sense of immediate relief was soon overtaken with my anxiety about seeing Mary. I was all a jitter with nerves. Rather than expose my friend to any unpleasantness, I decided to wait on the little bridge, but when I saw Mr Grundy's young ladies approaching from the Hall, I was struck with the sudden fear that if he saw me he would perhaps take Mary back into the house. I darted back to the cottage, sat in a corner by the window and waited until they had all filed past. Mary was not with them! I waited a moment or two and then hurried out to overtake them. I had to be quite sure whether Mary was there or not. Perhaps my anxiety had confused my sight!

'Miss Hammond!' I assumed it *was* Miss Hammond. She was a severe looking woman dressed in black. 'Miss Hammond, I am sorry for coming upon you like this, but is Mary Stock here with you? I am her mother,' I stammered finally by way of breathless explanation.

'She is at the front,' she said coldly, giving a haughty, forbidding nod.

Hurrying forward I saw Mary walking behind the unhappy Mrs Grundy. It had been the change from summer to winter clothes that had deceived me. Mary looked ill and frail. We spoke only a little. We both, no doubt, felt constrained by the lined haggardness of Mrs Grundy's presence. But I took Mary's little hand in mine and she gave it a gentle squeeze.

We were soon at the chapel and I was determined to be with Mary for another hour. I noticed Miss Hammond stooped in serious conversation with Mr Grundy who was sitting at the end of an ornately carved pew clasping his hymnbook in readiness to lead the singing. I hadn't noticed him before then. I took my seat next to Mary. Another glare from Miss Hammond; her thin lips were pursed so tightly she could have been blowing on hot broth. She was terribly agitated but I didn't care. Unfeeling woman! During the service Mary grew quite faint. A girl of perhaps fourteen came to her aid and asked her if she would like to go outside. Mary, moving closer to my side, shook her head. I remember nothing of the sermon, nothing of the man who gave it.

I walked with Mary as far as the wooden bridge. There we stopped. I thought it prudent not to go past the gate into the grounds of Parr Hall. The others walked on leaving us alone for a few precious moments. I promised her most solemnly that I would never desert her, not as long as I lived. She stood dry-eyed, small and thin in the wind. She nodded, only once, slowly, deliberately. And then she searched almost frantically for something hidden in her clothing. She found what she was looking for and gave it to me. It was a small sampler that she had made of a sunset. Fragments of simple cloud were saffron-yellow in an expanse of sky of lemon hues, which met a sea all golden fire. Painstakingly stitched under the scene were the words: *God's Hiding Place*. For how many days had she secretly carried it in the hope of giving it to me? My throat tightened. I could say nothing. The group of girls had stopped. I could see that Mr Grundy was growing impatient. Mary turned away from me to join them. I stood and watched as she walked towards the darkness of the building. 'Goodbye, Mary,' I whispered. 'Goodbye.' As if she heard me, she turned at that very moment and saw me still standing there in the road looking after her. She continued to turn and wave as she walked on up to the house. When the hedge intervened, she jumped up to look for me again – and again. At last, she quite disappeared. I waited a little longer, but I had had my last glimpse of her.

14th December 1818

There are times when the most ordinary of sights – skeletal branches dripping in the muggy stillness of fog, or the waxy red of yew berries – make my spirits lift. But there are also black days when I am reduced to a silent, brooding presence in the dark empty house; days of melancholy and inaction when my few books irk me, when my flageolet is dumb and resentful, and when Mrs Ball's company is cheerless. Weeks of almost continuous rain have kept me indoors. I know it will be a long time before I can attempt to see Mary again. I feel my idleness! I hear so little of what is going on in the world, or even in England! But I begin to dream of escape – or at least a temporary one. It is an old idea of mine. But first I have to endure the winter. It is a pity my bed is so small which makes it impossible for me to offer half of it to a friend for a night or two. In any case, my friends are few! I considered getting up a petition to be signed by my acquaintances testifying to my character in the hope I would gain more access to Mary. But who would sign it? Doctor Hawarden, certainly, and the Prices, Mr and Mrs Ball. And who else? My brother? The Armitages of Highroyd House? A governess is a wretched creature, a person with no equals in such a house and therefore quickly forgotten. My past students? Those who are still living in Up Holland and toil in dim hovels or in hungry wet fields? The butter man at the dairy on Garnett Lees perhaps? If I went on a journey, who is there to miss me? I am determined to go, but wonder how I can contrive to do such a thing alone.

I must write to Mary as cheerfully as I can.

Garnett Lees, Up Holland
14th December 1818

My dear Mary,

I hope you feel a pleasant surprise on receiving this little parcel and my note. We have friends in the world!

The raisins are the best I could find but you are not to feel guilty if you do not eat the tough leathery skins. Nor indeed should you eat the skins of any fruit. And on no account eat more than three or four of the prunes in a day, a larger number will make you ill and spoil your appetite. Take every opportunity you can to be out of doors and eat only a little meat. You looked so frail the last time I saw you! You must take care of yourself.

Your holidays are very near. I hope you can enjoy them. If there is anything you need, remember to ask your father for it.

The steel pen is yours. I hope you will write to me with it. I am old-fashioned and keep to my quill!

The weather has been windy and wintry and I am afraid it will be a long time before I will be able to see you again. I am snug enough but I am looking forward to spring as never before! I am thinking of going on a little journey to Wales then, so I will have much to talk to you about.

Christmas is my birthday. Don't forget me on that day!

Goodbye Mary

30th May 1819
Standishgate, Wigan

This is the last time I shall write in this diary. I have no wish to write more. No need. It is complete.

I was shaken by Mrs Braithwaite's appearance – her sad eyes and her sad smile. Her rug work lay neglected, her needle and thread were idle. I tried not to notice the difficulty she had breathing or the large black safety pin at her waist gathering in the dress now too large for her. Soon she would be a wizened old lady. She told me of my uncle's death. He had died in January, but I had heard nothing of it! I was always fond of him and I felt the news cruelly. I had gained five pounds out of my aunt's legacy, after it had been tampered with, but my uncle's legacy to me would, of course, have been forfeited in its entirety to Mr Aaron Stock. I walked for some time in the churchyard after leaving Mrs Braithwaite. She had stood waving to me from her doorway, looking very frail and anxious in the weak spring sunshine. My uncle's grave was next but one to my mother's. Pale-eyed jackdaws were nesting high up in the masonry of the church where they squawked and clacked gently. I could still hear them from inside the church. I knelt in the quiet emptiness before the altar but I could not collect my thoughts and was unable to pray. Wales! I had ten minutes to meet the coach.

★

I was unnerved and tried to force myself to be calm. To panic would not help at all.

The storm the night before had brought hail and had sent people reeling in the streets as if drunk in the furious wind. But it had cleared by morning leaving the day fine if cold and cloudy. I had set out as early as possible to see the Llanberris Lakes by way of Pentir carrying Williams's *Tourist Guide* and believing I was paying strict attention to my map. I realised, too late, that I had turned left after crossing a bridge near two miles off, instead of going straight on, and found myself on a barren expanse of hill covered in rough gorse and bracken, and streaming with rushing white water. Grey misty light blurred the distance. The cold wind marbled my cheeks and I pulled and tied my bonnet tighter. Underfoot was as soft and spongy-wet as water meadows. My thoughts were reckless – and a little bitter. Not a person in England knew at that moment where I was. Imagine the anxiety about me if I had been loved by a large family or if I had been affluent and famous! My husband had much to answer for!

There was a scream – needle sharp.

My eyes lifted to a red kite on spread, unmoving wings in the piercingly cold air. And higher, beyond the kite, Snowdon was cloud-darkened and misty. The sun did not touch its green blackness. '*Yr Wyddfa*,' Jane, my landlord's niece had said during the storm in her guttural native tongue so alien to my ears. We were snug before the hearth. The wind roared in great gusts and volleys and I was afraid the chimneypiece would not hold. Jane's dark eyes glinted russet red from the rich firelight. Her uncle sat beside her clutching a blackthorn cane. His hair in the warm glow of the fire was as white and as soft as cotton wool. She continued in English, 'It is the resting place of Rhita Gawr, a giant who wore a cloak made from the beards of the many kings he had killed.'

I fell, muddying my dress and gloves.

Even if someone were to be found in such a place, it would be hopeless to ask my way. No one could understand me, nor I them. I was a child in that strange country that had once been inhabited by giants. I was silenced, struck dumb. Since I left the Prices in Liverpool, almost a week before, I had been in a state of helpless, childish fear of what *might* happen to me. I knew no one on board the steam-packet to Bangor. The fare in the steerage was only five shillings, which suited my frugal plans, but I was obliged to be constantly on my guard to prevent familiarity. I am forty-two years old, thin and bony, and I still had to pretend to be blind to the leers and deaf to the coarse jests from women's enemy. Landing at Garth Ferry, I was frightened of the porters who unbidden reached for my bags. I was conscious only of hands – hands grabbing, appealing, beckoning, snatching. I understood nothing of what people were saying. At last I was rescued by a respectable looking woman who took me to a little huckster shop where there were rooms so clean and neat I engaged them for a fortnight for six shillings a week. Old Mr Pritchard and his even older housekeeper spoke very little English. We made signs, performed charades and laughed at the noises we made at each other in our poor attempts to communicate even the simplest idea or request. Only Jane who is in service at Penrhyn Castle spoke any English. My bed though was dry and comfortable and I was convinced there were no bugs or fleas. A window overlooked a small orchard that would soon be white with apple blossom. I kept my portable inkhorn and my journal on the sill.

I managed to ramble a little around the town and nearby country. I crossed the Menai in the company of four skittish horses and two wild Welsh cows to see the pillar erected in honour of the Marquis of Anglesea beyond the new bridge that Telford is building. The ferryman was a very singular individual. Short, corpulent, he rolled about the boat like a hogshead. His laugh was as rough and as coarse as his features. However, the crossing was made safely for two pence and I walked as far as Plas Newydd. I did not, of course, attempt to enter the grounds. I did not want to see anything that was not open to everyone. I spoke to no one and sought no company. The open road was enough. But I wanted to see the cromlech, *Bryn Celli Ddu*, mentioned by Williams. He would have it that it was close by behind the house, but I couldn't find it. It must have been enclosed in trees or perhaps it was not what I imagined it to be and so I failed to recognise it.

I was an object of curiosity in Bangor – why, I could not discover, especially when there must be so many visitors. I dressed plainly in a small slouch straw hat or bonnet, a nondescript grey stuff jacket and petticoat and I carried a white net bag. I dreaded the market place. People turned one and all to look at me when I asked the price of anything. Perhaps it was because I was a stranger, and alone; then it may have been because I was a woman taller and thinner than most and plain featured. Surely not ugly enough to attract attention! But few of us really know how we appear to others.

Another scream, more distant this time, the kite was plunging about in the sky.

With difficulty I clambered and slipped over rocks and the boggy ground and at last reached the top. I could see the lakes! They were a bright purple; the clearness of the air, I suppose, gave them that hue, and the hollowness of their situation. An exhilarating lightness of being coursed through my blood. I was in no danger of becoming lost now. I sat on a rock, resting and admiring. I breathed in the rainy smell of the air; listened to the rush of water. As I sat there the sun opened like a fan through the clouds and fell onto the bluffs and crags of Snowdon. *Yr Wyddfa* – the dark tomb of the giant – was bathed in distant white light. The tiny mechanism that had caused this transformation was nothing more than the chance shifting of cloud in the western sky. But I felt in that moment of light an unlooked for contentment as if I had moved a little away from myself. I looked at the alien mountain a long time, so absorbed in its menacing beauty that I forgot about my fatigue and my wet boots and the long walk home.

★

I walked to Aber and back. I was free to follow my own course without censure whether it was through streets or fields or on mountain paths. I bought a penny loaf in the village and ate it in the churchyard under the shade of an ancient yew tree. A young foal and its mother were my only visitors. Tentatively they came to look at me. 'You need not fear me,' I said quietly. 'I would not intentionally frighten any living creature.' Behind the closed gate it was quiet with the soft sound of birds and the mare cropping the grass. Wood smoke from a cluster of nearby cottages lifted almost vertically in the calm warm air. The church itself, like others I have seen in Wales, was comfortless and shabby within. A bell rope dangled down the outside wall as if from a gallows. I saw for the first time the manner of decking a Welsh grave. Many were trimmed with what had once been green and beautiful, but it had withered and was mouldering like those beneath. We are mortal and so, soon forgotten. I sat a long time at my dinner on a smooth gravestone of local blue slate. Below me hills fell steeply into Conwy Bay and to the north loomed Great Ormes Head. A single chaffinch hopped beside me and gathered a fallen crumb off the flat gravestone. Otherwise there was just the distant bluish water, and clouds, and grass and silence. It was beautiful and frightening, that silent vastness that had nothing to do with me. *It is what it is,* I thought. *It will not be what I want it to be or what I think it is. I can change nothing.* I looked at the mossed gravestones, wind-pitted, weathered, shunned and alone under the shade of yew, holly and mahonia. The dead. Here and about they had looked at the night sky, had walked through woods and fields, had gazed into the eyes of those they had loved. They had worked and suffered, had loved what they could not understand. I raised myself off the grave. The horses lifted their heads in unison and then lowered them again to the grass.

★

The road was very lonely. I felt somewhat afraid but as it proved, unnecessarily. On my right, the bay was in full tide, a crinkled soft blue beside me. My boots disturbed small green grasshoppers that clicked and whirred away. One or two clung to my dress for safety, one to my hair. The still, salty air was sticky. There was a laugh and the blue reek of tobacco smoke. Two men were lying at the side of the road basking in the sun. It was too late to draw back. They had seen me. I gave them no more than a quick glance and a lifeless smile as I passed them. One had a bundle of printed papers, which I suppose he was going to cry through the streets of Bangor, describing some wonderment or other for a halfpenny each. The other in a sweated flannel shirt with the collar unbuttoned had the blue eyes and dark hair of the Irish. He had nothing about him that hinted at his employment. They stood and greeted a man with a barrel organ on his back coming from the gateway of a large house and walked at his pace. Burdened as he was, I thought I would easily outpace them and soon be out of sight of them. But no, I turned and found the organist had left them, and they were close behind. They did not speak, but I could clearly hear the tread of their heavy steps. I preferred to have them in front of me, so I stood and pretended to look over the wall across to Beaumaris. It would have been easy enough to rob me in such a place and throw me into the sea. There was not another living soul, not so much as a sail on the empty bay. They looked quietly at me, but not rudely, nodded, and were gone!

Still, I waited a further twenty minutes or so at the spot. Nor do I believe my fears were completely unfounded. Men do so much injury to women as my own experience can testify. And daily the newspapers bring further instances. Soon after my arrival in Wales there had been a horrible crime. A young man, John Roberts, now said to be insane, had gone to the house of his late employer, a widow who lived on a farm in the mountains. Without the slightest warning he attacked her, breaking both her arms and mutilating her dreadfully in other ways with a billhook. She had died the following morning. He also cut the servant man and girl with the hook for trying to save their mistress. Jane had seen him being conveyed through Bangor on the way to Caernarvon Castle and had been terribly upset.

★

After three days of wet and stormy weather, I left Bangor and went to stay in Caernarvon. The earlier blackness of Snowdon, I was told, was a forerunner of the furious wind and rain. And it was from Caernarvon that I wrote to Ann Price.

Love Lane, Caernarvon
2nd May 1819
Dear Ann,

I am comfortably settled in Caernarvon after spending a fortnight in Bangor, so I now hope to hear from you soon.

Mr Price's reference to Mrs Evans was of great service to me. I soon found out Mrs Evans's daughter who was extremely helpful. She took me to many places to procure safe lodgings. I had hoped for a view of the Menai from the window but seeing more of the town I realised that it was not possible on account of the walls. However, I have fixed on a snug place for four shillings a week. Mrs Evans was quite willing to take me in herself, but I did not like the closeness of the situation. I am in Love Lane! And I love the lane well. I have a fine view of the castle, the river and shipping, and a side view into Castle Square.

I walked here in pleasant sunshine from Bangor, but since then the days have been mostly wet and gloomy. Today has been the first day that I have been able to venture beyond the town. I set out for a long walk along the Beddgelert Road half inclined to ascend Mynydd Mawr. It was a perfect day for such a climb, not too cold and the air was glass-clear. But I had left it too late, and instead I walked to the foot of Cwellyn Lake. It was unexpectedly beautiful and I sat upon a rock that commanded a full view of it. The sun shone brilliantly upon the mountains, all except Snowdon. The sun seldom touches it. Why, I don't know. It is very little higher than several mountains near it but they are not so continually shrouded in darkness.

The family I have left in Bangor and the one I have come to can speak very little English, but I find most in the town, especially the younger people can, in a manner, communicate with me. Perhaps in another hundred years Welsh will have disappeared for in the national schools the children are taught only in English.

Please thank Mr Price for his useful reference. I remember my good friends in Seymour Street fondly.

Yours gratefully,

Ellen Weeton

I put down my quill and in that moment knew that before I left Wales, I would stand on the summit of Snowdon! I would have to go alone for I knew no one and I was not at all sure how to go about it. After consulting my map, I decided it would be best to go to Llanberis or Beddgelert for a night or two, even though I hated an inn as much as a butcher's shop.

★

An intense silence settled as the little mail cart that had brought me from Caernarvon jolted away. The poor woman who had been my fellow passenger lifted her arm in a forlorn farewell. Her little girl, dark-eyed, pale, waif-like, solemn, was huddled beside her. The woman had not seen her husband, who was a sailor, for more than two years and was now compelled to return to her native parish. If the man had stolen a sheep or a horse he would have been pursued by the law and hanged. But he may cruelly desert his wife and her misery will be of no concern to the parish officers for as long as she asks for no more money! With these thoughts I sat on the battlement of Aberglaslyn Bridge eating part of the bread and butter I had brought with me, and then walked slowly to a spot near Llyn Cwellyn. The light was constantly changing; the weather was uncertain. The quiet lake water was a luminous pale grey under an almost colourless sky. The last two days had been brilliantly clear, but my timidity had prevented my bringing enough courage to the sticking place sooner. Even now I was irresolute. I had passed an anxious night of intermittent sleep. Disturbing dreams had come. I had seen the dead. I had had the helpless feeling of falling. Straining upwards to the surface of morning consciousness, I had brought with me the lingering sensation of having held a frightened bird in my hands. Its head had been between the thumbs of my cupped hands. I could still feel, as if it had been lived experience, its warmth, the hardness of its fragile bones, its tiny heart beating madly against the safe nest of my palms. A slight breeze stirred the trees and blemished the stained reflections at the edge of the lake. Turning, I looked up at the cloud shadows plunging down the slopes of Snowdon. My heart quickened. '*Yr Wyddfa*,' I said aloud, 'the final resting place of the giant.' Yes! That would be something! Something real, something perfect! With a trembling eagerness, I began my ascent.

★

I had left my watch behind for safekeeping but it must have been about two in the afternoon. A great space was opening around me. Huge rocks piled up, grey-green and black with wetness under a sky of fast moving cloud. Wild goats wandered sure-footed amongst them cropping the wet, springy turf. I took off my bonnet, lowered my head and drank comfortably from a clear rushing stream. I had brought no cup. The water was alive, purifying.

'Hey! You must keep to the copper path. See, along there!'

I looked up sharply. A short distance away a gentleman in gaiters and holding an alpenstock was descending with his guide who was calling out to me. I knew the way perfectly well from hours of studying my map. I had purposely left the regular path to quench my thirst.

'I can manage quite well by myself now,' the gentleman was saying. He perhaps assumed that I had come to meet and engage the guide.

I did not look at them, but walked as fast as I could hanging down my head. The guide continued to shout directions so insistently that twice I called out, 'Thank you!' When I was a considerable height above them, I turned and saw the guide trudging off home, but the gentleman was still looking up after me standing with his hands on his sides as if in complete astonishment! Hopefully he had not seen me clearly. I have no ambition to be pointed out and stared at in the street: 'That is the lady I saw climbing Snowdon, alone! A most singular female!'

★

I reached the lesser summit. I was now higher than I had ever been before in the world. A sea of mountains rose in every direction wave after wave rippling out into the white haze of distance. Immediately to the east, was a deep precipice falling away almost to the valley below. I dared not look down, standing, but laid myself flat and looked at the roads far below me winding through grey hills and grey lakes like white threads. No house or cottage could be seen, nor another human being. It was possible that I had the whole mountain to myself. A deep quietness engulfed me, perhaps because of my fatigue and the clean coolness of the moist air. Sitting up I thought of the cluster of wildflowers I had casually arranged in a bowl and had placed in the light of my window in Caernarvon. I thought of their wilting petals falling noiselessly on the hard wood of the sill, the faint scent in the chilly, empty room. Their quiet existence unnoticed. I thought of Tom and of my husband – with a compassion that surprised me. I thought of Mary. I looked at the clouds and rocks and heather without desire and without fear.

★

I had not expected this. There was no mention in either Bingley or Williams of such a path. I had thought that when I reached the top the summit would be broad. There was no crossing lower down. I must either return the way I had come or climb along the narrow rocky ridge before me. I hesitated. If I slipped to the right nothing could save me. It would be an eternity of falling. It was too much for my head to bear. I pulled my bonnet down close over my right cheek. On my left there were some rocks to hold on by – I began to cross. I looked at nothing except the next step, the next outcrop of stone that I could grasp. It was perhaps a hundred yards, perhaps two hundred; I was too terrified to be certain. I breathed again, tremulously, exultantly. The summit. I was now exposed to a rough wind. Had it blown the contrary way it would have been madness to brave the ridge. It snatched at my bonnet, tore at my dress, watered my eyes. My ears ached. I found a canvas bag forgotten or abandoned by some climber lying in the crevice of a rock, and strewn about it were what appeared to be samples of heavy copper ore. I kept one to remind me of the place where I had found it. My shadow had lengthened. It grew cold. I could not stay there in that place, but nor could I face those cliffs again. It would make my journey even longer but I decided to descend on the Llanberis side.

★

A shower of fine rain swept across the slope clearing the sky. The heath was sodden and the rocks were as slippery as polished slate. I fell often, but not seriously. The ruined keep of Dolbadarn Castle appeared below me, a rivulet, a bridge, cottages, the lake – the water was a pale, molten gold in the slanting light of the falling sun. I reached the road. A young man was cutting turf. Beside him stood a much older man, perhaps his father. Nearby a girl, thin, barefooted, tended the remnants of a good fire. I could have easily avoided them, but did not. A dog, as large as a mastiff, leapt to his feet with a growl, but was instantly subdued by a rasping command from the old man. I forgot to be afraid. The dog sniffed at my boots and at my hands, seemed satisfied and rejoined the girl beside the fire. The old man said something in his own tongue. Saw my incomprehension, smiled, gestured. His face, shiny with sweat, shone in the amber-yellow light with the pain and joy of living. The girl coughed, a dry, chronic cough and she moved closer to the dark smudges of smoky flame. Her striking blue eyes never left me. I crouched beside her. She was painfully thin. Finding some coins I squeezed them into her hand. Her dirty fingers instinctively closed on them. The younger man called out to me and raised his arm smiling. It may have been a farewell, or an expression of thanks. The girl was showing him the coins I had given her.

★

Below Dolbadarn I was able to walk briskly and easily through an open grassy field towards the lake and village. A beating whirr erupted all about me. I stopped, gasped. Small birds were lifting from the long grass with a wild fluttering of tiny wings. The sun lit up their burnished stubble brown as they twisted and turned in panic before dropping to the earth and disappearing once more. I smiled at my momentary fright and trudged on. The last red glow of the clouded sun had set the surface of the lake on fire. *I am not free and never will be. Nothing can mend the past. But I need not be afraid of the future. I will live according to my nature for its own sake. I can live no more deeply than that. To be alive is enough – if I can love enough.* I felt for the stone I had brought from the summit, but instead touched the sheet of paper I had put in my pocket that morning. I had taken the precaution of writing my address on it, both to my lodgings in Caernarvon and to my husband's house in Wigan, so if an accident should befall me, whoever found me would know where to apply. I opened its neat folds, tore it into tiny pieces and let them fall into the water and amongst the reeds that fringed the darkening lake. I breathed in the lingering twilight, again and again. In that moment, I was as happy as mortal can be. I turned and walked towards the village of Llanberis.

★

I made my way safely back to Garnett Lees and to the company of Mr and Mrs Ball. But I was able to revel in the quiet contentment I felt to be back amongst the farm's old trees and summer flowers and its wind-combed fields for only three days. I received a letter from Mr Gaskell, my husband's attorney in Wigan, requesting that I see him in his chambers at my earliest convenience. I suffered an agonising, debilitating anxiety. If I were to lose my quarterly payments, how could I live? Where could I go? How could I continue to see Mary?

★

Doctor Hawarden, who had kindly agreed to accompany me, supported my arm firmly as the attorney's clerk, Mr Ackerly, ushered us through to Mr Gaskell's office. The tired eyes and stony features of Mr Ackerly, did nothing to lessen the sickening dread that almost overpowered me. I had met him once before under equally trying and bitter conditions when I was forced to sign the deed of separation which so empowered my husband against me.

The ponderous desk of old oak was varnished by the sunshine which came spilling in at the window. Formal courtesies and a little unanchored talk quickly faded into an insipid silence. Mr Gaskell was elderly with a gaunt, furrowed face, but as he lent back into his chair his eyes were as bright and as hard as frost. I could not meet them.

'It is incumbent upon me, Mrs Stock, to inform you of certain changes in your situation which I trust you will act upon.'

I was capable of little more than studying the fragile, vulnerable skin on the backs of his hands. Was it possible that an executioner could have such hands?

He continued in a neutral voice. 'I have in my possession a copy of your husband's latest Will, in which he makes clear his intention that in the event of his death, the house at Standishgate will become the property of his daughter Mary.'

My head was bowed; I lifted my eyes briefly and nodded.

'Such a normal course of procedure hardly warrants this interview,' Doctor Hawarden said with a note of calm asperity in his voice.

'Indeed,' said Mr Gaskell. 'But of further relevance is the fact that Mr Aaron Stock has vacated the premises leaving his housekeeper, one Alice Bromley as caretaker. Your husband has moved to the district of Ashton-in-Mackerfield where he has ventured heavy investments in a colliery. The house is vacant and you are in need of a house Mrs Stock.'

'Impossible,' said Doctor Hawarden firmly. 'Ellen would be in perpetual fear of his return. The uncertainty would be unendurable.'

'That is not the understanding I have received from Mr Stock, Doctor.'

'Are we seriously expected to believe such a change of heart is possible given the man's history?' asked Doctor Hawarden almost querulously.

A corvine laugh erupted from the general hubbub of the street below as if by way of answer. Mr Gaskell threw a frigid scowl at the sun-filled window before proceeding in the same measured tones.

'Aaron Stock is a man of considerable means. As well as being part owner of Stanley Colliery he has recently purchased a residence at Seneley Green. He does have an enviable business acumen all said and done. As for matters of the heart, Doctor, his personal affairs in Wigan have reached such a level of complexity that he wishes only to escape from them – permanently. And he is prepared to pay for such freedom. You have my assurance of this.' He raised a sheaf of stamped papers and loose red ribbon from his desk in seeming proof of his statement before letting them fall noisily.

Doctor Hawarden nodded meditatively. 'Now that is more in keeping with our man,' he said quietly.

'And Mary? What of Mary, Mr Gaskell? What is to become of her?' I pleaded.

'Mr Grundy of Parr Hall has informed me that monies owing to him from Mr Stock have been in arrears for some time. All communications forwarded to Stock by him have been assiduously ignored. Mary is also in need of a house, Mrs Stock.'

Doctor Hawarden continued to ask several particulars but I heard nothing. 'Mr Gaskell, is it possible to organise a suitable conveyance for me?' I said interrupting.

'Yes, if you wish, my clerk will see to it immediately, Mrs Stock.'

★

Leaving Doctor Hawarden, I crossed the street as if on the edge of a waking dream. The buildings of mellow red brick, the interlacing cries and the acrid smells had no more reality for me than a watercolour sketch. I looked up at a chalk-blue sky and shut my eyes for a moment. I was going to bring Mary home.

Author's Note

In 1925 the historian Edward Hall discovered in a small bookshop in Wigan a well preserved quarto volume. Instantly recognising its historical value he bought it for the princely sum of nine pence. It was one of nine volumes of Ellen Weeton's Letter Books. Page after page contained letters in a clear legible hand that she had carefully transcribed from the originals and had kept by way of a journal.

The extant volumes – numbers two, three and seven, and a volume containing two works, *Occasional Reflections* and a fragment entitled *The History of the Life of N. Stock* – were painstakingly edited and published by Edward Hall under the title *Miss Weeton* in 1936 and were reprinted in two volumes as *Miss Weeton's Journal of a Governess 1807–1811* and *Miss Weeton's Journal of a Governess 1811–1825* (David & Charles Reprints, South Devon House Newton Abbot, 1969). The latter two volumes have been my primary source in depicting the historical backgrounds in *Standing on the Giant's Grave*. Another book I found particularly useful should also be acknowledged: *The Skilled Labourer 1760–1832* by J L Hammond and Barbara Hammond (Longmans Green, London, 1919).

Standing on the Giant's Grave is an historical account in the sense that I have attempted to be faithful to what is known about Ellen Weeton's life, but it is a work of fiction in that I have created for her an inner world of emotions, dreams and illusions. Therefore, while nearly every character in the novel has some basis in historical fact they are all essentially fictions.

Little is known about Ellen Weeton's life beyond her own writing. It would seem though, that her fortunes improved soon after her journey to Wales. Ellen was reunited with her daughter Mary, and lived at Standishgate at least until 1844. It is likely that she spent her last years with her daughter's family in Liverpool where she died at the age of seventy-two in 1849 from typhoid fever. Her brother Tom's ambitions came to an abrupt end when a certain Mrs Bevan successfully exposed him for forgery and misappropriation of funds in a matter relating to her will. No longer Clerk to the Magistrates he seems to have retired from the legal profession in 1837. He died on 5th March 1845. Her estranged husband, Aaron Stock, became the owner of Stanley Colliery and lies buried in the churchyard at Ashton-in-Mackerfield.

Finally, I would like to thank my editor Eifion Jenkins for doing what he does so well.

Standing on the Giant's Grave is just one of
a whole range of publications from Y Lolfa.
For a full list of books currently in print,
send now for your free copy of our new
full-colour catalogue. Or simply surf into
our website

www.ylolfa.com

for secure on-line ordering.

y Lolfa

TALYBONT CEREDIGION CYMRU SY24 5HE
e-mail ylolfa@ylolfa.com
website www.ylolfa.com
phone (01970) 832 304
fax 832 782